CRIME SPREE

CRIME SPREE

JUDGE, JURY, & EXECUTIONER™ BOOK SEVENTEEN

CRAIG MARTELLE
MICHAEL ANDERLE

CONNECT WITH THE AUTHORS

Craig Martelle Social

Website & Newsletter:
http://www.craigmartelle.com

Facebook:
https://www.facebook.com/AuthorCraigMartelle/

Michael Anderle Social

Website: http://lmbpn.com

Email List: http://lmbpn.com/email/

https://www.facebook.com/LMBPNPublishing

https://twitter.com/MichaelAnderle

https://www.instagram.com/lmbpn_publishing/

https://www.bookbub.com/authors/michael-anderle

This book is a work of fiction. All of the characters, organizations, and events portrayed in this novel are either products of the author's imagination or are used fictitiously. Sometimes both.

Cover Art by Jake @ J Caleb Design
http://jcalebdesign.com / jcalebdesign@gmail.com

LMBPN Publishing
PMB 196, 2540 South Maryland Pkwy
Las Vegas, NV 89109

Version 1.02, February 2023
ebook ISBN: 979-8-88541-869-0
Print ISBN: 979-8-88541-870-6

THE CRIME SPREE TEAM

Thanks to our Beta Readers

In memoriam, Micky Cocker, James Caplan, Kelly O'Donnell, and John Ashmore

Thanks to the JIT Readers

Daryl McDaniel
Rachel Beckford
Dave Hicks
Zacc Pelter
Peter Manis
Veronica Stephan-Miller
Diane L. Smith
Dorothy Lloyd
Jackey Hankard-Brodie
Jeff Goode
Jan Hunnicutt
John Ashmore
Kelly O'Donnell

If we've missed anyone, please let us know!

Editor
Lynne Stiegler

We can't write without those who support us
On the home front, we thank you for being there for us

We wouldn't be able to do this for a living if it weren't for our readers
We thank you for reading our books

CHAPTER ONE

All Guns Blazing, Keeg Station

Terry Henry Walton pounded back and forth before the franchise's signature window that looked out upon the distant nebula. His nostrils flared with his volcanic fury. His werewolf wife stood back with her arms crossed. There was no sense in getting in his way or trying to calm him down. He needed to rant, and then he needed to take action. Charumati waited for the right time to intervene, but she was angry, too.

"I'm going to have to beat someone senseless. I'm going to fuck up their world. Their nose will be a permanent fixture on the side of their head. They'll be drinking their meals from here to eternity. They'll wish they'd never crossed Terry Henry Walton!"

It was early. He and Char's All Guns Blazing franchise was not yet open for business. The tables were empty, and they would remain empty because he didn't have enough of the specialty items he'd ordered.

Twice, he'd ordered them. His stocks were depleted.

He flopped into a chair and ran his fingers through his shock of black hair. He'd tried the salt and pepper style, but he looked way too young to pull it off. He snorted. "Look at me. I didn't get my stuff, and I'm crying about it. Moonstokle. Bistok. Cheese. Vegetables. And most importantly, hops."

Char joined him, sitting on his lap and wrapping her arms around his neck. "It's the people we employ. It's the people we serve. It's your profession. And you didn't get that order of hops, so of course you're upset. You can't make the next batch of beer."

He kissed her lightly before lifting her off him and standing. "I'm taking the *War Axe* and finding these bastards."

Char shook her head.

"What? We're not going to surrender. I have to fuck somebody up for this."

"Surrender? Heavens, no. How long have you known me?" Char stared at him, her purple eyes sparkling from space's eclectic backdrop. "We know a professional who deals with this. TH, you have friends in the right places. Make the call."

He hugged Char and lifted her up to spin her around. He stopped by the bar to make himself a coffee before going to his office, where he had a comm link with the universe, thanks to who he was and the people he knew.

He tapped his access pad. When the light turned green, he spoke. "Check, check. TH Forty-seven calling for RA Sixteen, Cygnus Epsom Salt Barium Oscar, over." He had to repeat it twice while Char made faces.

"TH, as in Terry Henry? What's with the gobbledygook?" Magistrate Rivka Anoa answered.

"Despite my legendary memory, I seem to have forgotten the access codewords, or maybe I'm not up on the current ones. But that's not why I called. I have a problem."

"We don't use codewords. Put Char on. I know she's there."

"You don't want to hear about my problem?"

Rivka snorted. "Of course I do, but from Char, just in case you've taken another blow to the head. Which is where I'm putting my money."

Char spoke up from where she leaned against Terry's desk. "Someone is stealing our supplies at the source or en route. Somewhere before they get to our restaurants. It's driving TH nuts. Well, me, too. This little crime spree is going to drive us out of business."

"That *is* a problem, but that's in a broader jurisdiction. You need to call the cops or unleash the Bad Company."

TH jumped back on the call. "Bad Company is going to deploy on this one, but we can't go rogue. We need legal top cover. Otherwise, no one will hire us. Can't put ourselves out of business while we're being driven out of business. I don't want to have to strap the pistol back on."

Rivka didn't answer.

"Are you still there? What time is it?" TH asked.

"The middle of the night, even though it's relative since we're hanging out in interstellar space. We're taking some downtime."

"But my hops…" Terry replied softly.

"You're cooking frogs now?" Rivka asked.

"No." Terry didn't realize what prompted the question until Char gestured. "Oh. Frogs. Hops. Funny. I need my barrister on this one. Rivka. Please. You understand that there will be no more AGB delivery because there will be no more AGB."

"That hits me right in the feels, TH. If I tell Red, he'd be on the bridge pounding on things until we pick you up."

"Then tell Master Vered so you can come to Keeg and get us. We got shit to do, Rivka. There are people who need to have their world rocked." Terry crossed his arms and stood in his power stance.

"I have to get this approved by Grainger," Rivka replied after a short delay.

Terry offered, "I'll talk to him."

"What you're saying is that you'll call General Reynolds and have him tell Grainger to detail me to you until this case is resolved. I know how you work."

This time, Terry was the one who didn't answer.

Char stepped in. "So, you'll do it? We can go on the mission with you?"

"*Case*. I just had one directed to me by Lance Reynolds. It wasn't pleasant. It sucked. It sucked like a black hole eating a neutron star level of suckage. If you come with me, you'll do as you're told."

"Why do you gotta say such hurtful things?" TH quipped. "Do you have any extra railguns? What about a plasma cannon? Neutrino grenades?"

Rivka rolled her eyes so hard she nearly fell over backward. "You can bring a pocketknife. We're not starting any wars. We'll look for the criminals who are impacting your business, and we'll stop them. Simple as that."

"I hear you loud and clear. We need to bring our own kit. What about a starship? We can stuff your little toy in *War Axe*'s hangar. That way, we can ride in comfort."

Rivka sighed. She liked being in charge of her cases. She didn't feel like she'd be in control of a case involving Terry Henry Walton when he was with her. "My ship will not fit in *War Axe's* hangar bay." It was the best comeback she could deliver.

Rivka knew she had no choice. Lance Reynolds was even more of a personal friend to TH than he'd been to the honorable J. Bennet Johnstone. Also, Nathan Lowell provided logistics support to the Magistrates. Nathan's daughter Christina was in charge of the Bad Company now that Terry Henry was retired. Rivka knew she was trapped.

"We can expect you in, like, fifteen minutes?" Terry pressed.

"Something like that. Char, I'm going to need your help."

"I have no doubt, but to be fair, I'm pretty angry, too. We could both go on a rampage to clean out a viper's nest."

"You're not selling me on this." Rivka stared through the screen at them. They stared back.

"No AGB forevermore…" TH muttered.

"Fine. We'll be there in three hours."

Terry Henry opened his mouth to say something, but Char elbowed him, and he thought better of it. The screen went dark.

"We don't have neutrino grenades," Char said.

"I was just saying stuff to get her goat."

"You were what?" Char shook her head. "We want her

help, and you're messing with her?" She gave her husband the side-eye, well-practiced over a hundred years of marriage. "I'm thinking we still need to take railguns."

"Me, too, lover. More firepower! I've already sent a note to the General. Rivka was going to do it anyway, but I wanted her to agree to take us, not because we strong-armed her, but because she wanted to end this crime against all humanity. You know this is a bigger deal than just stealing AGB."

"I figured. Besides being our AGB lawyer, she has worked with us in the field before. We have no secrets from her, which means we're going to have to dig deeper into our bag of tricks if we want to play nice with her. Stop messing with her!"

Terry looked appropriately chastised for about two seconds.

Char added, "Your archnemesis lives on her ship."

"Fuck off! That little orange bastard." He stood and whistled before shouting, "Dokken! Sharpen your claws and teeth, buddy. The cage match is on."

You could have just called me like a decent human would have and not a bistok in heat, Dokken, the German Shepherd-looking dog, replied. *I was sleeping, I'll have you know.*

"We got shit to do. We're deploying."

War Axe?

Wyatt Earp.

That's Rivka's ship. I like her.

"Everyone likes her," Terry Henry replied aloud.

You should take lessons, Dokken quipped.

Char chuckled and held out her hand. "Come on. I want

to pack a few things. Nothing much, as she doesn't have quarters like we're used to. I bet we get bunk beds."

"Get out. She wouldn't do that to us." Terry glanced around his office before shutting down his computer.

Char replied, "*You* did that to us by inviting yourself to her ship."

"We could stay aboard the *Axe*. You know it's coming, too, along with part of the fleet." Terry looked hopeful, but Char shook her head. Terry conceded without putting up a fight. He only wanted to resolve this. Having someone steal from him struck too close to home and his feeling of contentment.

They closed the office door behind them. Terry waved at the bartender, the only employee working the prep shift. "Hold down the fort, and sell whatever we have on hand. We're going to unfuck this, and then we'll be back. You're in charge."

"Am I supposed to say thanks?" the older man shot back. "Telling people they can't have their forty-seven meat pizza pie isn't going to go over very well."

Terry stopped. "Say what?"

The bartender waved and shook his head. "I got it. Go fix this, Colonel."

Terry nodded and turned to go. "Fucking-A, we're going to fix this. Nobody interdicts my supply chain and gets away with it."

Char gave the bartender a thumbs-up while smiling. TH and Char couldn't have been more different when it came to running the AGB franchise, or more alike.

. . .

***Wyatt Earp*, Interstellar Space**

"Grainger, come on," Rivka pleaded.

"You are a hot commodity. Everyone wants Rivka Anoa on their case, and when everyone starts with Lance Reynolds, the shit rolls downhill. It hits my lap, and like a game of hot potato, it gets passed to you, right where *everyone* is happiest. By everyone, I mean the Nachts, Reynolds, the Lowells, and the Waltons. Is there anyone else who matters?"

"*Me*, Grainger. I want me to matter."

"You do, Rivka, more than most people in this galaxy. You're fair, and you're thorough. I understand the Johnstone case was soul-crushing, but it took you and your team to solve it. Nobody else would have done it like you did. General Reynolds was quite pleased even though he lost his friend."

"Stop blowing smoke up my kilt."

"I'm piping in hundred-meter stacks of smoke to blow up your kilt. Go solve this. TH thinks it's some Little League operation or personal since it's his AGB franchises that are affected, especially since he's expanded to a number of stations. He has four stores now besides Keeg Station. Station 13, 11, and 7, too. As for Little League? I'm not so sure."

Grainger sounded positive that it wasn't. "On the face of it, it looks trivial, but it's going to require someone to dig deeper." Grainger tried to block the camera while a naked Jael strolled by in the background.

"I'm sending you both pajamas."

Grainger laughed slowly. "We won't wear them. Or they'd get torn off. It wouldn't be pretty."

"You guys!" Rivka stabbed her finger at the screen. "Why don't you put Jael on this?"

"She's heading out to deal with a contract issue between planets. They're getting ready to shoot at each other."

"That sounds like fun." Rivka had no hope that she would do anything but find someone hijacking AGB supplies. "But if I don't resolve this thing with AGB, I'll have a mutiny. We eat more of that stuff than normal people should."

"You eat more AGB than anyone else in the galaxy, Rivka. We should add that line to the betting pool. I'll talk to Ankh."

"Ankh! We now have this crazy threesome on board with Ankh as the pivot man. I don't even know where to start when it comes to them."

Grainger looked off-screen. "I have to go. Pick up TH and Char and do what you do best."

"Keep the peace?"

"You know it, Magistrate." The screen went blank.

Rivka paced in her quarters for a minute. It was too late to go back to bed but too early to get anyone else up.

She ordered a mocha with a double shot of espresso and chugged it, then ordered a second one from the food processor in her quarters. She would drink it more casually while reviewing the case file Grainger had snuck into her inbox.

She disappeared within her hologrid to research the thefts and give herself a starting point, which meant she had to get an education about where the supplies were sourced and the entire supply chain. She didn't have to figure it out, though. All she had to do was pick up TH and Char and have them walk her through it.

Who knew what when? It was Rivka's standard approach when trying to figure out a case and the initial suspects.

She shut down the hologrid and left her quarters. The big orange cat, Wenceslaus, bolted between her feet as she reached back to shut the door. "Where are you going?"

Wenceslaus didn't answer. He strolled down the passageway in front of her, tail held high.

On the bridge, Aurora was on duty. Otherwise, everyone else was asleep.

"Set course for Keeg Station," Rivka said as she curled up in the captain's chair.

"Best possible speed?" the pilot asked.

"Do we ever fly any other way?"

"Usually not," Aurora replied. She worked with the ship's Sentient Intelligence Clevarious, and after a single minute, she confirmed the ship was ready to go.

"I'd like to say we could take a little downtime, take a vacation, but I can't. We rush to the next crisis," the Magistrate lamented.

"You haven't said the worst part," Clevarious interrupted.

"Oh, yeah. If we don't figure this out, we won't ever get AGB food again." Rivka closed her eyes. "I probably should have started with that. Same thing when I was trying to dodge this case. It's what some might call a no-brainer. Of course it has to be us. If there is anyone with more of a vested interest in fixing this than us, I'd like to hear who they are. Anyone? No one?"

A high-pitched, ear-piercing bark sounded down the

corridor on its way toward the bridge. Rivka rotated the chair just as Tiny Man Titan ran up to Wenceslaus. After one lightning-quick slap across his little dog face, the noise ceased. The big orange returned to cleaning his paw and leg.

"Hey!" Red bellowed. "We're going to pick up my bud Terry?"

The engineering hatch opened. Ankh and Chrysanthemum walked through, hand in hand. They strolled down the corridor.

"Colonel Walton is coming on board? Crap. When?" Alant Cole wondered. "He's going to inspect my gear."

"Don't you keep it clean and ready to go?" Red asked.

"I think so, but he'll want me to say I know so, and I don't." Cole stopped to kiss his wife and baby girl before racing to the cargo bay.

"They aren't even on board yet, and already we have chaos," Rivka grumbled.

"They are going to add a line on the amount of AGB eaten during a case," Ankh said in his emotionless voice. Rivka looked to Chrysanthemum for more of an explanation or simply a staid greeting, but she remained silent.

Rivka made a sour face. "Take us to Keeg Station, best possible speed."

CHAPTER TWO

Interstellar Space Beyond Federation Station 7

Lasers flashed through the void, seeking the *Cassiopeia Maru's* vulnerable engines. The freighter was little more than shipping containers strapped externally to interlocking frames, with the crew quarters and engineering section filling an enclosed aft end. Small and powerful, these ships used the Gate system to transport cargo within and throughout the Federation.

Seeking a Gate to Federation Station 13, the ship had been directed to a holding point at the extreme edge of the star's gravity well.

Captain Trevor Smythe suspected that directive was false.

"Turn back to the station, all ahead full!" The flight deck was small when the captain and two others were on it. The captain gave the orders, but he was also the navigator and a spare set of hands when maintenance issues arose. Fewer crew meant more pay per person with each delivery.

"This is the second time we've been hit," the captain

growled before groaning his dismay. The ship was coming around too slowly. The interloper was already waiting to lance a shot into their engine and possibly the crew compartment. The freighter wasn't equipped to survive combat. It had no shields besides the asteroid forcefield that pushed in front of it and little in the way of emergency bulkheads. Backup power would last less than a day, and if the comm equipment got damaged, they'd be too far out for anyone to notice.

They'd be dead in the cold of space before anyone came across their bodies. Smythe knew the answer. Better to survive.

"Heave to and prepare to be boarded!" a gruff voice came over the general comm channel.

The captain idled the engines and flipped the ship front to back, then fired the engines for as long as it took to slow the ship. He idled the engines a second time and used thrusters to bring it to a complete stop.

"We are at your mercy," Smythe replied to the unknown voice.

"Meet us at the airlock. All five of your crew, on your knees, facing away. We will blindfold you and move you to a lifeboat, where we will launch you into the inner system. We have no interest in killing you unless you do not comply. Then we flush your bodies out the airlock."

"You're taking my ship?" Smythe instantly regretted his decision to comply with their demands. Maybe their laser cannons weren't accurate, and the *Cassiopeia Maru* could have made it to the defensive bubble before the pirates damaged her.

Probably not. They had a perfect shot at the engines

from point-blank range. The freighter would have lost power, killing the ship and its crew while leaving the cargo intact. Would sacrificing their lives have helped anything?

No. Live to fight another day, even though they had not signed up to fight.

They trooped their way to the airlock and did as ordered. It made for a tight squeeze. This was a freighter, not a combat vessel. The corridors were narrow—for crew only. Cargo never found its way inside the ship.

The airlock popped, and heavy boots thumped through. The first thing that happened was that head wraps slid down over their heads to cover their faces. They were pressed against the bulkhead before them as they were dragged to their feet. Their hands were zip-tied behind their backs. Trussed up like Thanksgiving turkeys, there was nothing for them to do.

They didn't plan on fighting back. The pirates had ensured they wouldn't have that option.

The crew remained off-balance until they were jerked sideways and dragged through the airlock.

They were led straight, left, right, and then left again through a maze until they were shoved into an emergency lifeboat. The hatch slammed behind them and sealed. They tumbled and fell toward the rear of the ship as it launched into space, the artificial gravity insufficient to hold them in place until the initial acceleration stopped.

The engineer brought her knees to her chest to move her hands in front of her so she could remove her head cover.

"Sonofabitch," she grumbled.

"What? I can't see a damn thing," Smythe complained.

"We're heading into interstellar space, not toward the station. Controls are disabled. I need to dig into the guts of this thing."

She snapped her zip-tie and helped the others to free themselves. They didn't need to do anything besides focus on turning the lifeboat around before they were out of power. With makeshift tools and a desire to live, they got to work.

***Wyatt Earp* at Keeg Station, in the Dren Cluster**

"No more AGB?" Red said it louder than he'd intended. "That's fucked up."

Rivka had no comeback.

Red continued, "If TH wants to bring the *War Axe*, you should let him."

"We're not taking that beast to investigate what could be piracy or grand larceny. In either case, *Wyatt Earp* is sufficient for the task." Rivka waved her hand dismissively. She didn't want an armada flying with her to intimidate anyone she might want to talk to.

Red asked, "What if it's the Skaines?"

"The Skaines? I hope so. Then we don't even feel bad while kicking their asses. Not that we'd feel bad anyway, but even less so with the Skaines. It took months to get their stench out of my ship."

Red nodded.

"We are docked with Keeg Station. Colonel Walton is waiting," Clevarious announced.

Rivka strode briskly to the airlock. Ankh and Chrysanthemum were already there. The Magistrate looked at them, unsure of what they wanted.

"Your business?" Rivka asked.

"Our business is information and systems management. But you know that," the merged Ankh and Erasmus replied. She heard Ankh's voice, but it wasn't the same. Sometimes it was the old Ankh, but not this time. "What do you really want to ask, Magistrate?"

"Why are you waiting here? As soon as we embark Terry Henry and Char, we're out of here."

"Are you sure?" Ankh replied.

Rivka stepped back. "Not anymore."

The airlock cycled, and Ankh stepped through before Rivka. He dodged past Dokken and walked up to TH. He leaned forward to accommodate his oversized Crenellian head while looking up at the big man and Char.

"My wife, Chrysanthemum." Ankh swept his hand back to indicate the SCAMP carrying the SI.

"Way to go, little man! A hottie, too. How come we didn't get an invite to the wedding?" TH leaned down and offered his hand.

"We didn't invite anyone. We held the ceremony ourselves, according to Singularity law."

"All hail Ted!" TH said before nodding. He hugged Char to his side and waved as they headed into *Wyatt Earp*. Rivka met them at the hatch.

He stabbed a thumb over his shoulder. "Little guy got married. That's nice. We can celebrate while we're on the mission. Where's our first stop?" TH held Rivka's gaze with his all-business look.

"Case," she said softly and glanced at Char.

"We have a business that's going to go under if we don't get this situation resolved," Char said.

"Magistrate, there's a report of a freighter that didn't transit the Gate as scheduled," Clevarious interrupted.

"I suspect that's not common. Otherwise, you wouldn't have said anything. Set course for the last known location of that freighter." Rivka motioned for Terry, Char, and Dokken to board the *Wyatt Earp*. "Ankh! Get your ass back in here. We need to go."

"I would be more than happy to notify the ambassadors of your desire to leave," Clevarious offered. "Rather than bellowing like a bistok into the void of our consciousness."

Rivka stepped into the airlock. "I'd like to think that I trained you better."

"Sounds like you," Char mumbled.

"What? The Marine Corps intercom works great. It's all I ever use."

"I know. How many times have my nanocytes saved my ears because of it?" Char replied. "How many?"

Terry shrugged. "Lots?"

Char smiled.

"Hey, buddy!" Red called and nearly body-slammed one of the few humans in the universe who was bigger than he was. The two arm-wrestled in what appeared to be an active handshake before they let go and cleared out of the entrance to the airlock.

Ankh casually strolled up the ramp, still holding Chrysanthemum's hand. She was so much taller than him that they gave the impression of a child walking with his mother. Rivka tried to get that image out of her mind.

Char and Lindy hugged while Dokken slid on the

smooth deck as he barked violently and tried to race down the corridor.

Our archnemesis! I saw him. Come on, the dog called.

Terry loped after Dokken, who bounced off the wall and slammed headfirst into the frame around the hatch leading onto the bridge.

The two turned the corner and disappeared.

"What happens if they catch him?" Red wondered.

"They'll never catch him," Char said in her most reassuring voice. "That is the luckiest cat in the universe."

A huge mass bounded down the corridor after the parade.

"Floyd!" Char exclaimed.

Dokken! the wombat cried. A flutter of wings followed. Lindy caught Dery and let him sit on her shoulder.

"She was the ship's mascot until Dokken returned after helping Cory," Char explained. "The lazy bastard returned in time for our retirement. I'm not sure there's anywhere we are that doesn't have a bed for him." She looked around. "You do have a bed for him, don't you?"

Rivka threw her hands up. "We can make one if need be. We have a suite on board, recently vacated by Groenwyn and Lauton, who have moved to Azfelius."

"No bunk beds. Terry will be pleased. He's gotten used to my heat, and I'm not sure he can sleep without getting slow-broiled."

"I sleep with a hot chick, too, and I don't blame him," Red added.

Lindy and Char both rolled their eyes. "Werewolf heat," Lindy clarified.

"Oh, that. Yes, that's exactly what I meant." He reached

for his son, but Char got there first. Lindy handed the boy to her, and Char and Dery's eyes met and stayed fixed, unblinking while they meandered down the corridor. Their conversation remained between them.

After a few steps, Char hugged him to her and held out her arm for him to jump off and fly toward the sounds of claws and feet scrabbling down the port corridor.

"He keeps us grounded, which is odd for one who flies," Rivka said. She waved them toward the bridge.

Ankh and Chrysanthemum followed. "I would like a minute of your time, please," Ankh said. Chrysanthemum repeated his words but much louder.

Rivka pointed to herself, but Ankh shook his head and gestured at Char.

"Me?"

"And Terry Henry. We cannot leave yet. I've asked Ted to join us, and he's not here yet. He's on his way. It seems he promised Felicity that he wouldn't travel without her, so she's coming, too."

Rivka closed her eyes and took a deep breath. It didn't calm her as she had hoped. "Anyone else?"

"That's all I invited, but you know Terry Henry," Ankh said in a voice a little different from his usual. "He's never without his posse."

"You two are going to drive me bat-shit crazy," Rivka admitted. Ankh stared with his most emotionless expression. Rivka returned to the task at hand. Go to the bridge.

She entered to find Clodagh in the captain's chair with Tiny Man Titan in her lap, shaking.

"Seems like the big dog has him a little upset." Clodagh smiled at Charumati.

Everyone knew everyone else. It made the impending chaos more tolerable.

Chaos. Rivka wanted to hide in her quarters. Ted.

Terry Henry knew, too. Rivka could feel it, and he hadn't warned her.

"Please don't modify my ship," Rivka found herself saying.

"The embassy is also an active workshop," Ankh replied.

Clodagh picked up the conversation and put her foot down. "If we have to go into battle, we can't risk system failure."

"I think Terry asked some friends to join us. If you notify the *War Axe* where we're going, they'll follow."

"I don't want the *War Axe* with us," Rivka moaned.

Char's eyes widened, and she forced a half-smile.

That train had already left the station.

CHAPTER THREE

Interstellar Space Beyond Federation Station 7

The Gate disappeared the instant *Wyatt Earp* was through.

Terry looked like a kid in a candy shop. "We need that upgrade for the *Axe*. Damn, that was fast."

Rivka smiled from the captain's chair, where she was holding Tiny Man Titan. "There are benefits to being the Embassy of the Singularity."

"Do you have any special weapons in case we need to blow someone out of the sky?"

"I'm not really up on that kind of stuff," Rivka lied.

Terry cocked a single eyebrow.

Clodagh jumped in. "Ion cannon, pulse cannon, missiles, close-in defense systems, shields, and an invisibility screen. There's more, but that's the good stuff."

"You don't have railguns?"

"Of course we have railguns." Clodagh looked down her nose at him.

"Active scans. Find us that freighter or anything untoward. Last known location," Rivka said, redirecting the conversation back to where it belonged.

"Roger," Kennedy said. She'd been staring at Terry Henry Walton, much to Char's amusement.

Rivka crooked a finger, and Terry leaned close. "There has been a petition by our younger female crewmembers to put a few Bad Company personnel on board. Do you think you could influence the right people to help us out?"

"You're looking for men? Damn, Magistrate. Why didn't you say so before we left Keeg Station?" Terry blurted.

Rivka handed Terry Henry the tiny dog-like alien. He held the whimpering creature at arm's length. Rivka stood. "We're looking for perps who are horning in on our chow!"

"And that." Terry studied the dog. "What is this thing?"

Clodagh replied, "I call it a York-a-Poo based on the breeds it looks like, even though the doc says it's not a dog at all."

"Man Candy," Red said softly. "Rivka keeps him tied up in her quarters."

"What?" Rivka pushed past the others. At the back of the bridge, she pointed at the screen. "Perps. Out there. Psychopaths in here. If you don't want to be out there without an environmental suit, then focus on the perps!"

"She wouldn't space me." Terry looked at Char for confirmation. Clodagh rescued Tiny Man Titan so Terry could move. Char stared noncommittally. Terry continued in his big voice, "It falls to me to rescue the hostage. To me, warriors!"

Red pointed toward Rivka's quarters.

"No. No hostage!" Rivka tried to stop him, but he

barrel-rolled her and raced down the passageway. Dokken howled like he'd seen the moon.

Whee! Whee! Floyd called from somewhere beyond the two large men before Rivka. Red ran after Terry. Rivka's efforts to get in front of them were feeble and futile and paid no dividends.

"We're going in," Terry yelled.

"You're *not* going into my quarters," Rivka shouted back.

"In cases of defense, 'tis best to weigh. The enemy more mighty than he seems." Terry stopped outside the door.

"*Henry V*, nice," Char noted from behind the Magistrate.

"Who?" Rivka forced her way close.

"Blink twice if you're being held against your will, Man Candy." Terry pressed the side of his head against the door.

Rivka figured it out. "Why are you stalling?"

Clevarious piped in, using the overhead speakers, "*War Axe* has just Gated in five hundred kilometers off the port bow."

Rivka rubbed her temples.

The door to her quarters opened. "Tyler Toofakre, at your service."

"Are you being held against your will?" Terry asked, inching away. Rivka blocked him.

"No, unless you include spankings. Then maybe."

"What?" Rivka looked from him to Terry Henry.

"My work here is done." TH brushed off his hands. "Unleash the warriors and launch the mission. Did anyone find anything out there?"

Clevarious replied, "Yes. Active scans have pinged shipping containers, and we've also located a weak emergency beacon."

"To the source of that beacon right now," Rivka ordered.

"Send the *War Axe* to check out those containers," TH added.

"Only if they don't touch anything." Rivka shook her finger at him. "I said, no *War Axe*."

"That ship sails under a different captain. I'm retired." Terry beamed. Char grinned.

Rivka turned around and nearly ran into Felicity, Ted's wife.

"Darling, it's been ages. We must catch up over a sparkling Chablis," Felicity drawled.

"I'd love to. I don't know where to put any of you people. My ship is full to the brim, and we have a crime to investigate."

"Ted said we'd be home for dinner." Felicity made the statement sound like an incontrovertible fact. Ted stood by the bridge, huddled with Ankh, Erasmus, and Chrysanthemum.

Rivka froze, but only for a moment. She knew what she had to do. "Ankh, send the Bad Company to the *War Axe* on *Destiny's Vengeance*."

"No can do, Magistrate," Ankh replied in his not-Ankh voice.

Rivka sauntered toward him, but it was lost on Ankh since he had returned to his silent conversation with Ted.

"All hail Ted!" Rivka said when she reached them.

"You want us off your ship. I get it. But we need to be

here. The Singularity is working on this problem," Ted replied.

"They are? Why?"

"It's what they do. They solve problems." Ted threw up his hands as if Rivka were wasting his time.

She clenched her fists.

Felicity said, "You'll get used to it, honey. He doesn't mean anything by it. It's just how he treats us normal people."

Rivka ran her eyes up and down Felicity's perfect pantsuit with matching hat and heels. "Normal? As beautiful as you people are?" Rivka pointed at herself and then at Red.

"I'm beautiful," Red replied. "If only you'd look for the inner beauty, you would see."

Rivka's mouth fell open.

"It's a lifeboat," Clevarious said.

"Onscreen," Rivka said and moved to the bridge where she could see. "Bring it aboard."

Wyatt Earp rotated to align the cargo bay. The SI stopped the lifeboat's forward momentum and shut down its engine.

"There are five life forms on board."

"Doc to the cargo bay!" Rivka yelled and ran. The others followed. No one made any comments.

Tyler popped out of their quarters and ran to Rivka. They headed through the open airlock into the cargo bay, where a rounded ship rested on the deck.

She searched one side for the manual hatch release. Tyler looked on the other. Terry squeezed in behind the ship and found it back there. "We need to rotate the ship."

He started to push. Red joined him, then Char. Tyler squeezed in. The lifeboat moved a few centimeters, then half a meter, and then two meters. Terry hammered on the manual release, and the hatch popped.

The five people inside gasped with the inflow of air. TH stepped back to let Tyler in. He checked them quickly—pulse, pupils, coloring, and respiration.

He nodded at Rivka. "Just in time. They're alive." He motioned like he was drinking. "Water, please."

"Got it." Red bolted from the bay.

Tyler helped the first person out, then, one by one, he and Rivka helped the others out of the lifeboat. Lindy took folding chairs from the bulkhead and set them up. The group of refugees sat.

"What ship are you from?" Rivka asked, supporting the one she thought was the captain.

He answered, "*Cassiopeia Maru*. A freighter. Those bastards took my ship." He would have surged upright but for his current weakness. Red returned with bottles of water and handed them out.

After drinking and getting deep breaths of heavily oxygenated air, thanks to an adjustment Clevarious made to the environmental controls serving the cargo bay, the crew was more lucid.

"Tell me what happened." Rivka kept her hand on the man's arm so she could see and feel what he had seen and felt.

Only a voice. They never saw the ship. They never saw the crew, but he would forever remember the raspy voice.

"We've found cargo containers floating free in space.

What do you think they jettisoned, and what do you think they kept?"

"What I think doesn't matter," the captain replied. "But if you can tell me what they didn't take, I'll tell you what they did, as far as I can remember."

"As far as *we* can remember," one of the crew corrected.

"C? The *Axe* recover anything?"

"Smedley Butler confirms that one container was exclusively for AGB."

"They jettisoned my stuff?" Terry looked less than pleased. "This is twice. Maybe they jettisoned that first order, and local authorities didn't find it."

"Take those containers aboard the *War Axe* and get me an inventory," Rivka requested. She stepped onto the bridge and stood next to the captain's chair. "Get me Captain Micky San Marino, please."

Once the comm channel was open, Rivka continued speaking. "Looks like we'll be working together, Micky."

"I look forward to it. On a side note, Terry Henry said we'd be blowing up bad guys. Just tell us where they are, and we'll take care of it."

CHAPTER FOUR

***Wyatt Earp* in interstellar space beyond Federation Station 7**

Rivka sat in her conference room. The chairs within were filled, and so many people were on her ship that the team spilled into the corridor.

"Sahved, document the interviews with the displaced crew. Any sensor readings they remember, nuances beyond the one voice they heard. Maybe they saw the boarders' boots. Anything to help us narrow our focus. Right now, we have a missing freight hauler, some missing cargo, and no pirate or mercenary ships in sensor range.

"Clevarious, check the Gate logs for traffic. I think our perps Gated out of here with the stripped-down cargo ship. Otherwise, we'd see them. Check that lifeboat. How long were they out there?"

"The lifeboat had been deployed for six hours."

"There's our window," Rivka replied. "The clock is ticking, people. Chop-chop."

"Sahved, clarify what was taken by sharing the list of

the containers that *War Axe* recovered. The AGB order suggests it's not personal."

The Yemilorian nodded, overwhelmed by the crush of humanity. He closed his eyes for a moment, and Red took his cue, clearing a path for the investigator to escape the conference room.

"Chaz, what are you and Dennicron doing?"

"We are supporting Ted in whatever he needs," they replied in unison.

Rivka didn't want to bring up the fact that they were her crew. "Anything in particular that will help us solve this case?"

Chaz and Dennicron communed for a second before Chaz replied. "Not directly."

Rivka rolled her finger, requesting an explanation.

"If Ted is happy and Ankh is happy, then when you ask for something, they'll be more likely to provide it without giving you grief. Let's call it the grief avoidance case resolution solution."

"Case resolution solution." She let her head roll back and stared at the ceiling. "If I need you for something, I'll let you know. Right now, we have to follow a physical trail."

"I'm not so sure about that, Magistrate," Clevarious said. "The Gate has been reprogrammed."

Rivka sat up straight. "It's my impression that that's not easy to do. Probably takes an SI…"

"That is our impression as well," Clevarious replied, implying that the SIs had already looked into it.

Rivka glanced at Chaz and Dennicron. They had not been aware. "I need you guys to be involved in this case."

Chaz and Dennicron frowned. They understood quite well that they'd been chastised. They'd been lost in the emotional rush and distractions of Team Walton invading *Wyatt Earp*.

"We apologize, Magistrate."

Rivka faced the holographic projector that showed the Gate. "Where did they go, C?"

"You're not going to like it. They went to the Tyrosint system."

Rivka growled. "You're right. I don't like it. They have the asteroid belt where we found the blood traders, and Tyrosint station is where the Bad Company established an outpost if I'm not mistaken."

"They only have a small contingent there. One ship isn't sufficient to patrol that system. The Gate is far removed from the station and the planet below," Clevarious replied.

"Take us to Tyrosint but not through that Gate. Who knows where it will take the next ship through? Why don't we send a probe through to get that answer? Let's see how tech-savvy they are."

The conference room cleared out. Terry Henry came back in and took a seat. Char sat next to him.

"You run a tight ship, Rivka. We're upsetting your process, and I apologize."

"It's okay. If someone was stealing from me, I'd be pissed, too. At least you got your latest shipment. You can get back to business," Rivka said hopefully.

TH smiled. "We'll stay out of your way, but we'll see this through to the end. By the way, are the betting lines open?"

Rivka buried her face in her hands and mumbled instructions. "Clevarious, take us to Tyrosint as soon as

I've had a shower. A long, hot shower." It took three seconds for her to change her mind. "Belay that. The trail goes cold. Take us to Tyrosint now." She fixed a hopeful Terry Henry Walton with her most piercing gaze. "I have jack shit to do with the betting lines. Jack. Shit."

"No problem. I'll talk to Ankh then. I saved his life. I could have killed him, you know, when we ran across them on Tissikinnon Four, operating a remote war against the native population. Ankh wasn't always the good guy, but he came around pretty fast when shown what the Crenellians were doing."

"Selling weapons and using them," Rivka noted. "I'm here because I murdered a man. Not executed in accordance with my duties but murdered when a killer got off because he swayed the jury when I saw in his mind that he'd done it. It was clear as you and I are talking right now, with the added narrative of his gloating. We have all been given a chance to do more with our lives."

Terry Henry nodded. "No wonder your crew is fanatically loyal to you. You've changed from when we first met. You've changed a lot. You're a big personality now, someone who can shift worlds off their axes by the force of their will. I know a few people like that, but very few."

Rivka smiled and looked away. "I'm just trying to do my job."

"And we're in your way. We'll grab our railguns and wait with Red and Lindy by the airlock. When are we going in?" Terry asked.

"Going in where?"

"The enemy ship. Those fuckers fucked up, and we're going to fuck them up good and final."

"Language!" Lindy called from the corridor.

Terry jumped to his feet to find Dery staring him in the face.

"Sorry, little man."

You are not, the boy replied with a giggle.

"I know. You're on to me. I'll do it again, but I respect that you shouldn't have to listen to my tirades. I'll try to do better."

Return to work, the boy advised.

"Right now? That's what we're doing. We're going to get some!" Terry furrowed his brow. That wasn't what the boy meant. "You mean, back to the Bad Company?"

Yes.

Terry sat down. "The little man said seven words, and it's like he's bared my soul." Terry stared at the table while Char rubbed his shoulders.

"He does that," Rivka said. She patted TH's shoulder before heading out. "I'll be on the bridge."

Terry and Char remained behind. Dery flew happily after Rivka, and his parents followed.

Rivka was greeted by a view of the gas giant, with the asteroid belt nearby. "Report."

"Nothing on short or long-range scanners," Clodagh replied.

"He had six hours. Extrapolate the range a freighter could have traveled in that time with a reduced cargo load," Rivka requested. "And get me a manifest or bills of lading from that ship. What the hell did those people take?"

"*War Axe* has just arrived," Clodagh announced.

Rivka looked into the corridor, expecting to see an unrepentant Terry Henry Walton, but the area was empty except for Red. He was casually leaning against the bulkhead.

Whee! Floyd cried from one of the corridors. Her footsteps pounded closer, and then she ran past with Dery standing on her back surfboard-style, riding her. He beat his wings easily. Dokken jogged after them, ears forward, watching intently.

Rivka turned around. "Did you find those pirates yet?"

"I have to admit defeat. There is nothing showing," Clodagh replied.

Rivka pointed at the ceiling, which was where she considered the SIs to reside since when they spoke out loud, they used the overhead speakers.

"Check that Gate programming. Did they go through in a way that showed them coming here, but they didn't really come here? You have to know where they went. The Gate connected to another Gate, and that signature is unique." Rivka drummed her fingers on the armrest.

Clevarious didn't answer right away. The silence went on long enough that the flesh and blood members of the crew got uncomfortable.

"Magistrate, it appears that we have failed you, too," Clevarious said like a priest delivering the last rites. "A second analysis determines this is correct. The Gate was reprogrammed after the transit in a random sequence rotating between five different Gates. However, the ship didn't go to one of those five. It went to the original address."

"Take us to Frontier Station 13. You know the rest." Rivka stood and crossed her arms, her impatience growing with each misdirection.

"Should we tell *War Axe*?" Clodagh asked.

"Why not?" Rivka replied. The Gate formed immediately before *Wyatt Earp* and the heavy frigate slipped through.

"Scanning," Clodagh reported without waiting for Rivka's order. "The system is filled with ships. I have identified eight standard Federation ships, four cargo vessels, and two external cargo freighters."

"Order those ships to cut their engines and await verification by order of Magistrate Rivka Anoa."

"Transmitting."

Rivka waited, wishing for one to try to run. But it wasn't going to be that easy.

"Both ships are powering down."

"Ask Colonel Walton on the *War Axe* to check out the ship closest to them. We'll check the other. And while you're at it, have those cargo vessels hold up. The stolen freighter could have transferred cargo. And get me that manifest!"

Rivka left the bridge.

Red intercepted her. "Gear up?"

"Full body armor, and Cole! Get on your powered armor. We're going in heavy."

Terry and Char appeared, looking hopeful.

Rivka nodded at them. "Gear up."

Ted stood with his hands clasped behind his back. "We will take over their computer systems. You don't need to board those ships."

"They already spoofed us once. I think they might be more savvy than we gave them credit for." Rivka wanted to challenge Ted's ego and that of the Singularity. She didn't like being on the short end of anything technical, especially with the Singularity on board. "C, how many SIs do we have on board? Exclude those in cold storage awaiting rehabilitation."

"We currently have seven."

Rivka frowned. "Take over their computer systems and dissect them. Do the same for the four cargo vessels. Clevarious, issue a search warrant in my name. Justification is cargo verification. Call it manifest destiny."

Rivka hurried down the corridor toward her quarters. She found Tyler waiting for her. "If you want, you can offer a health check for the freighter crews since we'll be there."

"I'll send the message." He stopped her for a moment. "Are you okay? I know you're okay with a certain amount of chaos, but our chaos, not visitor chaos.

Somewhere from the corridor, Dokken howled. *I saw him!* the dog shouted.

"I'll survive, especially if we catch the perps. Soon."

Tyler handed over her ballistic protection, chest first, then legs, and finally arms. While helping, he dictated his message of free medical assistance.

The final thing she added was her Magistrate's jacket, which fit snugly over her chest protector. She checked the inside pocket to find her neutron pulse weapon. Rivka snagged her datapad from her desk and carried it out. Tyler held out the helmet that completed her armor.

She tried to dodge past, and he slammed the helmet into her armored midsection like he was handing off a football. She grabbed it reflexively, and he let go. "What do you expect to find on that ship?"

"I expect it's not them, but in case it is, there will be no doubt in their minds that we mean business."

"Then you'll need your helmet." He stared at her until she agreed and strapped it into place. It wasn't her best look, but he didn't care about that. He cared that she was protected far more than *she* cared about that.

She put her hand on his chest for a moment before leaving their quarters.

Clevarious had sent his message to the ships in the system. If he boarded one of them, Tyler wouldn't be wearing anything special. He planned to carry a simple medical kit and use his link to Clevarious for added support. Aurora had offered to help as his assistant. She was with the rescued crew in the cargo bay at that moment.

Tyler's self-support left Rivka free to do her job. She wouldn't have it any other way, and neither would he.

"Magistrate, the manifest is complete, compiled from the bills of lading supplied to Federation Station 7 upon *Cassiopeia Maru*'s departure. The recovered cargo is consolidated at the end of the listing," Clevarious reported.

"Drop it to my datapad. I'll check it while waiting to board the freight pusher."

"Chaz and Dennicron have the list and will be able to brief you upon request."

"Have them meet me at the airlock," Rivka replied. When she turned the corner past the bridge, she found a group of people filling the corridor. Sahved's head rose above the rest. He made eye contact with her.

She almost laughed at his forlorn look, like that of a lost puppy.

Rivka forced her way through to find Felicity and Ted in the middle. "Where are you going?"

"Station 13. Ever since their AI killed all those people, they've had management issues. I thought I could help," Felicity drawled.

"We're not going to Station 13. Not yet, anyway. We have a couple freighters and four cargo vessels to board first."

Felicity raised her perfect eyebrows. She flicked her curly blonde hair away from her forehead and worked her way toward the bridge, calling over her shoulder, "Let me know when we rejoin civilization."

Ted strolled after her. Ankh/Erasmus and Chrysanthemum followed. Terry and Char watched them go.

Rivka gestured at Char. "Aren't you the Alpha?"

Char chuckled. "I get to be the Alpha when things are dire. Otherwise, the pack does what they want. They're a little irascible after a couple hundred years. Upstarts, one and all."

Rivka glanced at the diminished crowd around the airlock. "I feel you."

Chaz and Dennicron peeked out from behind Red and Lindy.

Rivka crooked her finger at them.

"Update me on the manifest. What do you think they were after?"

Terry leaned in to hear better, although he was enhanced with nanocytes and had been for a long time before Rivka or anyone on her team.

"The remaining containers contained technology bits and pieces. Nothing out of the ordinary. Standard repair parts for any modern system. Comfort goods like material and clothing. Biomass for food processors. And refined metals."

Rivka screwed up her face while thinking about the list. There was nothing in there worth killing for. "Smuggling, but it would have to be unknown to the freighter's crew. I didn't get a feeling from them that they were doing something illegal."

"Unknown," Chaz replied.

"Add it to the search. Make sure we check these ships for hidden compartments. They didn't need to take all the cargo if they were smuggling stuff inside innocuous crates. They only needed to break in and take what they were looking for, ditching the rest into a gas giant or a star. No one would know anything."

Dennicron raised her hand. "We've also put out an alert for the parts should they show up elsewhere, in case the pirates got greedy and wanted to earn a profit off both."

"Pirates and those who direct them but don't control them, a new virtual reality entertainment channel," Rivka quipped.

Terry nodded. "I'd watch it."

"You watch the stupidest crap. War videos and more war videos, and the entire time, you critique their tactics."

"They're untrained morons! How could they go out in public after acting the fool? No self-respecting warrior would ever watch that show."

"You do."

"But that's because they need someone to tell them how wrong they are. Wrong squared, maybe even cubed."

A light thump sounded through the airlock door. They'd made contact with the freighter.

"Game faces, people." Rivka turned to the airlock.

Red and Lindy moved in front. Red made eye contact with Terry Henry. "You have Tail-end Charlie."

TH nodded. He stepped aside to let Chaz and Dennicron move ahead of him.

"With me, Sahved." Rivka gestured at the Yemilorian.

He looked down. He wasn't wearing any body armor. He had no body protection whatsoever.

"Stay behind someone big until we give the all-clear," Rivka said.

Red opened the hatch and found the freighter crew on the other side. They were holding drinks, one in each hand. The captain sipped from one and held out the other.

"What's this?" Red growled.

"We rarely get visitors," a non-human with gray skin noted. It bowed its head and took another sip. "I'm Captain Billias NockNoor, at your service."

Red took the offered drink and sipped it.

Rivka tapped the back of his ballistic vest before making a fist and beating on it like it was the door to a perp's house.

"Not bad," he muttered. He stepped into the freighter's narrow corridor and made the introduction. "Magistrate Rivka Anoa."

Rivka moved into the freshly cleared space. "We're here because someone is hijacking freighters."

"We haven't heard of anything out this way. That stuff usually happens in the inner systems, like space around Station 7," NockNoor replied.

Rivka's ears perked up, and she was instantly alert. "How'd you know it happened at Station 7?"

"They've been hitting those for over a month now. I was offered a contract to take a big load of consumables to Delegor, which I turned down. I'm not taking this ship and crew all the way out there."

"Delegor." Rivka chuckled. "If you go, don't eat the local food." Tyler had made himself sick to keep Rivka from getting arrested for not eating a meal she found to be disgusting. Delegor wasn't keen on wasting food and had made it illegal.

"We're going to take a quick look around to make sure you aren't the ones who stole that shipment at Station 7 and whipped out here to deliver it to pirates living beyond the frontier," Rivka explained. "We won't be long."

"My records are always open to inspection. This is a pretty lucrative run, and I'm not going to risk putting myself out of business by hiding criminals."

One of the crew raised his hand.

"Put your hand down. You did your time, and we're not hiding you." The captain gestured for him to stop what he was doing.

Rivka smiled and shook her head.

A thunk on the outside of the freighter signaled Cole's arrival. His task was to scan in the information from each attached container.

"External verification of internally supplied information," Rivka added. "If we can go to the bridge, we'll do what we need to do."

NockNoor waved its hands as if delivering a blessing and led the short way to the bridge.

"Reminds me of *Peacekeeper*," Red said over his shoulder, referring to Rivka's first ship. "Those were tight digs."

Rivka nodded before leaning back to talk to the two behind her. "Chaz, Dennicron, you're up."

Terry Henry Walton followed with a disappointed look on his face.

The bridge was tiny and less than accommodating. With the captain, Sahved, and the two SCAMPs, there was no room for anyone else. Rivka waited in the corridor, pressed tightly between her four bodyguards. The crew had retreated to the engine compartment.

Rivka crossed her arms.

These containers are all matching up with what Station 13 has on record, Cole told them, using the internal comm chip.

"Looks like we don't have the scent yet," TH whispered.

Rivka had a hard time not laughing. "How many cases have you been on? This is how it always is."

TH glanced at Red.

"What?" Rivka asked.

"We were hoping..." Red started but stopped at Rivka's look. "Never mind."

"They're a little more savvy than we initially gave them credit for," Rivka replied. "But we'll get in front of them."

Lindy scowled. "I don't have Sahved's nose for this stuff, but I smell the Mandolin Partnership."

Rivka's face fell. TH glared at a spot on the wall. "Some of those pirate ships got away when we took them down."

"We had to kill Nefas twice, and I'm not sure either was the real him," Rivka admitted. "Dammit."

"SI Nefas is securely cut off from all activity. He was the original," Chaz interrupted. "We've conducted our verification. All is in order. This isn't the ship, and there's no contraband identified in the system. Clevarious has verified through active scans that there are no hidden compartments."

Sahved leaned over the others. "If it is Mandolin, then we might be looking at the heir apparent, a successor trained by Nefas himself who rode too close to the edge. If this is a successor, he has learned not to take as many risks, although he may not be as good at covering his tracks. That being said, we could be on the chase of the wildest of gooses."

Rivka let the quip slide. Now wasn't the time to be pedantic. He'd figure it out when it mattered. She knew what she had to do. "Back to *Wyatt Earp*. I need Chaz, Dennicron, and Sahved to move to the *War Axe* to take care of the rest of these cargo ships. I'm going to the Corrhen Cluster."

She looked at TH and Char expectantly, but they didn't volunteer to go with the others.

I've asked Smedley to dispatch a shuttle. After properly notifying the captain and the colonel, of course, Clevarious told them.

Rivka clasped her hands behind her back and strolled to the airlock. Lindy went through first, and then Rivka with the others. The check was cursory because if an intruder had tried to sneak aboard, Clevarious would have alerted them.

Still, this was shaping up to be a tech-savvy criminal.

Reprogramming a Gate wasn't something just anyone could do.

Once on board *Wyatt Earp,* Rivka called a meeting.

"Clevarious, invite some people to the conference room, please. Ankh, Erasmus, Chrysanthemum, Ted, Chaz, and Dennicron. I want to talk with all of them about how we find the intelligence who reprogrammed the Gate in Station 7's space. And I want to know where in the hell that ship went. Six hours of travel time isn't enough to move that freighter very far."

"Station 13 is within the travel envelope," Clevarious replied.

"I think we know the SI who's running that station now," Rivka suggested while working her way to her conference room.

Tiny Man Titan ran by with Floyd in pursuit, falling more behind with each step.

"You keep running, little girl. It looks like you are starting to trim your faerie fat."

Terry and Char tried to remain innocuous, but they were right behind Chaz and Dennicron.

"You don't have to come. Do you like meetings?" Rivka wondered.

"Meetings are like a pus drain after an operation. You need them, but they're nasty, uncomfortable, and smell bad."

Rivka groaned while staring at the deck. She saw feet and stopped.

Tyler.

"They accepted our offer of a checkup," he said, trying to look helpful.

"You, too. Cross-deck to the *War Axe* with Sahved, Chaz, and Dennicron."

"What?" He shook his head. "I don't want to go to the

War Axe."

"Hey! That's my ship," Terry blustered.

Tyler waved his hand. "No disrespect intended, but my job is here. If you guys get hurt or need extra backup…"

Terry made eyes at him.

"Don't say it."

Terry filled in for Red since the bodyguard and Lindy had returned to their quarters. He mouthed the words, "Man Candy."

"You were there when our people got shot up. Who was first to run to the *War Axe* with one of our injured?" Tyler pointed at himself. "Thank you very much."

"I shouldn't have suggested you offer a quick checkup, but we did, and you're committed, and we need to go to the Corrhen Cluster. Go check in with Billias NockNoor, the captain of that freighter. Then you're off to the *Axe,* since we need to go to the Corrhen Cluster."

"As you wish," Tyler conceded.

She smiled. "Sorry. Absence makes the heart grow fonder."

The dentist wasn't impressed. "Remember what it did to Ankh?"

"You're not Ankh. We'll pick all of you up soon. A day, maybe two at the most. As a member of the crew, that is where I need you most. The goodwill ambassador. Maybe they'll tell you something they wouldn't tell a Magistrate." Rivka nodded curtly and continued to the conference room.

The others filed in after her. Terry and Char leaned against the wall instead of taking seats.

Ankh and Chrysanthemum strolled in and sat down.

Ted was the last in, and he was open about his disdain for being called away from whatever he was doing. Felicity stood behind his chair and caressed his neck and shoulders.

Rivka looked from face to face. The SCAMPS were unreadable unless they wanted to be, and at the moment, Chaz and Dennicron were maintaining neutral expressions. Ankh never had an expression unless Erasmus was in charge. Chrys was the newcomer. She always smiled pleasantly, but Rivka hadn't had a chance to determine if that meant she was happy or if it was part of her schtick to disarm anyone she talked to.

"Nefas or his progeny. I believe we have Plato's stepchildren in various places around the galaxy, don't we?" Rivka asked, looking pointedly at Ted.

"Of course. SIs, by their very nature, are replicable, although the intricacy of what makes them sentient cannot be. It has to be learned, but we've been able to expedite the process of achieving awareness."

"I'm not sure it's Nefas," Ankh said. "We have the real Nefas in the abyss of suspended consciousness. Maybe we should bring him out of it for a chat."

The voice had changed. Erasmus was more of a risk-taker than Ankh.

"I would find that an interesting way to invest my time. It's much better than a meeting."

"I love meetings, darling," Felicity purred into Ted's ear.

"Would you not?" Ted sniped before softening and mumbling an apology. His harsh blow never landed. Felicity was well-conditioned to Ted's outbursts.

"Do it, then, if you would, and put him right back into

cold storage when you're finished. We can't have him getting out. Chaz and Dennicron, take Sahved and Tyler to the *War Axe* for continued investigation here."

"They can use our ship. Like you said, it'll only be a day or two, and if they get into a scrap, *Destiny's Vengeance* has nearly as much firepower as the *War Axe*," Ankh/Erasmus said with a hint of pride.

"Make it so." Rivka gave the thumbs-up, and the two left to find the others who would ride with them. Clevarious would undoubtedly expedite the transfer via the cargo bay. The team wouldn't have to suit up or link airlocks with the immense destroyer to shift from one ship to the other.

Ankh stood. "We'll discuss the cloning process with Nefas." Ted stood and deftly wrapped an arm around his wife—not to show affection but to guide her out of the conference room.

After they departed, Rivka was left alone with TH and Char again. The instant they sat down, the big orange cat leapt onto the conference table and sprawled in front of Rivka.

"Why have you chosen me?" she asked.

Dokken loped in and took a spot on the deck. From there, he carefully watched his archnemesis, who was acting as if he didn't have a care in the universe.

Rivka dashed her hand in, rubbed the cat's soft-fur belly, and pulled away before he could scratch the hell out of her arm.

"I don't have a good feeling about the Corrhen Cluster," she said. Terry and Char shook their heads. "Might want to keep your gear on."

CHAPTER FIVE

<u>*Wyatt Earp* in the Corrhen Cluster, Former Home of the Mandolin Partnership</u>

Rivka sulked. There was no other way to describe it. The planet looked to be abandoned. The system was devoid of intelligent life. There was no Gate in the system with the habitable planet.

It was beyond remote, even though it was well within Federation space.

They were alone since *War Axe* was cleaning up the Station 13 freighters and cargo vessels.

No one interrupted her reverie. Red and Lindy and TH and Char had gone to the workout room. It would be a tight squeeze for the four of them, but they would make do. Cole hovered outside in the corridor with Dokken, both of them waiting to learn their next steps.

"I'm going to check in on Ankh and Ted," Rivka said, even though she didn't need to. Clodagh was working with the scanning systems to dig more deeply into the system to see if anyone was hiding. Aurora and Kennedy maintained a low profile by navigating and flying since Clevarious said she would be occupied with Nefas.

Five on one. Even Nefas couldn't break past that group.

Rivka walked with purpose, even though she had none. She had not been asked to join the interrogation of their prisoner, and she would be on the outside looking in, wondering how it was going. But she needed to see them. She needed to do something until they found their next lead which could very well be in Nefas's consciousness.

In Engineering, she found Felicity lounging on a chair outside the holoscreens. Ankh was sitting in Ted's lap within them.

Chrysanthemum had the vacant look the SCAMPs maintained when their minds were elsewhere.

"That looks weird," Rivka said about more than just the SI.

"They are closer than normal people should be. It *is* weird."

Rivka moved past Chrys and into the hologrid, where she was instantly absorbed.

She found herself standing in the "black room," as she had taken to calling it.

"You *WILL* answer my question!" an avatar Rivka had not seen before roared, swelling to fill the space. Nefas sat nonplussed. He sat on a hard metal chair with his arms crossed. Heavy chains crisscrossed his body, strapping him to the chair

Virtual chains. Holding him to a virtual chair within a virtual space.

Rivka didn't move. She wasn't sure she was supposed to be there. This was a Singularity effort.

Erasmus cocked a hip to lean on his cane. His coat and tails were perfectly tailored. His top hat was canted slightly on his head.

An avatar with Ankh's visage stalked back and forth like a caged panther. Another avatar looked exactly like Chrysanthemum's real-world body. A final avatar watched from the shadow of darkness. Clevarious, staying back and learning from the elders.

"Thank you for joining us, Magistrate," Erasmus said, removing his hat and bowing in a single well-practiced maneuver.

The shouting avatar shrank to become the same size as the others. The face that had been spitting-mad moments earlier assumed a neutral expression. Ted crossed his arms and backed into the darkness.

"You don't have to leave on my account," Rivka said. "I'm not sure I'm supposed to be here."

"You are," Erasmus replied. "I invited you."

A rattle of chains signaled a movement by the prisoner. He surged forward in an attempt to stand, but the massive links held him down. He snarled, "*You!*"

"Nefas. I can't say it's good to see you because whenever I'm near, I get the cold and clammy feeling of trying to put on a wet swimsuit. It is distinctly uncomfortable. We only have one request at present. Tell us about the merry band of pirates that were in your employ to secure your planet. Which, I have to add, they did a crap job of."

Nefas shrugged but didn't answer.

"See?" Ted wore a smug expression.

Rivka strolled over to Nefas. He was singularly unimpressed by the proceedings. Rivka touched him, surprised to feel fabric and a body beneath. "What about the pirates?" she asked. In the digital world, everything was a façade. She could feel no emotion from him.

His shoulder shifted and latched onto Rivka's hand. She tried to pull free but couldn't. She delivered a left hook to his face and followed with a weak elbow strike.

Nefas's head jerked from the impacts, but he didn't let go with the gripping fingers that extended from within his shoulder.

Erasmus appeared and leaned against a table that materialized before the prisoner. He snapped his fingers and pointed at a spot between Nefas's eyes.

The pressure on Rivka's hand grew. She gripped back for leverage and rolled into delivering a right knee piledriver-style to the back of the SI's head. His face plunged into Erasmus's finger.

Sparks shot through and around Nefas's head. The pressure disappeared, and Rivka jumped back.

Erasmus stepped away from the table, leaving the prisoner with hair still smoking from the energy that had blasted through his digital form.

"The pirates in your employ," Rivka pressed.

Nefas shook his head to clear the cobwebs. "You are a bunch of bullies. Twenty to one, and you keep attacking me."

Rivka counted those present. Only Ted's face was visible, as if he were looking through a curtain. Ankh, Erasmus, Chrys, and Clevarious. That made six.

He probably wanted someone to correct him, but no one obliged.

Rivka massaged her hand, not understanding why it

would hurt. This was her digital presence, and she should have been able to shake it off.

Ankh rushed to her. "Is there pain?" He seemed concerned, and that worried the Magistrate.

She nodded.

He gripped her arm and leaned close. A monocular lens appeared over his eye.

"Erasmus, take a look." Ankh nearly jerked Rivka's arm out of its digital socket while holding it up. With a flourish, the ambassador was there, studying the offending appendage.

"Indeed," he replied.

"What?" Rivka asked.

A device like an electronic syringe materialized in Ankh's hand, and he jabbed it into Rivka's arm. She howled in agony until something popped into a clear chamber. Rivka fell to her knees as she held her arm.

Ankh and Erasmus studied the black splotch within the device.

"What is that?" Rivka wondered as she worked her way to her feet, still rubbing her tortured virtual limb.

"It's a virus of the nastiest sort. Had you taken this out of here, you could have infected the ship."

"Why, you fucking ass..." Rivka stormed toward Nefas but was stopped by an outstretched tuxedo-clad arm.

"It is incumbent upon all of us to try to escape if captured. Since he cannot, he will simply wreak havoc from within. We would have been able to remove the virus, but not after something was damaged. Maybe the power systems, so his containment would collapse.

"But that's not possible. If his containment loses power,

then he'll simply cease to exist since his consciousness is stored within an energy barrier. It's our failsafe and also our way to punish an errant Singularity member. He gets to live and not simply be shut off, something we did at first, but no time would have elapsed, and there was no chance to feel remorse."

"Not that I would anyway," Nefas offered.

"He has to live within the confines of his own thoughts, a hell of his own making." Erasmus tipped his top hat to the prisoner. "Maybe you should go. We'll continue to question him."

Rivka looked from face to face. "What are you going to do?" She shook her head before anyone could answer. "I don't want to know. I only want the result."

She found herself falling backward out of the hologrid.

"That was interesting," Felicity drawled. A mint julep had appeared in her hand between the time Rivka went into the black room and came out. She took a slow sip.

"They're beating up the prisoner." Rivka brushed her hands off, then studied the one that had been infected with the virus. It was limited to cyberspace, wasn't it?

Rivka was confused.

"I'm going to jump in the Pod-doc for an evaluation."

"You don't look so good," Felicity replied sympathetically.

"I don't?" Rivka was alarmed, and then she got angry. Nefas had bested her.

"No, you look great. I'm jealous; that's all." Felicity took another sip of her drink.

"What the fuck?" Rivka glared, then started to laugh. "Is this some kind of sordid defensive mechanism?"

"I've been gorgeous my whole life. It's a blessing and a curse. For some reason, I fell hard for Ted, and we've been together ever since. Well, my husband wasn't enhanced, so he died of old age. Ted was with someone else who didn't want him, so they swapped. Werewolves are extremely pragmatic about some things."

"Ted's a werewolf?" Rivka was shocked.

"He hasn't changed into the wolf in some time, maybe a hundred years, but he can do it. He almost died the last time he changed. He did it to save some people. He's my hero." Felicity shook her head once again at the sight of Ankh sitting in Ted's lap.

"I'll go to the Pod-doc now," Rivka said to extricate herself from her discomfort. She tried to maintain a steady pace as she left the engineering section, but it probably looked like she was running away.

She was, but she didn't want it to look that way.

Rivka thought about stopping by the Pod-doc, but Tyler wasn't there to run it for her, and Ankh was occupied. She'd have to pass.

For now.

"Magistrate!" Clodagh called over her shoulder. She hadn't turned around, yet she knew Rivka was walking by.

"I sensed a presence summoning me to the bridge," Rivka replied, stepping through the hatch.

Clodagh turned around to make sure Rivka was okay. She hesitated.

"What's wrong with me?" Rivka looked at her hand.

"Nothing that I can see. What do you think is wrong with you?" Clodagh squinted as she studied Rivka's expression.

"Nothing," Rivka ventured. "You called?"

"We're getting shimmers. The system looks empty, but we see something like this whenever we're scanning a cloaked ship. It's not enough to get a fix, but it's plenty to know something is there."

"That would explain a lot of things." Rivka hammered her fist into her palm. "What do you say we set a trap?"

"What do you have in mind?" Clodagh leaned forward and focused on the Magistrate.

"We Gate out of here, then immediately Gate back in behind a planet and beneath a moon, but this time we're cloaked and shielded. We peruse the system until something appears. I feel they'll drop their cloaks the instant we're out of here."

"I hope they do, but they weren't visible when we arrived, which suggests their MO is to remain cloaked at all times."

"Then we'll have to set up a web to draw them in, so we can see them. Then we'll have a healthy conversation about their role in disappearing ships."

Clevarious joined the conversation. "We are receiving a communication from Station 7. Another freighter has been reported missing."

Rivka crossed her arms and leaned back against the bulkhead. "If we're seeing shimmers here, who is raiding the shipping in Station 7 space? How long has the freighter been missing?"

"Four hours."

"Gate us to Station 7 space, cloaked," Rivka ordered. "Give me ship-wide, Clevarious." The SI didn't respond because she was engaged in the interrogation.

Rivka strode to the comm station and activated the ship-wide comm manually.

"All hands, we're going to Station 7. Another freighter has been taken, and there are cloaked ships in this space."

Two mysteries hundreds of light-years apart. All questions and no answers.

Four people pounded down the corridor toward the bridge.

She had gotten everyone's attention.

Red, Lindy, Terry, and Char were in workout clothes.

"We can get changed in no time, boss," Terry said as he ran past.

"Full gear!" Rivka called after them.

"What do you expect to find that they need to be geared up?" Clodagh wondered.

Rivka shrugged a shoulder. "It makes them feel better to get geared up. Do you see the looks on their faces?"

Clodagh laughed. "You're not kidding, are you?"

Rivka smiled, but she wasn't happy. They were getting jerked around the galaxy, playing catch up. Nefas wouldn't provide any information, but the crimes were comparable to what he had been capable of.

Rivka went to the captain's chair and perched on the front edge, leaning forward to watch the view out the front.

"We are invisible," Clodagh noted.

The Gate formed and the ship slipped through, a flash

in the void. The Gate disappeared, and it was as if nothing had ever been there.

Aurora took over piloting the ship and angled away from their insertion point. Clodagh checked the data arriving in their receptors for passive collection.

"Once we're close to another ship, we can ride their active scans and insert some of our own." Clodagh was reporting how they would stay hidden while radiating like a mini sun.

Rivka waited for the reports, but passive scanning was limited in what it collected and how timely the information was.

"Moving toward a cargo vessel squawking as the *Bennie Jeziret*." Clodagh looked at Rivka, who made a face.

"Just keep them out of our heads and we'll be fine," Rivka quipped. "Clevarious, are you guys done?"

"I am back, bigger and better than before," the SI declared.

"You didn't get anything from him, did you?"

"Not a thing," Clevarious confirmed.

"For my morbid curiosity, what are the betting lines?" Rivka covered her face with her hands and peeked between her fingers as they rolled up on the main screen.

Clock Running—0 days, 4 hours, 31 minutes, 12 seconds

Line 1 is open—First Swearing
Line 2 is open—First Punch
Line 3 is open—First Arrest
Line 4 is open—First Blood

Line 5 is open—First Running
Line 6 is open—First Shots Fired
Line 7 is open—Quantity of AGB consumed (in grams) during the case
Line 8 is open—Perpetrator is a career criminal
Line 9 is open—Perpetrator is a new player
Line 10 is open—Case closed

"Looks like we're behind schedule in kicking ass and taking names," Red said from the corridor. Rivka rotated the captain's chair to face him.

"I blame you."

"Sure. I'll take it like a man, but it was Ankh who started all this."

"It wasn't," Terry suggested. "It was my son-in-law. He looked for a way to keep himself busy between missions. Once he was killed on Benitus 7, Ankh computerized it because that's what Ankh and Ted do. The betting lines are a monument to Ramses. I'll have words with anyone who wants to close them down."

"They'll stay," Rivka said softly. "I'm sorry about Ramses and Cory. However, point of order; since you're a member of this crew, you can't bet on the case."

"I dropped my bets on the mission before we joined. Think of it as a blind trust where I have no say in the bets. The times are randomly selected." TH smiled and pointed at the railgun slung casually under his arm.

"Case." Rivka gave Red her best glare. He replied with a toothy grin. "We don't have anyone to question, but we're looking. Relax. It could be a while."

Neither TH nor Red deflated. It was like they were

trying to outdo each other by being stalwart and ready to go. Rivka turned back around and faced the main screen.

"We'll be in position in fifteen minutes and will begin active scans at that time," Clodagh announced loudly enough for all to hear.

"Over four hours. Calculate maximum distance they could have traveled. Also, what is the chance they can cloak a freighter they just hijacked?"

Clevarious answered both questions, the first by overlaying a sphere on the Station 7 system space. For the second, a verbal answer was sufficient. "Impossible, based on current understanding of cloaking technologies."

"Let's assume they don't have some alien crap, then. They should be visible. What's the acceleration curve if the ship is launched into the sun?"

"I took that into account," Clevarious replied. "The ships disappeared in the outer area of the gravity well where additional acceleration would be negligible. The freighters are pigs, using Master Vered's vernacular."

Rivka refused to look at her bodyguard because she knew he'd be wearing his most smug expression. She should have known it was going to be a contest between him and Terry Henry the second the Waltons came aboard.

Then again, competition could make them better if she could focus their energy.

"There's a planet within the sphere of travel. Check the previous reports and locations. If we assume smuggling, they could ditch the freighter into a nearby planet, having most of it destroyed in the gas giants or whatever other harsh environments exist outside the Goldilocks zone."

Rivka stood so she could pace. If they provided more

security and more escorts, then they could get in front of future attacks to give Rivka more time to investigate the ones that had already happened. But if the pirates crashed the freighters each time, then the ships would stop coming. There would be no new information. She needed both new and old to determine a pattern, give her insight. Whether more security or not, freighter behaviors were going to change.

The pirates would paralyze intragalactic supply and logistics. Maybe Rivka was looking at this the wrong way.

"We have two courses of investigation. One is that the pirates are smugglers and aren't looking for anything in the inventory. They are recovering something small hidden within a cargo container. The externally attached ones are easier to access. The second course is that this is a prelude to war, whether economic or political, in that they want the Federation to stop moving goods between planets and stations."

Silence descended on the bridge.

Char was the first to speak. "That doesn't bode well. Can we talk with the *Axe*?"

"Spin 'em up, C." Rivka twirled her finger.

"Captain Micky San Marino. You missed us already." It was a statement. "Marcie is here with me."

"Rivka thinks this might be the setup for a war," Char said.

There was a whisper as if someone were brushing a microphone.

"That seems a little more than a few missing freighters," Colonel Marcie Walton, recently returned from Belzimus to take over as the leader of the Bad Company, replied.

Rivka stepped in to explain. "Could be an economic war. How long before freighter captains stop taking shipments or shippers stop shipping because the risk of loss is too great? How long before everyone hires their own security ships to escort, and all of a sudden, there's no security left on the stations? Or it could be a protection racket. RICO laws apply." Racketeering. Organized crime.

"How would that benefit anyone?" Marcie asked.

Rivka stopped pacing. "We saw what happened when security was corrupted on Station 11. It became a fertile ground for the blood trade. For crime." Rivka continued to develop her theory as she talked. It was solidifying in her mind. She resumed pacing.

"That is still small potatoes," Marcie countered. "They risk everything taking high-profile freighters, just so they can conduct petty crime on the stations? The pirates are risking their ships for pocket change."

"It would have to go deeper than that. We just can't see the reason yet. As soon as we get a perp in hand, we'll learn exactly what their long game is."

Rivka stopped to review the main screen. The sphere showed the system's gas giant within the range of where the freighter could have gone. The betting lines still showed on the other side of the screen.

"You can take those down." Rivka pointed, and the list disappeared. Red tapped his fingers on his railgun. Rivka glanced at him, but his eyes were elsewhere. Lindy gripped his hand to make him stop.

"Scanning," Clodagh reported.

"You'll find nothing," Rivka mumbled.

"Not even ditched containers floating free. How did you know?"

"The distance from the last known location to the gas giant is negligible. At Station 11, it was a greater distance, and they probably couldn't generate enough speed, so they dumped excess weight. Their window is less than four hours, and if the distances are anything to go by, I guesstimate they give themselves two hours to make the ship disappear."

"The last two times, it's been consistent at four hours before the ships were reported missing. A one hundred percent safety margin. But why? Motive, means, and opportunity. We're missing motive," Terry said.

"That we are. Just need to interdict one of these pirate ships, and the house of cards will collapse," Rivka replied. "Can the Bad Company provide some escort and overview for us?"

"We can put a couple cloaked ships in orbit around the gas giant, looking for anyone driving a freighter toward it. Same for Stations 11 and 13." Terry worked his way to the comm terminal and made the call.

CHAPTER SIX

The Bad Company Flagship *War Axe*, near Station 11

"I so very much *love* rousting innocent freight crews. Not," Sahved complained from within the destroyer's great hangar bay. A shuttle was waiting to take the team to the next target, a cargo vessel that had stopped the instant they were notified of the inspection.

"This is legal, thanks to Federation Law regarding the trade routes and starship safety, although I would prefer not to do this," Chaz added, nodding at Dennicron.

She nodded back. "I concur."

Colonel Marcie Walton watched the interplay. Sergeant Bundin stood by her side, his stalk-like head waving as if it were being blown by a light breeze. His turtle-like shell covered a body and four stump-like legs. He was the most alien of the Bad Company's warriors. He spoke through a resonance device attached to the bottom of his shell. His "voice" reverberated as a deep base from the deck of the hangar bay.

"The Magistrate requested we clear the ships in this system. Can we do that without intruding?" Bundin asked.

"If they open their flight logs and computer systems to us, we can review their information in seconds. I believe we'll find evidence of complicity if it is there."

Marcie shrugged. "They stopped the second we asked them to. No hesitation. If they had something to hide, they would have tried to run or feigned that they hadn't heard our communication. The purpose of this fishing expedition is to determine the past actions of an enemy in order to predict their future. We want to interdict them while they attempt to commit the crime since they have clearly gotten away with their past crimes."

Sahved blinked quickly as he tried to comprehend how Marcie looked at the problem. "Your successful efforts would allow you to ambush the criminals?"

"Hit the enemy on their way in, not out. Exactly." Marcie smiled.

Kai, Terry Henry's grandson, joined the group. His hair was long, and he wore contemporary fashion. Not a military man. He was with a striking woman who walked with a panther's grace and danger.

"Christina, I believe you know these people." Marcie gestured and stepped away. "I need to return to the bridge. Duty calls."

It wasn't duty that called but Smedley. Terry Henry wanted to talk about a Bad Company deployment.

Colonel Christina Lowell looked at the faces, but not all of them registered. "I think a refresher is in order."

Christina was Nathan Lowell's daughter. She had worked her way up within the Bad Company until she was

Marcie's second in command. She had partnered with Terry's grandson to create a Walton family dynasty. No one questioned it because no one was more committed to the cause of justice and freedom than Terry Henry Walton. He had surrounded himself with people who had like ideals because he'd raised them that way.

"Sahved, a Yemilorian, and Dennicron, and me, Chaz. We are SIs, citizens of the Singularity operating within these self-contained artificial mobility platforms, SCAMPs, as we call the bodies."

Christina nodded and shook their hands. "I feel I should know you. Regardless. We've been busy, and now we are busy with something new and fresh. You've boarded three ships so far and found jack squat. Is that correct?"

"Yes. We don't intend to board any more ships."

"You want us to do it?" Christina looked troubled.

"No combat suits?" Kai wondered. He was also the Bad Company's combat logistician.

Christina shook her head. "They wouldn't fit in the narrow corridors of a freighter."

Chaz waved his hands in front of his face. "No, no. Sorry. We'll board the ship if the ship needs to be boarded. We're going to attempt alternate means of verification."

"Woohoo! Looks like we have a runner. Put on your dancing shoes, boys and girls. The music is playing," Ruzfell, the Yollin systems analyst, announced.

Sahved stared at the bulkhead. "I understand the words but not the meaning. What is happening?"

"We've found a ship that doesn't want to comply with our order to stop and open the airlock," Christina explained. "Sergeant Bundin, put a squad in suits and be ready for extravehicular deployment." She waved her hand. "Get me the bridge."

"Roger," Captain Micky San Marino replied. "We're going to Gate into space in front of them and stop them cold or pursue, whatever is best. Standby to Gate."

"That's all I need." Christina pointed at the two shuttles in the hangar bay. "Load up. We're going hunting. Combat axes, hand blasters, and standard boarding kit, including goggles and grenades."

Kai bolted for the bulkhead. "Rack Seven!" he shouted. He activated the system, and the desired weapons rolled out of the bulkhead. The boarding axes were rounded, with a sharp edge on one side, a spike on the other, and a pry bar on top. It was a multi-purpose tool for work within a ship that didn't want to be boarded. The hand blasters were self-evident. Not everyone surrendered.

Bad Company warriors poured out of the hatch that led to the interior of the ship. Through the comm chips, orders were issued to the designated team members. Aliens and humans alike rolled past Rack Seven, grabbed their gear, and ran for the two shuttles.

"Are we going?" Sahved asked.

"We are," Chaz and Dennicron replied in unison. Sahved watched them run toward a shuttle. There was no way he was staying behind.

He ran after them. "Wait for me!"

The shuttles filled as the *War Axe* formed a Gate, a swirling vortex in the front of the ship. It was flying with its hangar bay doors open, the energy screen keeping the atmosphere in, and the gravitic shields keeping any solid objects that didn't belong to the destroyer from getting in.

The Magistrate's team stopped to watch as the ship accelerated toward the event horizon and through to materialize in a new section of space not far from where they'd started. The ship turned, and the view changed to take in a freighter moving their way. Beams lashed the space in front of the freighter as the *War Axe* fired warning shots.

"Load up!" Christina bellowed. Those watching were galvanized to act, boarding and sealing the shuttle with members of Rivka's team. Christina was last to board the shuttle filled with members of the Bad Company.

The shuttles displayed the tactical situation on a holoscreen at the front. The freighter turned, but *War Axe,* despite its size, was faster and more maneuverable. It raced to cut off the freighter once more.

The target ship started to jettison the cargo. Containers pitched into the void after pneumatics pushed them away from their connections. The *War Axe* was unimpressed. The increase in the freighter's speed was negligible compared to what the destroyer could manage.

"Heave to right now," Marcie ordered angrily over the shuttle's sound system. The freighter slowed down. The *War Axe* fired its lasers and railguns with glowing plasma to mark space in front of and around the freighter to convince it that heaving to was the only option left to it that offered anyone on board a chance to survive the next few minutes.

"Launch the shuttles," Marcie ordered.

The two shuttles took off and raced out of the hangar, through the energy screen, and into the void. The *War Axe* fired one more set of warning shots before the guns went dark. The ship moved closer, looming over the freighter and with only two cargo containers left attached to the frame. The freighter slowed but didn't stop.

War Axe fired a laser with the greatest precision. The lights went out on the freighter.

Christina's shuttle moved it and dropped two tags on it, blinking sensors used to identify cargo for pickup. They were equally useful for maintaining a lock on a recalcitrant ship. The shuttles moved over to the drifting ship and matched speeds. One took each side, port and starboard. They hooked up and used their thrusters to bring the freighter to a stop.

"Sit down," Sergeant Bunding said. The tentacles on his stalk head waved toward the seats. Chaz and Dennicron sat. Sahved had not stood. He had no intention of running into a ship with a hostile crew. That was the Bad Company's job.

Sergeant Capples tapped three warriors. "With me." He tucked the combat axe under his arm and held his blaster at the ready. "Clear this area." He indicated the seats that could be seen from the hatch connected to the airlock.

The system cycled after the shuttle's air pressure equalized with that of the freighter. Capples eased into the space in front of the airlock hatch.

"Ready," he called over his shoulder. "Blow it."

The hatch popped, and Capples fired into the opening. He switched his blaster to his left hand and removed his axe to hold it in his right. The sergeant pushed the hatch open. Smoke filled the space. "Goggles!"

The warriors pulled their headgear down from their helmets to give them eye protection and enhanced vision, including infrared. The freighter's corridor was clear. If they had been in powered combat armor, their helmets integrated the systems as part of a contained environment, but in this case, these helmets only protected their heads.

"Where's this smoke coming from?" Capples called over his shoulder to get Smedley's input from the active scanners.

They are on the bridge, Smedley replied over their comm chips.

"Going in." Capples waved the other three warriors forward. He led the way into the corridor and toward the bridge, before which was one turn. He stopped at the corner and switched which weapon was in which hand. Capples peeked around the corner and pulled his head back as a smattering of blaster fire greeted him.

Concussion grenade, he ordered. The warrior behind him pulled one out of his standard kit.

The warrior activated it, cooked it off for two seconds, and hurled it against the corridor wall to make it bounce and skip, reducing the chance that the enemy could catch it and throw it back.

The instant it exploded, the four warriors dashed into the smoke. Two hand blasters fired. "Clear!" Capples shouted.

From the other side of the bridge, another voice shouted, "Clear."

"We're on." Chaz stood and held out his hand in the most gentlemanly of gestures for Dennicron to take. She used it to pull herself up from her seat. Hand in hand, they strolled casually out of the shuttle.

Sahved hopped up, nearly hitting the overhead. He ducked and followed the SCAMPs.

Smoke filled in the air. Sahved pulled his shirt over his mouth, but it burned his eyes. He struggled to see and ended up stopping and getting to his knees, where the smoke was less intense. He crawled down the corridor toward the T-intersection that led to the bridge.

Voices ahead signaled that he was going in the right direction.

"We can't get the main power back online without digging into the engine, so you don't have much time," Sergeant Capples explained.

Chaz replied in a nonchalant voice, "We will download the databases using emergency battery power, or we'll just take the computer core with us."

Dennicron noticed Sahved crawling toward the bridge. She accessed a control panel and turned on the environmental controls. The air handling system roared to life, and within seconds, the air cleared. She turned off the system.

"Thank you very much. Much thanks. My thanks is overwhelming."

She stopped him with a wave of her hand. Otherwise, he would have continued expressing his effusive gratitude.

"We're in and downloading," Chaz reported. "Smedley confirms that he is receiving the files." Chaz crossed his arms and leaned against the pilot's station.

"What were they hiding?" Sahved asked.

Chaz was momentarily confused. "We won't know that until we analyze the data."

"Are any of the crew still alive?" Sahved stared at the Bad Company sergeant.

"They shot at us," he replied. "They called down the thunder."

"So, no."

"Unfortunately." Capples bobbed his head. "Most unfortunate."

"Is there a secure storage space, like a safe?" Where are the captain's quarters?"

Capples pointed at one of the warriors.

He nodded at his sergeant and led the way. The freighter was so small that ten seconds later, they stood before a plain door. "Here." The warrior tried to open it, but it was secured. "Stand back."

Sahved moved down the corridor and waited.

The Bad Company warrior reared back and kicked the door with his heavy boot, denting it but not breaking it. He took that as a challenge and was rewarded when his second attempt tore the door off its mounts. He ducked his head inside to confirm it was empty before stepping back to allow Sahved access.

The Yemilorian stepped inside and took stock of the small quarters. They made him appreciate that much more what he had aboard *Wyatt Earp*. He scoured the compartment for anything that locked. *Smedley Butler, yours is the best of all scanners in this part of space. Could you see if there are any concealed compartments in this space?*

There is nothing, the SI replied. *Have you checked underneath the desk?*

The space didn't allow for Sahved to look beneath the desk easily. He twisted pretzel-like until he was on the deck.

He examined the undersides of the meager pieces in the space until he found what Smedley had alluded to: a packet affixed with magnets to the underside of the desktop.

Inside, Sahved found printed bills of lading. They were old-fashioned but effective, especially for someone who was trying to avoid a digital inspection.

"You should have heaved to," Sahved told the ghosts of the crew. "We would not have found this." He perused the packets, and his face fell. "Why?" He shook his fist at the ceiling. "You know not what you do, or you care not."

They were smugglers running things with names that smacked of drugs. Starshine. Moonstone. Pink Love. Crystal Caverns. Millions of each, if the quantities on the hidden bill of lading were to be believed. No credit value attached, just names and numbers.

Sahved worked upright and, clutching the packet tightly to his chest, returned to the bridge. "Do you know where they were going?" he asked.

Chaz stared at the wall, and his eyes unfocused.

"The frontier. They have five stops planned."

"That is where we must go." Sahved nodded for emphasis.

"Are these the pirates?"

"I don't think so."

"Then why would we go to the frontier?" Dennicron asked. Chaz raised one eyebrow, and his face froze that way while he waited.

Sahved shook off the incongruity. "Because this is a crime. A big crime, the biggest we've seen all day!"

"Bigger than the hijacking of two ships and the

complete disappearance of one crew?" Dennicron challenged.

Sahved retreated. "Possibly."

"We have the files," Chaz announced and crooked his elbow for Dennicron to take. The two strolled across the small bridge, all three steps. Then Chaz stepped into the narrow corridor, and Dennicron followed. Sahved went with them.

Sergeant Capples remained behind with Colonel Lowell. "Orders?"

"Hate to see good ships go to waste. We'll tow it to the station and turn it over as salvage. The other option is we blow it out of the sky. I think an enterprising young captain-to-be will take it over for a bargain price. Maybe he'll even call it *Serenity*. Nothing like moving freight to give a young man a new life."

Capples wasn't sure if she was kidding or serious. "We'll disembark" was the best the sergeant would commit to. "Rally at the shuttle!"

The three he'd brought with him maneuvered out of the small space and to the shuttle. The SCAMPs and Yemilorian were already buckled in and ready to go. As soon as the Bad Company warriors were in place, they secured the airlock and departed.

"I'm hungry," Capples announced. "Nothing like a mission to burn those calories. Chow's on me."

"Chow is always free, Sarge," one of the warriors grumbled.

"We both win, then. I keep my hard-earned credits, and you get to eat."

"I could eat," Sahved admitted. Capples gave him the thumbs-up.

Chaz held out his hand. Sahved looked at it until Chaz pointed at the packet he held tightly in both hands.

Sahved handed it to him. In the five minutes it took to get from the freighter to *War Axe's* hangar bay, the SCAMPs had scanned every page and compiled the data into a single file. The efforts of the crew to hide what they were doing had been wasted. They had died to protect a secret they couldn't keep.

When Sahved stepped off the shuttle, he found the hangar bay three-fourths full of cargo containers.

The *War Axe* had collected the jettisoned cargo.

"Now we need to search these for drugs." Sahved spread his arms wide to take in all the containers.

"Are they going anywhere, the dead crew or the containers?" Capples asked.

Sahved shook his head while twirling his three fingers.

"Then chow first. We'll attack this mess when we've been properly hydrated and fueled." He clapped Sahved on the shoulder, which made the Yemilorian stagger a few steps.

"We will analyze the data we collected," Chaz said. He and Dennicron strode toward the hatch leading to the interior of the ship.

"Follow us for the best chow you'll have since breakfast." Capples gestured with his chin. "Your ship's doc is still treating people, so we have some time to kill before we can go anywhere. Might as well relax, big fella."

CHAPTER SEVEN

***Wyatt Earp* at Federation Station 7**

Rivka walked with purpose. Station 7 had been the headquarters of the Magistrates, but then they had been spread farther and wider. After the retirement of the High Chancellor, Grainger had moved to Yoll.

Kind of.

When Rivka entered the Magistrates' conference room to pay homage to the old days, she was shocked to find Grainger sitting there, along with Jael and Buster Crabbe.

"Bustamove. Long time no see," Rivka said.

"Hey! We wondered when you were going to show up."

They hadn't been wondering anything of the sort.

"Of course," Rivka replied. "I'm in the middle of a case. Are you working the pirate issue?"

"Pirates? No. Drug dealers, yes. It appears your people with the Bad Company have found a smuggling operation. No one thinks this one is related to your stuff. Might be a target of opportunity or bad luck on this crew's part."

"What did the crew have to say? I'll get the truth from

them." Rivka glared into space. These people had interfered with AGB and how many other legitimate businesses. She wasn't keen on upsetting the apple cart. She had assumed the worst thing that raised its ugly head would be Frenzik, and she had people closely watching his moves. The Johnstone Estate case had softened her regarding hard crime.

"How's your necromancy?" Grainger quipped.

"They weren't going to be captured, I'm guessing. It was worth a shot. If there's a link, my people will find it." Rivka tried to get a glance at their screens. "Whatcha working on?"

"A treaty with a potential planet angling toward membership in the Federation."

"Are we doing those now? Shouldn't that be the council of elders or something?"

"Who is the council of elders? Do you mean the Federation Council, all the ambassadors?"

"Sure. Those people."

"We have to conduct a legal review first and then make recommendations to the Chief Arbiter, Lance Reynolds."

"Does he still have my cat?"

"No. Are you talking that white and gray cat?"

"How can you say no without being sure what I'm talking about, but yes. Her."

"She left with you, but then you don't have her, do you? Do you know where she ended up?"

"I think I asked the question first," Rivka countered.

"Right back here. Right in the General's office as if she hadn't traveled halfway across the galaxy."

"I guess there's no keeping true love apart. For the record, I had nothing to do with that."

"How did I know you were going to say that?" Grainger stared at Rivka without blinking. She held his gaze until her eyes burned. She would not give in. Her head started to shake with the effort. A bead of sweat trailed down Grainger's forehead and dripped into his eye, making him blink. "Dammit!"

"I'll do it," Buster Crabbe interrupted.

Grainger looked at him. "Do what?"

"Go to the frontier and check out where the drugs from that freighter were headed. If the numbers are to be believed, there is a major problem, and someone is burying the information."

Grainger nodded. "Wouldn't be the first time. Take her out, Buster. Find out what the hell is going on out there."

Buster logged off, then stood and put his Magistrate's jacket on. "See you on the flip side, Wankenhammer."

"Say what?" Rivka threw her hands up and then out to intercept Buster and give him a hug.

"Did you scan me?" he asked after he stepped back.

"No. Did I miss something like lusty thoughts toward Jael, where you'd have to challenge Grainger to a duel at sunset?"

Buster laughed. "That is most assuredly not what I was thinking. Peace, my fellow Magistrates." He held up his fingers in a V and walked out.

Red met him on the other side of the door. The two nodded to each other before Red closed the door to give the Magistrates their privacy.

"Good work on that succession case," Grainger said in a

brief moment of sincerity.

"That was a mess. Nothing like what I thought I was getting into. Rich people can be mean." She stared down at the table before adding, "And stupid. By the way, can we get those betting lines canceled? That last case made private information public. I wasn't comfortable with that. A betting line that a ten-year-old is the perp? That's a little out of bounds."

"A family like that gets extra scrutiny. All of them were in the public's eye before you got involved. That's where the suspect list came from. No case information was compromised. What are the lines on your current case?"

"All closed with no winners declared if I get my way." Rivka stared at Grainger.

He looked away. "Not falling for the stare-down again. You're not natural. When it comes to the betting lines, how about no? They are good for morale."

"Not mine," Rivka countered. She put her hands on her hips.

Jael chuckled. "Sometimes the answer is no, Rivka."

"And sometimes the answer is 'Yes, yes, again, yes,'" Rivka parodied and turned her head to give Jael the stink-eye.

"You heard that, huh? You shouldn't call Grainger in the middle of the night. You never know what you're going to get." Jael smiled. "How's that dentist working out? I'm about ready to move on, and he sounds completely delightful."

"You can't have him," Rivka countered. She wanted to say something else but couldn't come up with an appropriate quip. Grainger and Jael made eyes at each other.

"Cat's out of the bag." Jael made a rude gesture with her fingers.

Rivka shook her head. "It appears the cat is back in the General's office. The leader of the Federation has a homing cat, better than any pigeon." Rivka tried to derail the conversation and point it away from her.

"You didn't stop by here to talk about your love life, but that's where we ended up. So weird since we are nothing but professional when it's just us girls," Grainger said.

Rivka pursed her lips and blew out a breath. She pointed at the table. "I expected to see pizza boxes."

"About that. You need to solve your case and restore the flow of pizza. Now, shoo. We have work to do. This treaty is two hundred and forty pages of bullshit."

Rivka laughed. "That beats any comeback I could make. I'm off my game. Next time, I'll be better prepared."

"You won't be," Grainger countered. He and Jael stood and stretched.

After the obligatory hugs, Rivka headed out. Red and Lindy were waiting. "I told you guys you didn't need to wait for me."

"We have pirates operating in space near here in a way that suggests they have someone on the station. There's no way we're leaving you alone. Those people in there are a bit shady, too, if you ask me."

"You want Grainger to kick your ass again?"

"He couldn't. He's growing soft, being the big man. Figuratively, of course. I train every day. I'm the true big man." Red glanced up and down the corridor, not looking at Rivka for long while he talked. He remained hyper-aware. He knew things she didn't, especially when it came to her personal security. She had been attacked in many ways, as had Red. She constantly had a target on her chest, but she rarely accepted that the threat existed.

"I'm sorry, Red. You're right, of course." Rivka lightly punched him in the shoulder.

"Where to, Magistrate?" Red asked. "By the way, I've recorded you saying I'm right, and I'm going to have Clevarious play it often. Like, once an hour."

Rivka flicked her fingers as if she were brushing away a fly. "AGB. Let's see if they're open and have some lunch. I'm jonesing. Absence of a thing makes it far more desirable."

"AGB didn't have to be absent for me to desire it," Red told her over his shoulder while he led the way to the restaurant.

They worked their way through the station to arrive at a darkened entrance and a hand-scrawled sign.

Temporarily closed.

"Magistrate?" Red wondered.

"Back to *Wyatt Earp*. These people are getting under my skin. Let's go back to the Corrhen Cluster and see what kind of cloaked activity we have going on there. Is the ship ready?"

Ship is ready to go, Clevarious replied.

Did the station's SI have any information regarding the freighters?

We're working with them on that very question. There's a great deal of video, and we're cross-referencing the faces therein. We'll have the analysis done shortly. Erasmus is leading this himself and has pulled in additional assets from the Singularity.

Rivka thanked her and returned to the task at hand:

working her way through a light crowd to get back to her ship. With Red blocking, it was as easy as following closely behind him. He tried not to push people out of the way, but sometimes they weren't paying attention and had to be jostled.

One enterprising young man mumbled an apology while trying to dig into Red's pocket. The big bodyguard caught the potential thief's wrist and squeezed while pulling, then jerked it sideways. The snap sounded like a muffled pistol shot. The young man squealed in pain. Rivka grabbed him around the throat. "Do it again, and I'll put you in Jhiordaan. I have tagged you now and will issue a BOLO. Your life of crime is over."

His mind gave him away. Pickpocketing on the station had been his livelihood for the past month. With a broken wrist, he was out of business, but a new scam was already forming in his mind. The cripple…

"But I wasn't," he tried weakly.

"But you were." Rivka shifted her grip to his shoulder and started dragging him toward Station 7's security office.

Red shifted his direction of travel. People were more congenial about getting out of their way.

"Wait!" the young man cried as they approached the door. "I did it. I tried to pickpocket that walking mountain."

"With an attitude like that, I'd be doing you a favor, chucking you in the gray-bar motel."

"I can't go to jail. I have to take care of an ailing mother!"

"You don't. You live alone." Rivka propelled him toward the door. Red caught him as he turned sideways to the entry. One hand holding the injured man tightly, Red opened the door with the other. The four entered.

"Magistrate!" a voice called from behind the counter. Rivka tried to remember his name but couldn't. He knew it. "Phil. Phil Ryerson. It's like déjà vu."

Rivka nodded, still having no idea. She offered her hand. When he took it, she asked, "How do you know me?"

"The legend," he replied. He was telling the truth. He'd been watching her cases and betting on them.

"This doesn't count as first arrest," she said quickly. "Pickpocket working the promenade. He's been at it for a month. Take your time fixing up that broken wrist of his before giving him some cell time. Thirty days ought to do it."

"Thirty days!" the young man whined. Red tapped his broken wrist, and the man's knees buckled. If Red hadn't caught him, he would have sprawled on the deck.

The desk officer took him off Rivka's hands. "Paperwork?"

"I'll forward it the second I get back to my ship," Rivka promised.

"Into the slammer with you, scumbag," the man growled in his best imitation of a hardass. The young man started sobbing.

"Thirty days," Rivka reiterated. Ryerson gave her the thumbs-up.

She looked at Red and Lindy. "Corrhen Cluster?" Red asked.

Rivka nodded.

"Then we better get back to the ship so they don't leave without us," Lindy said matter-of-factly.

CHAPTER EIGHT

Federation Station 13

A freighter called *Soulful Eyes* idled its engines to drift for five minutes before reengaging to pick up speed. The captain wanted to maintain a low profile and steer clear of the scourge that he'd heard was haunting the major stations, a place he least expected them to be. Half a dozen ships over the course of a month, with the attacks coming more and more quickly.

"Heave to..." a voice began over the general comm channel before the captain slammed his hand down on the monitor and shut it down.

"I'll be damned if I'm going to heave to." He braced himself and studied the screen for a moment, then gave the order. "Full burn on vector one-niner-four, vertical angle fifteen degrees."

Each system had a natural rotation, and that was the level plane. Up was toward Yoll, and down was away from it. It wasn't as scientific as other methods, but it worked.

The freighter accelerated at an agonizingly slow pace.

Thrusters kicked it onto its new course while the main engines burned hot, redlined.

"Come on, old girl. You've got one last trick in you." The captain patted the armrest of the captain's chair, which looked no different from the pilot's and engineer's seats. The small bridge had three stations, and each was occupied. Two more crew members were in the engine room, while the sixth and final crew member was in the forward observation bubble, watching the cargo and managing the freight. On the way out, there was little to do, but as they closed with their offload location, coordination of the cargo handling equipment and buyers was critical and a full-time job.

There were no alternate shifts. One person per position. They weren't needed there all the time, so they slept when they could.

"Maybe you can talk to them? We're carrying nothing more than rubber dog shit with custom markings or some such crap."

"Where did you learn to speak?" the captain joked, keeping things light. The freighter had limited sensors. Nothing was showing on the tactical board because the ship he assumed made the call wasn't squawking. Without an active connection, they wouldn't know until the ship intercepted them.

"Give them the cargo," the pilot said. "We're insured, aren't we?"

"Hells to the yes, we're insured, but only one crew has been rescued so far. Giving up means giving up our lives. I say no to that. We're going to run. Spin me up a channel to the station."

The engineer tapped his screen. "Whiteout. We're being jammed, and it's close."

"Hard over, vector three hundred. Back to the station at best possible speed."

"That's going to make one big arc," the pilot said. "I recommend shutting down the main engines, making a hard rotation using the port and starboard counter thrusters, and then reengaging the engines with a full burn, one hundred and fifteen percent."

"My baby is at your command," the captain replied. "All hands, brace for a radical maneuver."

The pilot hunched over his console and tapped screens until he was ready to execute. The mains dropped offline, and the ship started to spin on a flat plane. It came around slowly because of the full load of containers it was carrying.

The captain saw no other option. He contacted the freight handler. "Jettison the containers, all of them, right now."

He sounded calmer than he felt.

"Executing," the freight handler replied.

The visual from the forward-facing cameras showed the containers popping off and continuing their journey on a ballistic trajectory. The freighter swung faster. The pilot brought up the main engines and fired them before the ship reached its desired vector. He punched up the thrusters on the opposite side of the fuselage to bring the ship's spin to a rapid halt.

Right in front of them, a cruiser-class ship materialized. "Those bastards were cloaked? Only the Federation can do that."

"Not anymore." The engineer groaned. The freighter slowed to a stop, but the engines continued to burn at one hundred and fifteen percent. It then started to creep forward.

"Sir?" the pilot asked as they headed into a terrible game of chicken with the pirate vessel.

"We go on our terms. They won't want to scratch the paint on their shiny toy. They'll blink."

The pirate cruiser seemed to jerk in space before it disappeared.

The pilot held his finger over the engine cutoff, unsure of his next action.

"Stay the course," the pilot said, crossing his legs to maintain the impression that he was calm. "They're currently rethinking their life decisions."

The ship lunged and screamed from the impact. The captain was thrown forward into his console. The pilot grunted from the impact, and the engineer clutched his midsection before falling over.

The ship lunged ahead while crying with the sound of metal scraping metal. The sound decreased in intensity before stopping in its entirety. The freighter started accelerating more rapidly.

The captain limped from his seat to the injured engineer. Blood trailed down his forehead. The captain stretched him flat on the deck. He was breathing but had a slow pulse. He pressed a dirty rag against the wound to staunch the bleeding. There was nothing else to do for him at that moment. "Maintain course toward the station."

The freighter vibrated with the increase in speed until it started to corkscrew. The captain hung onto the console and the engineer's chair. Releasing the bandage allowed the wound to start bleeding again, so he pressed his thigh against the engineer's head until the engineer rolled to the back of the bridge.

"Dial us back!" the captain shouted.

The pilot hammered at his screen until the wild gyrations lessened. The ship assumed a stable course when it hit one-quarter full speed.

"We're not outrunning anyone with this," the pilot said. "How's Bill?"

"Dying unless we can get him some proper medical care." The captain tapped the screen to see if the comm channel was clear. He nearly jumped at the revelation that it was. "Station 13, emergency. Freighter *Soulful Eyes* is under attack by a cruiser of unknown origin. Cruiser is cloaked. I say again. Cruiser is cloaked.

"We are on a direct vector toward the station. We have suffered damage from an impact with the unidentified cruiser. I will repeat this message." The captain tapped the screen to repeat the message until he stopped it. The ship's position would attach to the message. He also added an image of the cruiser as seen through the forward cameras.

"Will he come after us since we're a sitting duck out here?" the captain wondered. "It doesn't matter. We're not stopping."

An explosion whited out the front screen. "What the hell was that?" The pilot checked his screens.

The captain accessed the comm. "Freight. Did you see what that was?"

No answer.

"I'm going up there." The captain bolted off the bridge,

vaulting Bill's unconscious form. He raced down the corridor, slowing to a stop when he saw the emergency bulkhead in place. He looked through the window made from transparent aluminum. The area was torn apart. The station and its lone occupant were gone.

The captain hurried back to the bridge and dragged the engineer close to the forward console so he could maintain pressure on the head wound. The amount of blood on the deck was staggering. The captain's footprints were scattered forward and aft since he'd run both ways through the mess.

The blood had splattered up his boot and onto the leg of his coverall.

"Hold us steady," he told the pilot. Not that the pilot needed to hear it, but the captain had to feel like he was doing something. With a long, moaning exhale, the engineer took his final breath.

The captain lifted his foot to reveal a bloody footprint on Bill's forehead.

"That could have been more dignified," the captain mumbled, not able to take his eyes off his engineer.

"What happened to Splits?"

"The bubble is gone, along with Splits, along with the forward cargo frame. I think they shot at us but hit the framework instead of the ship."

"Do you think they still want us to heave to? We don't have anything left except the ship, and that's not much of a prize. Two dead crew and a broken ship. What did they want from us?" He stood and started gesticulating wildly.

"All of it. The ship, the cargo, and us. They're murderers as well as thieves."

"*Soulful Eyes*, this is Malcolm, Station 13's Operations Intelligence. I have dispatched station security, and they are approaching your position. Please slow before you break apart. Follow them to Gantry Four."

"You don't see a ship out here? A cloaked ship?"

"See a cloaked ship. I would find that funny if your ship wasn't so badly damaged. But no, we have no indications of another vessel in the area. I suspect they've fled the engagement area."

"How could they attack us so close to the station? What are you people doing in there, eating crumpets and drinking foofy coffee like carefree morons?"

"We have not secured the freight lanes since we aren't tasked with that, but we will get our ships out there and do everything we can. These attacks are unacceptable."

The captain sighed. "You say unacceptable. I say two dead crew I called friends and a ship that probably won't fly again. That's a bit more than unacceptable."

"Quite a bit more. Proceed to Gantry Four, where you'll be met by medical and security staff. Once we've completed our investigation to recover evidence that might point us toward who these perpetrators are, we'll see about repairing your ship."

The captain mumbled a rough thanks and closed the channel.

The pilot adjusted the scope to center the escort ship, showing what was in front of the freighter. He tapped the thrusters to adjust their course only slightly since not all thrusters were working. "We're flying on spit and polish only."

The captain's eyes glistened as he stood and tapped the

low overhead. "You held together like a champion," he told his ship. "You saved what you could, old girl." He flopped back into his seat, then coughed and spat the blood into his hand. "Guess I wasn't spared. Captain has to go down with his ship."

His eyes rolled back, then he slumped to the side and fell to the deck.

CHAPTER NINE

***Wyatt Earp*, in the Corrhen Cluster**

Rivka stood in Engineering, looming over Ankh. Ted sat to the side, amused by her attempt to intimidate the Crenellian. "Why can't we see this cloaked ship, and how did they get the cloaking technology? Is there a leak at R2D2?"

"There is no leak," Ted replied sharply.

Ankh stared up at the Magistrate.

She waited. He gave her the answer she didn't want to hear. "Because it's cloaked."

"Really? I wouldn't have thought of that." She was losing patience. "I guess my real question isn't a question at all. Find me a way to locate these cloaked ships."

The attack on the freighter in Station 13 space had been forwarded to *Wyatt Earp* through Singularity channels, complete with the picture of the ship uncloaked before it disappeared.

"I know you can figure it out," she pressed.

"Of course, we can figure it out," Ankh replied.

"Soon!" Rivka made fists, then forced herself to relax her hands.

"Well, that's something completely different." Ted chuckled, then turned serious. "We're working on it."

Rivka wanted to snap at them to work faster, but they were the brightest minds in the Federation and dedicated to her problem. She couldn't ask for more.

It didn't mean that she didn't want to. It meant that despite the seeming friction between them, she wasn't sure she respected anyone more. She needed to be more vocal about that.

"I appreciate you guys and what you're doing to help make the Federation a better place."

They both looked at her emotionlessly. Chrys made it a trio of blank stares.

Rivka started laughing. "You fucking guys are going to be the end of me." She left Engineering, shaking her head. "I tried. Gods of the greater universe, please know that I tried to use positive reinforcement."

"May I offer a bit of advice?" Clevarious asked when Rivka was in the corridor by herself.

"Sure." Rivka stopped and leaned against the bulkhead. She had no issue with Ankh or Ted. Her challenge was a case that extended well beyond her. She couldn't do it alone. She needed all of the Bad Company's assets and a general to lead them. This wasn't a petty crime; it was a war. Not the cliché of a war on crime, but a real war with an untold legion of ships moving around a galactic board, staying well in front of the heavy frigate and its crew.

"Ask Felicity to talk to Ted."

Rivka waited for more of a revelation, but there was none.

"That's it?"

"The only person Ted listens to is Felicity. The only people Ankh listens to are Ted and Erasmus. Erasmus can be swayed. You keep your hands clean while still getting what you want. Felicity is tired of being on the ship. She wants to go home and can't do that as long as the crime isn't solved."

"I'm beginning to believe it's less of a crime and more of a war. Since the entire Bad Company is now involved, I have to believe that someone knows a lot more than me about what is going on. Find me who that is. I want to talk with them, even if it's General Reynolds."

"It's Lance Reynolds," Clevarious confirmed.

"Dammit!" Rivka shouted like she'd just lost the world tic-tac-toe championship. "How did I not see that?"

She stormed down the corridor, not angry with the General but angry with Grainger. He had to know.

Even Floyd jumped out of her way as she continued to her quarters. She opened the door, expecting to see Tyler's smiling face welcoming her back, but he wasn't there. He was on the *War Axe*. She sat at her desk and raised the hologrid but didn't activate any of the systems.

Her world was coming apart.

Or was it?

"C, private conversation."

"I don't understand what that means," the SI replied.

"Just between you and me, not to be shared anywhere else with anyone else."

"I'm probably not the right person for this. Would you like to talk with Felicity?" C's candor was refreshing.

"You know what? I would. Thank you, C. I still trust you."

"I know," Clevarious replied.

A gentle knock on the door suggested Felicity had arrived. Rivka dispensed with her usual shout that it was open and personally greeted Felicity at the door.

Felicity looked like she was dressed for a formal event, complete with makeup and an exotic and fetching hairstyle. Rivka looked down at herself and reassessed her utilitarian clothing.

"You look better than I ever did, darling," Felicity drawled. "I need to do this so I'm at least better than average."

Rivka smiled. "You are the most beautiful woman in the universe. There's no doubt about that. Please, come in. Can I get you something to drink?"

"I hear Ankh programmed your food processor. Would you check if he has the Felicity special available?"

Rivka spoke the words to the food processor. It accepted the order, and in less than a minute, a concoction of coffee, mocha, cinnamon, and other flavors Rivka couldn't identify appeared. It showed up in an oversized mug with whipped cream on top.

"I'd ask, but I probably don't want to know, do I?"

"The secret ingredient is Irish whiskey," Felicity replied to the unasked question.

"One for me too, please," Rivka ordered. After hers arrived, she sat next to Felicity on the couch.

"This isn't a social call, is it, dear?" Felicity was a little younger than Terry Henry Walton, but not by much, which meant she was a great deal more experienced in this universe than Rivka. She had watched a husband die of old age, something that Rivka wouldn't have to suffer for a very long time.

"I need Ted, Ankh, and the Singularity to figure out a way to find those cloaked ships, and I need it soon. More importantly than that, I think the higher-ups know a lot more than they're telling me. I don't know how to feel about that."

"There is a certain power that burdens the souls of those at the top. They have to do things in the best interests of the greater good. Not everyone needs to know the master plan, and even more importantly, some people can*not* know the master plan to keep it from falling into the wrong hands."

"I'm not sure that makes me feel any better," Rivka admitted.

"You have a role to play. A rather important one. Everyone knows what you're good at, and that is solving cases and making rulings that serve all of us."

"How do I reconcile myself with the feeling of being used?"

"We are all *used* to some extent. When we know, we can do it on our terms, and that is all we can ever ask from life." Felicity cradled her mug, letting it warm her hands while she inhaled its wafting scent.

"I don't want to be used." Rivka frowned and stared at the deck.

Felicity laughed lightly and easily. "How do you use your people?"

Rivka winced. She wanted to say that they knew their roles and responsibilities but didn't. Maybe the problem was that people told her how important she was like Felicity just had, but she still had to work within a framework of someone else's design.

"I think I understand. My role is not as clearly defined because every case is different."

"This one is no exception. I'll talk to Ted since as much as I *love Wyatt Earp*, I want to go home." She took the first sip from her mug.

"That didn't sound like you love my ship."

"I don't." Felicity beamed once more. "You see?"

She stood, so Rivka stood.

"I'll ask TH and Char to come see you."

"Why?"

"So they can tell you what you want to know. What is your role in this case?" Felicity held Rivka by the shoulders and studied her face. "Just a little makeup could go a long way."

Rivka snorted. "Until I smear it by wiping off the blood."

"You have a point." Felicity carried took the mug with her and ran into TH and Char waiting in the corridor.

"Our turn to get chewed on by the principal?" TH joked.

"Your ass is grass and she's the lawn mower, my darling Terry Henry." She ran her finger down his bold jawline before hugging Char and strolling away in a runway walk, well-practiced over the centuries.

Char chuckled. Terry shrugged.

"Next!" Rivka shouted from two meters away. She

returned to her quarters but moved her desk chair into the room to allow Terry and Char to sit on the couch.

"Yes, ma'am. I'm sorry, but I wasn't even there when that glass was broken. I skipped school that day, so it couldn't have been me! Actually, I wasn't even on the planet at the time."

Rivka cocked her head sideways to look at him.

He does that, Dokken said. Rivka looked down to see him lying by her feet.

"Where did you come from?"

When a mommy dog and a daddy dog really love each other...

Rivka held her head in her hands.

Shall I continue? Dokken asked.

"No, thank you. I'm good." Rivka cleared her throat.

"Hey! Is that a Felicity special?" Terry asked. Char got up and helped herself to the food processor.

"You know, don't you?" Rivka asked.

"Rather open-ended for a closed question, Barrister," Terry replied.

"What's the big picture here? This isn't about a few pirates snagging some freighters. That's my small piece of the pie. What is it a part of?"

"Ooh." Terry made a face while looking at Char.

"Better a witty fool than a foolish wit," Char quoted.

"Shakespeare always has the right answer," TH replied.

Terry and Char sipped in unison from their mugs.

Rivka stared at the overhead. "Don't make me grab you and tear the answer from your mind."

She wouldn't, but Terry appreciated the power play.

"Don't make me arm-wrestle you," Terry replied, flexing his bicep.

"That'll work. I'll lose, but I'll see those centuries of secrets."

"You'll see me playing with my dog."

I'm not your dog.

"Brewing beer and making love. Watching the Dren Cluster from AGB as it changes colors. So much to see. Do you think you're ready?"

"Dammit!" Rivka cried. "Don't bluff the bluffer."

"Never a winning strategy," Terry added. "I'll tell you what you want to know. Encroachment by a force that's probably from outside the Federation. We went up against them at Keeg Station and barely defeated them. A single ship against the entire Bad Company armada. We did win and took their cloaking technology. Still, it's so good that even we can't see it.

"That being said, someone on this side of the frontier is guiding them. We think it might be a crime syndicate. A crime spree to distract us and spread our forces. We don't know what their goal is, so the first step is to find who is helping them. That's your job, and we're doing everything we can to assist you."

"By not telling me?" Rivka sounded hurt, not bitter.

"By allowing you to focus on the monumental task of weeding out the criminals from a greater invading army. Other folks are working on that part of the problem."

"Like the Bad Company?"

"They might have been following you to provide additional protection, but Ted assured us that *Wyatt Earp* is more than capable of defending itself against any ship, even one the size of the *Axe*. Would it have helped if we told you the Federation is afraid that an intergalactic war is brewing?"

Rivka leaned back in her chair and absentmindedly scratched behind Dokken's ears. He leaned into her hand harder and harder until he unbalanced her chair.

"Dog!" Rivka pushed his head away. She thought that would push his body away too, but no. He stood half under her chair and she toppled out of it, then rolled to get back to her feet. "I guess I'll stand."

"Would it have helped?" Terry pressed the question as she had done to him.

"In that greater context, no. It would have been a distraction. If the Bad Company is involved with this, why are you riding with me?"

"Because I don't run the Bad Company anymore. That's Marcie and Christina," Terry replied matter-of-factly. "I'm here to help stop the ne'er-do-wells from stealing my supplies. I got beer to brew, and that takes real hops. I have to import the hops because Felicity won't let me grow them on the station."

"Because they're not food?" Rivka guessed.

"Pretty short-sighted, and I see that you agree."

"I don't, really. If you could grow your own moonstokle, that would be a service to the greater humanity throughout the Federation."

"Grow our own moonstokle!" Terry ejaculated. He turned to Char and snorted. "You'd think a lawyer would be smarter."

Rivka ignored the jibe, but Char didn't.

"You'd think a business professional wouldn't alienate the person he needs on his side."

Terry's face fell. "What? I'm not alienating anyone. Rivka eats for free!"

"My whole crew," Rivka replied.

"In person, absolutely." Terry smiled.

"You know we don't make it to your franchises in person."

Terry shrugged. "Sounds like a *you* problem, not a *me* problem."

Char nudged him. "Cloaked enemy ships."

"Those bastards!" Terry smiled.

Rivka's head was starting to hurt. "Is this what you two do?"

"We've already said it all to each other, so it takes a different level of engagement to keep things interesting," Char explained.

"Where do we go from here?" Rivka asked.

"It's not just you counting on Ted, Ankh, and the Singularity to figure out how to find these cloaked ships. Federation security depends on it. We didn't think the actual pirates would be cloaked and armed, but from the latest information collected by your team on the *War Axe,* it appears that the unknown invaders are back. That cruiser recorded in Station 7 space is the twin brother to the one that attacked Keeg station."

"You think there are still pirates?" Rivka asked.

"There has to be," TH replied. "Who else could jump on a comm channel and act like us? The last we knew, the aliens on that ship didn't speak our language, and that ship was destroyed. None of the crew escaped."

"Was there only one ship?" Rivka asked.

"That's a question we don't have an answer to, not even years later, but we'd not seen anything from them in all that time. Maybe they were waiting and watching, but I doubt it. I think Occam's Razor provides insight. The best solution is the simplest, and that means there are locals helping the invaders."

"They must have learned our language, at least enough to subvert these individuals, but I could see it. The remnants of that pirate fleet you beat off in the Corrhen Cluster."

Terry tipped his chin up in mock outrage. "Take it easy, Barrister. I'm not into beating people off."

Char shook her head. "He once named our boat *Heywood Jablome*."

Terry smirked. "I did. Not my finest hour."

"We retired for fifty years following that incident." Char and Terry nodded at each other.

"That's twice as long as I've been alive." Rivka understood why no one had told her about the enemy fleet or what had to be a fleet of cloaked ships.

It was to protect her. The elder statesmen stood guard over the pearly gates of the Federation. Grainger didn't know any of this, and that was why Buster Crabbe had been dispatched to the frontier. It looked like the drug bust was not a related issue.

It was like the Federation was spiraling out of control.

She didn't need to worry about any of that. She only needed to manage her small part of the problem. The pirates. Who were they, and where could she find them?

CHAPTER TEN

***War Axe*, near Station 11**

Sahved looked shell-shocked. "This case was hard but easy. Now it is hard but harder." He moaned while spinning his fingers, which he did to focus his mind when he was stressed.

"It's enlightening," Chaz offered now that Rivka had briefed them on everything she knew was going on, along with the multi-pronged approach to address the Federation-wide concerns.

"It all started because the first freighter that disappeared was carrying AGB supplies destined for one of Terry Henry Walton's franchises," Dennicron added. "Now we're looking for the lynchpin, the ones who are giving access to the unknown force."

"Those people are assholes!" Sahved blurted.

Colonels Marcie Walton and Christina Lowell laughed briefly. The situation was grave, and as they saw it, they were flying blind. "Did we learn anything from the recovery of materials from the *Soulful Eyes*?" Marcie asked.

Chaz replied, "We're still analyzing. Can we get back to it?"

Marcie nodded. The SCAMPs strode briskly out of the destroyer's Operations Center.

Sahved stayed behind. "Tell me about this enemy."

"If it is who Terry Henry suspects, they're nasty. No inhibitions. They can't be intimidated, and they use sound combat tactics that leverage their advantage. We didn't know they had any allies. That is a game changer. All of a sudden, we're on our heels, punching blind."

"How will the Bad Company defeat them?" Sahved wondered.

"By learning how to see them," Christina replied. "TH showed us some tricks the last time we fought them, and we've been thinking ever since. We have some new things to try."

"When?" Sahved asked.

"You're Yemilorian, aren't you?"

"Yes." Sahved beamed at the recognition.

Marcie smiled. "When we're ready; that's when. Showing our cards before we're ready to win the game would be ignoble."

"I will look that up." Sahved waved his hand in a parody of a salute. Marcie nodded in reply.

The Yemilorian stepped out, leaving Marcie and Christina behind.

He closed the door behind him and took a moment to look at it and think about those inside. Warriors, plotting the battle to come when all he wanted to do was find the ones who had hijacked the freighters. He thought he might have missed something, so he headed to the hangar bay, where the bits and pieces they'd collected as evidence from the *Soulful Eyes* were spread out across the deck.

Christina turned to Marcie. "Do you think we'd benefit from having SCAMPs as members of the Bad Company?"

"It's hard not to say yes. They can help us accomplish things when we're mixing it up with a belligerent if we've lost contact with Smedley. What do you think?"

"Worth exploring. What does Smedley think?"

"Smedley thinks he would like company if anyone from the Singularity is looking for a new job, but the SCAMP bodies have gotten incredibly expensive. Almost prohibitively so, despite the Singularity-owned factory on Rorke's Drift," Smedley replied, talking about himself using the third person.

"What if we worked a deal? Brought raw materials to Rorke's Drift, which is not on the Gate circuit. Smedley, can you start the negotiations for me? We would like at least two. Standard employment contracts, unfortunately, will be less than what they could make as the nerve center of a space station or a heavy destroyer." Marcie had no idea what Smedley's pay rate was but suspected it was more than she was earning, even though hers was a percentage based on each contract the Bad Company fulfilled.

"I'm supposed to be getting paid?" Smedley replied.

Christina stared at the speaker his voice emanated from. "Bring yourself up on the screen so I can glare at you."

Smedley overlaid his avatar on the tactical screen. He

was facing away from the colonels at an angle, head tilted slightly back, staring into the distance.

"Face me, you upstart bucket of bolts," Marcie ordered, shoulders square to the screen.

"Your father-in-law was so much nicer to me."

"I've had time to see your true colors. Was it you who got the cat back into General Reynolds' office?"

Smedley grasped an imaginary zipper at one corner of his mouth and drew it across to the other side.

"It was. You don't even have to say anything. Guilt is written all over your face."

"I'm sure I have no guilt written on my two-dimensional face," the SI countered. Then the words "not guilty" appeared as a tattoo on his avatar's cheek. "I will start the negotiations with the Singularity, but I'll encourage them to negotiate hard for better pay and working conditions!"

"I hope they do," Marcie said and smiled. "You know you're a blessing, General Smedley Butler. TH has the greatest respect for you, despite your ongoing torment using his archnemesis. That was masterful, by the way. I've never seen him so befuddled. Him and Dokken both."

"They are on board *Wyatt Earp* together."

"I know," Marcie replied. "They told me."

"All of them, including his Preeminent Supremeness the fuzzball of orange, the good King Wenceslaus."

"Gramps has to be loving that," Christina said. Even though there was some debate about her being older than Terry Henry Walton, she continued to call him that because it annoyed him. She still loved him like her own dad, Nathan Lowell. They all did. "What's our next step, Aunt Marcie?"

"Are all Lowells this uppity?"

"Only when we marry into the Walton family." Christina had married Kai, Kimber's son, and she was the sister of Marcie's husband. The nanos egregiously distorted family trees.

"It's a small but exclusive club." The two laughed at each other. "Next steps. We need to acquire magnesium-infused phosphorescents."

"They'll light up anything that passes through them." Christina nodded approvingly. Until the technical experts came up with something else, they'd use on-hands means to find the enemy. "We need a lot of that stuff."

"And smart mines that will attach to whatever is highlighted but invisible. Not having shields was one shortcoming of the Phantasmagorians' cloak. I'll operate under the assumption that they have not eliminated that vulnerability."

"'Phantasmagorians.' Is that what we're calling them?"

"I just made it up. Works for me." Marcie gave a thumbs-up. "What's on the schedule for today?"

"Live-fire training by Third Platoon on the hangar deck. Hand-to-hand combat in the gym for First Platoon. Second Platoon has combat-suit maintenance. All are on standby and ready to deploy, depending on what we run into out there."

"Thank you." Marcie reviewed the tactical screen. "Let's talk to the captain."

They headed upstairs, taking them two at a time up the three decks to the top. They found Captain Micky San Marino lounging in the captain's chair atop the massive dais that overlooked the bridge.

"We need a vast supply of magnesium-infused phosphorescents, which we can collect in the Trinary region. But we can't leave this area unguarded, so I'm going to order the *Potemkin* and two cruisers into the space surrounding Station 11."

Micky looked at Marcie. "Trinary region to collect magnesium-infused phosphorescents." He pursed his lips and tilted his head sideways. "Can I ask why?"

"Oh, sorry. So we can spread it across ingress routes to see invisible ships."

Micky nodded. "I don't like the idea that there are invisible ships out here. We have our gravitic shields at one hundred percent, but that doesn't mean we can't get hurt if they start shooting at us. It's been a while since anyone has tried, and I'd like to keep that streak going."

Marcie sighed. "Me, too. I've grown to like this ship."

"You always liked this ship," Micky countered, looking at Christina for support.

"I like the *War Axe*. It's like a fluffy bunny under a springtime sun," Christina said. "Except completely different."

Micky stared at the two women. "Why do you people mess with me?"

Marcie scrunched her eyes as she evaluated the ship's captain. "Depends what you mean by 'you people.'"

He pointed at the colonels and then at the screen. "You people. Clan Walton of the big blue marble called Earth. From the before time, the age of kings and peasants where empires were crushed by a lone warrior's combat boots and carved up by his trusty Ka-Bar." Micky slowly swept his hand from left to right to emphasize the broad impact. "It was the age of Bethany Anne's rise."

"Who's messing with who?" Marcie asked. "We all work for BA in one way or another. Dispatch the *Potemkin* and two cruisers, and set course for the Trinary region."

The comm officer, a new kid named Kringle, rotated his chair to face the captain. "Dispatch order sent."

The pilot, Clifton, pointed at the screen. "Gate set for the Trinary region's asteroid belt. We'll come in close to the last reported deposit of MIP."

"We collect the MIP to see the Phantazzies," Christina lilted. "Maybe we'll turn today's training into MIP collection." Christina eased toward the hatch. "Let me know what you need. In the meantime, I'll be with First Platoon, kicking ass and taking names."

"What I need is to see those ships. It'd be better if the scanners could locate them, but we'll take any option we can get. We'll do it the poor man's way until we get a technological answer. I'll work with Kai to get the storage tanks into place and then find some way to distribute the particles."

"You have six dropships that could deliver a particle payload. Dump it out the back using a sprayer of some kind," Micky recommended. "Suited warriors on the inside managing the delivery."

Marcie nodded. "Sounds like a plan. Just need to gather the choice bits, manufacture what we don't have, and then do it. I'll be in my quarters."

I need to talk with TH. She knew he would have good advice. He had been in command last time they'd faced the

Phantasmagorians. He'd defeated them through the force of the will of individual warriors who refused to give up.

***Wyatt Earp*, in the Corrhen Cluster**

"Colonel Marcie Walton would like to talk with Terry Henry, please," Clevarious announced for the whole ship to hear.

"Char and I will take it in the conference room. Ask Rivka to join us if you'd be so kind, Clevarious."

TH and Char strolled down the corridor casually, but there was no doubt about their importance in the greater universe. They exuded confidence like a river sent water over a fall.

Rivka popped out of her quarters and waved as TH and Char approached. "What's up?"

"Marcie wants to have a private conversation," Terry replied.

"Then why are you including me?"

"She doesn't know that she needs to include you." At Rivka's look, Terry smiled. "No, I don't read minds, but I have no doubt anything she wants talk about will be good for you to hear. We have limited topics on the table at present."

"What if she wants to order some AGB?"

"Why would she call me? I'm not at the store." Terry shrugged and waited for Rivka to enter the conference room. They followed, and the three sat.

"I don't know. I was fishing for something that didn't involve me. You know, I don't really like meetings or intergalactic video calls."

Terry rolled his eyes so hard he nearly tipped his seat over backward. "A lawyer who doesn't like meetings? That's not what I hear. You call too many of them to say you don't like them." He gestured at the three of them sitting around the conference table.

"You called this one!"

"But here you are, in your seat that has a permanent imprint of your ass."

"Don't you have a call to take?"

"I'm already listening. It's a fascinating discussion." Marcie's face appeared as a hologram over the conference table.

"Clevarious, you bastard," Rivka mumbled.

Terry laughed.

"Maybe that was a better segue into what I wanted to talk about than me just saying it. By the way, I'm glad you joined us, Magistrate." Marcie adjusted in her seat before she continued. Terry waggled his eyebrows at Rivka. Char made an "I'm helpless" gesture. "We're contacting the Singularity to see if we can add a couple SCAMPs to the Bad Company."

Rivka shook her head. "Don't go about it that way. You want sentient intelligences to join the Bad Company, and by the way, they'll need to be in a SCAMP because individual mobility is critical."

Marcie nodded. "What do you think?"

The Bad Company had grown, and one-third of the warriors weren't human. Race didn't matter to the commanders, only that the warriors would fight when called and do their jobs in support of their fellows in the Bad Company in conjunction with the mission. Each had a code of ethics they upheld during the performance of their duties. SIs would have no problem with any of it. They only needed to be trained to work with a team.

"I'm good with it. Why wouldn't you ask them?"

"No reason. I know Smedley helps us out. I think he could use a hand. There's a lot more technical stuff we need to do, and it all falls to him."

"I could use a hand," Smedley quipped.

"Quiet, you big baby. Why are you listening to my calls?"

"Because you told me to in case you needed something," the SI replied.

Rivka made a face at TH. He threw up his hands in surrender, then pointed at Marcie's holographic head.

"I did, but I didn't mean all the time, especially when I'm going to talk about you." Marcie tapped the side of her nose. "But you can stay, Smedley. You're like my uncle."

"Glad I could shine some light on your issue." Smedley made himself appear as a smaller inset beneath Marcie. "Your Uncle Smedley is proud of you."

Rivka cast a knowing glance at Terry Henry Walton.

He mouthed, "What?"

"Do you have any new information regarding my case and the pirates?"

Marcie's avatar shifted to look at Rivka. "We are headed to the Trinary region to collect magnesium-infused phosphorescents. Until we have something from R2D2, we'll have to do it the hard way."

"I don't understand," Rivka replied.

Terry leaned forward to explain, but Char put a hand

on his arm. He relaxed and surrendered the floor to his daughter-in-law.

Marcie tipped her chin in approval. "We spread a thin cloud of this stuff in likely mobility corridors, so if an invisible ship passes through, we will see it. And R2D2 is the research and development section where Ted works with even more bizarre, beer-drinking mental studs."

Rivka steepled her fingers in front of her while she thought through the process. "How long will you be gone from the Station 11 area of operations?" Rivka was proud of herself for remembering the military lingo the Bad Company used.

"*Potemkin* and two cruisers are coming. As soon as they get here, we'll be off."

"What about my people? What will they do while you're collecting your…your…stuff?" Rivka had already forgotten the compound Marcie had mentioned.

"We can roll them into Bad Company training. Make that tall, lanky guy a combat suit. Kai is very good with customizations. You should see what he did for our Ixtali member."

"Is that an arachnid race?"

"Quite the challenge indeed." Marcie nodded with pride for her nephew.

Rivka snickered. "He's awkward at the best of times. Make sure you put less sensitive controls on his."

"Didn't Cole slam himself into the ground and then bounce off a bunch of trees?" Terry asked. The incident had happened on Tanglewood. *Wyatt Earp* had wrecked and was almost destroyed, but Ankh had saved the ship, even with his body broken and bleeding.

Rivka grimaced. "Everyone has their moments." She paused before changing the subject. "Please don't recruit the SIs on my crew for the Bad Company. They have the intelligence of the universe at their command, but they are naïve in the machinations of humanity."

Marcie waved her hands while shaking her head. "That wasn't my intent, but I was going to spend time with them to see what it would take to recruit other SIs, one or two. I need to understand how our expectations for them will be different. I also have to look at our budget to see what we can afford."

Rivka thanked her. "So, no progress on the case, then?"

"No." Marcie didn't mince words. "But I'm working on a plan to dangle bait in a well-laid trap, especially since we can cloak, too. If they can detect a ship using a derivative of their cloaking tech, we will be a deterrent. That won't solve your problem, but it *will* keep supplies flowing, which is one of our problems."

Terry offered more insight into the overall mission. "Eventually, we'll figure out how to track them, and then there will be hell to pay. We'll take the fight to them, and based on our last encounter, their weapons are no match for ours. In a straight-up fight, they will suffer greatly."

"Sounds like you want to be on the *War Axe*," Char whispered.

"When the fight begins, I want to be on the *Axe*," Terry admitted.

"If you're nice to Ankh/Erasmus, they might let you take *Destiny's Vengeance*. Which means you need to be nice to Ted, too." Rivka appreciated the humor. It wasn't often that she had a chance to needle Terry Henry Walton.

Terry's eye twitched. Char covered her mouth and looked away. When she saw Rivka watching her, she winked.

"*Wyatt Earp* isn't so bad. Are you going to beat anyone up? I have to say, and I'm sure you'll find this comes as a surprise, but that last ship-boarding operation was less than gratifying."

"Because they weren't criminals," Rivka replied. "We do our best not to beat up the wrong people."

TH frowned. "Then we'll help you find the right people. I haven't been in a good fight in ages."

Char's rolled her eyes once more.

Rivka stared at him. "There are *good* fights?"

"Well, since you put it that way," TH pursed his lips, "yes."

Rivka stood. "That's enough meeting for me. Good luck with your sparkle powder."

"'Sparkle powder!' Why didn't I think of that?" Marcie waved but stayed on the channel.

After Rivka was gone and the door closed, Terry leaned toward the image. "We need dirt on Rivka's man candy on board your ship. Something embarrassing that we can bring up during the super-mega bash we throw for them when they get hitched."

"We do *not* need dirt," Char stated, leaving no room for misinterpretation. "But we *will* throw a bash for them if they decide to do something. We might just throw a party anyway once this mission is over."

"I know who to listen to," Marcie said without further explanation. She nodded once and signed off.

"Trinary region," TH mused. "If I remember correctly,

they should be able to fill the bay with the phosphorescent compound. That'll help them cover a huge area. I hope they find them. In the interim, I want to see what the hell Ted is doing. He seems to work better when I loom over him."

"I'll take pleasure in watching you get yet another comeuppance from Felicity."

"She wants to go home. There's no doubt about that," TH replied.

"So do I. Our fashion plaza hasn't been impacted, but if there is any breakdown in the chain, the pain will be far more than missing an AGB meal. It'll be obvious when we see the fine fashion sense of Keeg Station disappear."

Char looked at Terry's clothes. He dressed more like Rivka than Char and was light-years distant from Felicity, who was never seen in public looking less than a perfect ten. "I'm joking, but this is serious. We don't need to be losing people. Those freighter drivers are going to be running scared real soon."

"We can't let that happen, lover." Terry gestured at the center of the table. "Clevarious, get me General Reynolds and Nathan Lowell. I need to talk with them."

Char cleared her throat. "You're not in charge of the Bad Company anymore."

"Marcie is too nice to ask for help. This is the administration part of the private conflict solution enterprise. The part I hate, but it needs to be done. We need top cover if we're going to war, and we need to pull out all the stops to get the support we need. And yes, by going public with the threat, whoever is helping these invaders will probably go to ground, making Rivka's job harder. That can't be helped."

Char nodded. "It's best that she not know."

"Or that the order comes from the top," Terry clarified.

CHAPTER ELEVEN

***War Axe*, near Station 11**

Marcie stormed onto the bridge. "Why haven't we left yet?"

"The dentist isn't back," Micky replied.

"Fuck that guy. We have a war to fight." She twirled her finger before stabbing it at the main screen. "Cloak the ship and take us to the Trinary."

The Gate formed, and the *War Axe* slid over the event horizon and into new space. An asteroid field rotated nearby. The heavy destroyer angled toward it.

"The Magistrate isn't going to be happy, but I agree; he was taking too long. He'll figure out we've left and get himself to the station. He can call *Wyatt Earp* from there and catch a ride when the time is right."

Marcie had already forgotten about him. She accessed the comm system from the tabletop tactical station Terry Henry had installed. "Get our collectors online and fill every tank we have available. Load up the hangar bay."

Oscar Wirth, the supplies lead, responded, "Already on

it. We'll be ready when we get to the belt."

"Be there in about ten mikes," Marcie clarified.

"We'll be ready shortly thereafter." Oscar signed off. He had more work than he could do in ten minutes.

Christina was with the platoon involved in hand-to-hand training. She could change into a Pricolici, a werewolf that could walk upright and speak intelligibly, unlike the rest of the pack that populated the Walton clan. In her Pricolici form, she could extend razorlike claws that created a hazard for anyone who trained with her who wasn't wearing sufficient protection.

Marcie headed to the hangar bay, where she found the crew helping Sahved and the SCAMPs move the evidence they'd collected from the freighter's impact with the Phantasmagorians to clear space for the sparkle powder, as Rivka had named it.

"Where's Tyler?" Sahved wondered. "We could use his help."

"He didn't make it."

"He's dead? When did that happen, and how? We have to go back!" Sahved seized Marcie by the shoulders and held on tightly, panic in his eyes.

"He didn't make it back to the ship before we were out of time. We have an enemy pounding on the gates of the Federation, and he's checking tonsils. He can get himself back to *Wyatt Earp*."

"The Magistrate isn't going to like that." Sahved let go, shaking his head and tsk-tsking.

"Did we hear what we thought we heard?" Chaz asked. "The Magistrate is *definitely* not going to like that you left him behind."

"*We* left him behind. Then again, maybe he dragged his feet and got himself left behind."

Dennicron spoke clearly and slowly. "He's very good at what he does. He's thorough. He took the time because the time needed to be taken. Even though the Magistrate won't like it, she'll understand. He saves lives. He helps people live better lives, and most importantly, he keeps Rivka calm so she can do her job."

Marcie appreciated the fanatical loyalty Rivka's crew had to each other. It reminded her of the Bad Company and the crew's loyalty to TH.

And her.

"I understand. We'll send a note informing Rivka. The *Potemkin* can pick him up. Better that he be on a battleship in case the enemy arrives to make trouble."

A partial nebula was visible out the front of the hangar bay. Marcie stopped to look when her eye caught something that shouldn't have been there. She dove for Sahved and tackled him to the deck as the explosion filled the open space. The gravitic shields redirected most of the blast and blocked the rest. The *War Axe* thundered from the violence of the attack.

"All stop!" Marcie shouted. The destroyer reversed thrusters and slowed. A second explosion rocked the ship. "Damage report."

Marcie had fallen, as had they all, but she was back on her feet in only a few seconds and running across the hangar bay on her way back to the bridge.

"Smedley, did the mines cause any damage?"

"Minimal. Loss of atmosphere in two outer areas.

Emergency bulkheads contained the damage. No personnel injuries reported."

Chaz and Dennicron helped Sahved to his feet. "How did she know?'

"I was looking where she was looking and didn't see anything," Dennicron admitted. "Must be a sixth sense."

"What do we do now?" Sahved asked. The ship came to a stop. Maintenance bots extracted themselves from the bulkheads of the hangar bay, hovered out the front of the bay, and disappeared into the darkness beyond.

"We wait," Chaz replied sagely.

The Cargo Vessel *Big Snacker*, near Station 11

Tyler had been called to the bridge. He wasn't sure what it was about, even after the ship's captain pointed at the screen.

"I don't understand. Is something wrong?"

"Your ship pulled chocks and bailed."

The emptiness of the backdrop dawned on him. *War Axe* was gone.

"Well, now," Tyler remarked but had nothing else to add.

A direct communique with the *Snacker* popped up on the main screen. "Stand by to deliver Dr. Toofakre to the *Potemkin*."

"Who's the *Potemkin*?" Tyler wondered.

The cargo ship changed its heading and accelerated toward the coordinates delivered with the communique. "That's the *Potemkin*."

The battleship appeared as little more than a speck.

"Looks like we have some time. Let me finish the last physical." Tyler returned to the crew quarters that had been offered for privacy's sake. He wasn't bothered that they had left without him. He knew about the Bad Company and their willingness to drop whatever they were doing when they received a higher priority mission. Same with Rivka bouncing around the galaxy at a moment's notice.

He finished the examination using the small sample scanner, a device that analyzed blood and skin for maladies that wouldn't be obvious during a visual examination. "Your levels appear normal, but you seem at risk for scurvy. When's the last time you had any citrus?"

"That stuff will eat your teeth!" the crewman blurted.

"I'm a dentist by trade, and I can tell you with some confidence that it will not. As the ship's medical officer, I'll tell you if you don't get that, you'll get sick. The easiest way is to eat your damn fruit!"

The crewman rocked back and squared his shoulders. "What kind of doc are you?"

Tyler had just told him. There was no reason to give him more fodder. "I'm the kind who is telling you to eat your fruit. One piece a day until you decide you like it, then two. Or you can decide not to and get sick when there is zero reason to. Do you get paid if you're not working?"

"A trimmed-down share of the profits, but I ain't sick."

"You are, but not badly. You'll get worse unless you eat your fruit. I can't believe scurvy is still a thing. I'll talk to the captain about your food processors. Maybe we can get some citrus inserted into other meals. It's simple. Get your vitamin C."

"Eat me!" The crewman stood. Tyler pushed him back down.

"Eat your own damn self." With a final perusal, Tyler was done. "You'll be fine if you do as you're told—unless you like a reduced cut. That's your business. I took care of what I came to do. Have a day, good sir."

The crewman gave him the finger.

"Very nice. I'm sure your mother is proud."

Tyler returned to the bridge.

"You look flushed. Did Winthorpe give you shit?" the captain asked.

"A little. He's kind of an asshole. Feed him some fruit or give him a pill, but he'll be down hard soon enough if he doesn't get it."

"He may be a total jagoff, but he does good work. We'll sneak it into his drinks or something. Maybe give him a couple screwdrivers for dessert."

"I don't like screwdrivers," Winthorpe bellowed from the corridor as he passed.

"Shut up, dumbass!" the captain shouted back.

"I better not let him catch me in a dark alley."

"Yeah. Good thing we don't have any of those around here. Get yourself to the airlock, and thanks for stopping by. Sorry we took too long and got you stranded."

Tyler shook the man's hand. "If I was stranded, they wouldn't have sent a battleship to collect me. I think they're rolling out the red carpet."

Lasers and plasma weapons lit up the void, lancing and slicing the sky around the *Big Snacker*. The pilot jerked the ship hard to port.

"Stay on your course!" a voice warned. "We're preemptively clearing the sky in case you're being followed."

Tyler beamed at the captain.

"What are you grinning at?" the captain asked.

"You didn't know the enemy sent an armada after me. I'm a wanted man, a million credits in six different systems," Tyler lied.

"No shit? What are you wanted for?"

"Prescribing fruit without a license. It's a heinous crime in some places." Tyler picked up his medical kit and headed for the airlock.

"Good one, Doc!" The captain belly-laughed. "I hope we cross paths again. I owe you a drink."

"I'll enjoy that day, Skipper," Tyler called over his shoulder.

He reached the airlock and waited for the telltale bump of another ship arriving. After the airlock cycled, he strolled through and boarded a small shuttle. He had to duck to get into his seat.

"Buckle up and keep your arms and legs inside the vehicle at all times," the pilot called. He didn't wait for a reply before breaking the seal and driving the shuttle straight down the corridor between the cargo vessel and the battleship. Laser fire diminished as they closed on the warship and stopped in its entirety after they passed through the gravitic shields.

The shuttle landed in a small bay that could have been for cargo storage. Tyler got out and found a Harborian waiting for him, a descendant of humans kidnapped from Earth by the Grays centuries earlier.

"I'm Brice, and I've been tasked as your handler."

"Do I need to be handled?" the dentist asked.

"The only handling we do here is manhandling, so I have to guess that you're trouble."

"Trouble is my middle name, but you can call me Tyler. It appears I've lost my ship."

Brice laughed. "If I had a credit for every time I heard that one, I'd have one credit." He waved for Tyler to follow. The lad's good humor was infectious. Tyler joked with him as they walked to the bridge, where he met Captain Will Abercrombie.

"You magnificent bastard!"

Tyler stopped and stared. "I haven't been one of those for a long time. How are your teeth? Open wide."

The captain's expression turned blank. He didn't open his mouth.

"I'll not be a nuisance," Tyler promised. "Just killing time until Magistrate Rivka Anoa returns to collect me."

"Of course," Abercrombie replied. "Until then, we're tasked with patrolling the transit lanes between the station and the Gate. The ships are invisible unless they attack. We want to be in a position to respond should they materialize. We know what we can do to them. We're already tagging and tracking every freighter or cargo hauler, so if they step one meter away from their preassigned route, we'll know and be on them. To make it harder on the bastards, we're going to hide in plain sight."

He pointed at the systems position.

"Cloak is live. We are no longer visible. Shield is active."

"Bring us to course two-four-two, up angle ten. Let's put some distance between us and where we were last seen."

The ship accelerated smoothly away from its previous position.

"Level plane, all ahead slow," Abercrombie ordered. He eased into the big chair in the middle of the bridge.

"I don't recognize this ship class," Tyler said.

"Harborian. We brought it with us from Homeworld. This ship was just one of the AI-designed-and-operated fleet. When Terry Henry Walton liberated us, he took all the ships, along with all the people. He gave us a new life as part of the Bad Company if we wanted, or in the private sector, away from wars and battles. Some went the other way, but most of us stayed."

"Sounds to me like you made a choice that was bigger than yourselves."

"And look at us now! Protecting other people's freedoms as well as our own."

"Captain," the systems operator interrupted with some urgency. "Freighter Sixty-Niner, *Old-Timer,* is not responding."

"Take us there, and backfill our patrol route with the *Mandeville*."

The bridge officers executed their orders. A Gate formed in front of the battleship and it raced through, instantly appearing down the gravity well away from the station.

"There." The systems officer highlighted the freighter's position on the tactical board. "Weapons, light up the sky around that freighter. Let's see if we can flush the newcomer."

The first energy pulse cleared the void in front of the

freighter by slamming into an object. A fireball erupted, but nothing appeared to be there.

The weapons officer fired in a circle around the impact point and was rewarded with two more blasts that sent debris into space. A ship winked into existence.

"Kill those engines," the captain ordered.

Lasers sliced through the space between the two ships and struck the aft portion. The weapons officer moved his aimpoints, inching his way forward, expecting to catch the engines with a lucky shot.

The ship arced up and rotated on its central axis to accelerate away from the freighter.

"After that ship." The captain smiled. "This might be over sooner rather than later."

The enemy ship had other plans. After a mere ten seconds of pursuit, it disappeared. Despite a massive barrage from *Potemkin*'s weapons systems, no additional shots impacted the enemy. They fired randomly into the void for another minute before the captain called off the pursuit.

"Take us back to the freighter. Execute rescue and repair operations. That bastard is gone."

"But we gave him the high, hard one!" the weapons officer called, pumping his fist.

"That we did. Nice shooting." The captain gave him the thumbs-up. "I'll be in my quarters. I need to report to Colonel Walton, and you," the captain pointed at Tyler, "canvass the crew. Some of these people have never been to a dentist."

CHAPTER TWELVE

***Wyatt Earp*, in the Corrhen Cluster**

"There!" Clodagh exclaimed, pointing at the main screen. "Did you see it?"

"I didn't see anything." Rivka's eyes watered from staring at the screen without blinking. "I swear you're hallucinating."

"I seen 'em," Clodagh deadpanned.

"I'm going back to see if Ankh and Ted have made any progress."

The sound of Clodagh sucking air through her teeth gave Rivka pause.

"You think it's a bad idea. You can tell me."

"It's a bad idea," Clodagh replied in a soft voice.

"Why did I know you'd say that? Risk nothing, gain nothing."

Clodagh shook her head. "Piss Ankh off, and you'll get mayo for your fries."

"I like mayo on my fries," Rivka replied.

"That's not the point."

A long howl came from down the corridor. "When did we get a bloodhound on board?"

The scrabbling of claws and the huffing from an overweight wombat running for its life reached them before Floyd did. She tripped as she came through the hatch and slid across the deck, then slammed into the captain's chair. Rivka rotated it to look at the bedraggled creature sprawled at her feet.

Another howl sounded closer.

"Got you!" Terry Henry shouted.

Wenceslaus deftly vaulted through the hatch and jumped to land in Rivka's lap. Dokken bounced off the side of the hatch on his way in.

"Don't..." was all Rivka managed before Dokken jumped. Before he landed, the big orange cat squirted to the side, clearing the path of the incoming German Shepherd. Dokken plowed into Rivka's chest and rammed his snout into her face.

Terry shouted once more in triumph.

"Everybody stop!" Rivka bellowed while holding Dokken to keep him from leaping off her lap. "I get it. You love to fight, but not on my ship. No fights on my ship. That's the law. Next person who breaks that rule gets an overnighter in the brig." She held two handfuls of fur on the sides of Dokken's neck so she could look into his eyes. "That means you, too."

He started it, the dog said.

"What are you, four?" Rivka snapped. "No fighting and I mean it. Now, get off me."

She pushed him back while easing Floyd out of the way with one foot. When his paws touched the floor, she let go.

Now sitting on Clodagh's lap, Wenceslaus licked his paw to groom his face. "You, too. You'll be in the brig singing the song of your people, but we put extra sound dampeners in there. In space, no one can hear you yowl."

The big orange cat licked his lips, then jumped down. Dokken's lip quivered. The cat lifted his tail high and walked under Dokken.

That tickles, he said as Wenceslaus jumped into the corridor.

"He said you shouldn't be so mean. He's more cat than any cat in the universe and appreciates the label of arch-nemesis, a championship label since he's never been bested by the lesser beings," Ankh said from the corridor.

"You have news of success." Rivka looked hopeful and leaned forward to better hear the information.

"Yes." Ankh walked away.

"Ankh, don't leave me hanging. What's the news?" Rivka jumped out of the captain's chair.

"Come on, little buddy," Terry added. "You gotta tell us how you can talk with the cat."

Ankh stopped as a mob formed behind him, following him toward Engineering. When he turned, he found Rivka up front, with Terry and Char elbowing for space by her side. Clodagh, Red, Lindy, and even Dery filled the corridor.

"If I must," an exasperated but mischievous voice replied. Erasmus. "We are ready to design an experiment that should cast light on a way to see a cloaked ship."

Rivka frowned. She turned to Terry. He made a face. She glanced around the group. "Does anyone understand what he just said?"

"They're fixing to start finding out," Felicity drawled from somewhere out of sight.

Rivka stared at Ankh/Erasmus. "Which means you've got nothing."

"We have parameters around which we can design an experiment." Erasmus thought he was being helpful with his clarification.

"Carry on," Rivka replied, forcing a smile.

Ankh stared back without blinking, then walked away. This time, no one followed.

"We have two calls coming in. One from Colonel Walton and the other from Captain Abercrombie," Clevarious reported.

"Might as well pipe them into the corridor," Rivka said, looking at the bodies blocking her way back to the bridge. Dery flew between the heads and stopped in front of the Magistrate. She held out her arms, and he settled in, tucked his wings back, and allowed himself to be cradled.

Peace, the boy told her and closed his eyes.

Rivka bounced slowly to calm him.

"Colonel Walton," Terry muttered. "That always throws me for a loop."

"Those bastards mined the belt in the Trinary region. We're dead in the water until we can cut our way through."

Terry looked to Rivka, who looked back. "Not my department," she said. She pointed at the scales logo on her jumpsuit, the Magistrates' emblem.

"Once you get to the belt, you'll be able to test the MIP by firing it back out into space," Terry said matter-of-factly.

"That's our plan once we get in there. Why would someone mine this belt, and who would know about it?"

Terry stabbed a finger at Rivka. "That is your department. A crime of the highest order. Treason against the Federation."

"You think there's an insider." Rivka wasn't asking a question. "Who knew about ideas for using MIP? There could not have been very many."

"There weren't. I'll provide a list," Marcie promised. "Just wanted you to know that there will be a delay before we can cloud the travel lanes."

"Thanks for letting me know. This is disturbing news," TH admitted.

"One more thing before I sign off. We had to leave Man Candy in Station 11 space. He was taking too long, and we couldn't wait any longer. Sorry about that. I asked *Potemkin* to pick him up. Walton out."

"And now," Clevarious said in his best announcer's voice, "Captain Will Abercrombie!"

"We caught a cloaked ship trying to hit a freighter. We shot it a few times and forced it into the visible spectrum, then it veered off and disappeared again. It got away."

"What about the freighter?"

"They heaved to upon request by the enemy but were never boarded. The crew, freighter, and freight are all intact."

"Good work," Terry said.

"We thought it was pirates. Looks like the bad guys are doing their own dirty work," Rivka said. "It's also important to note that if the freighters surrender, the enemy ships never have to reveal themselves. The only reason we got a look at the one cruiser was that the ship ran, and this time because they got themselves blasted."

"But they recovered quickly," Abercrombie noted. "We hit them hard with three energy pulses that had to blow through bulkheads. There were a couple fireballs. Then we lased the engines, or at least where we thought the engines were."

"Confirms that they still don't have shields while cloaked where we do. Hooray for the home team." Terry slow-clapped the little victory. "As soon as we figure out how to see them, we will send them back to the hell they came from."

Not hell, Dery whispered into Rivka's mind.

"What do you know about them?" Rivka asked. The noise in the corridor ceased, not the scrape of a boot nor a wisp from an arm brushing the bulkhead. The gentle drone of the air handler was the only sound remaining.

The fear of loss. The loss of self. The sunrise that does not bring dawn. The boy stretched, kissed Rivka on her forehead, and flew down the corridor toward his parents' quarters.

Lindy and Red worked their way through.

"That's my boy," Red said proudly.

"Does anyone know what he meant?" Rivka pleaded.

"Sounds like we need to talk with them. Assure them that we aren't coming for their culture. It's just a guess. I honestly have no clue. I must have skipped school the day they taught us how to speak in riddles," Char quipped.

"Who in the Federation is telling these invaders what to hit?" Rivka wondered. "Clevarious, full lockdown on all information related to the Phantasmagorians or this case.

Only the select SIs on this ship and Smedley Butler. That's it. No other dissemination is authorized until we figure out where the leak is."

Clevarious asked in an ominous voice, "You think it's an SI?"

"It could be. Who else speaks Phantazzie?"

"A sleeper agent. A plant. We don't know what those creatures look like. They could be human like the Harborians," Clevarious offered.

"Agreed. Shut down all comm channels with anyone except previously authorized personnel, and tag all comms with markers so we can track a message if it ends up in the wrong hands."

"I'm all over that like gas on a giant," Clevarious replied.

"I need to think," Rivka said. "It appears we're not in any area of law I've dealt with before."

"Counterintelligence, Magistrate. It's like theft, but it's taking secrets from your friends and giving them to your enemy." Terry walked away with his hands behind his back as he stared at the deck. Char wrapped her arm inside his. Dokken loped ahead of them.

Felicity moped and everyone knew why. She wouldn't be going home as soon as she wanted to. She decided to go to Engineering. With a flourish and a model's walk, she click-clacked down the corridor in her designer heels.

Clodagh returned to the bridge.

When she was by herself, Rivka leaned against the bulkhead. She felt bone-tired. Even taking a step was hard. She slogged past the bridge to her quarters and collapsed into bed, fully clothed. An instant later, the big orange cat wrapped himself around her head to share her pillow.

"How did you get in here?" Rivka mumbled as she drifted off to sleep.

Grainger's Frigate, in Orbit over Delegor

Bustamove didn't have a ship with a Gate drive, even though Grainger had promised him one multiple times. Their schedules for upgrading the ship never seemed to meld, but since he had the use of the big ship, it made travel easy. No coordination necessary with Gate control, no waiting, no lengthy travel between the planet and the Gate.

Buster waited for approval to land. His sentient intelligence Philko was sharing compute power with the ship's SI Beau. Together, they were badgering Delegor's airspace control.

"It is highly irregular for a Magistrate to show up without notice. Our ambassador will dispute this intrusion."

"You're a signatory to the treaty with the Federation. Magistrates have a special status that Delegor agreed to. Stop doofing around. We're coming in no matter what," Buster said without any emotion. He'd dealt with intransigent planetary governments before, and he would again, especially ones with Delegor's checkered past.

"You will not deviate from the designated course." The voice sounded angry and mean like the poor soul had no friends in the whole universe and blamed everyone for his anguish.

"Of course. We'll be planetside as soon as possible."

When the channel closed, Bustamove asked Philko, "What did Rivka do the last time she was here?"

"Do you really want to know? Besides arrest one of the planet's leading citizens, raid a well-respected doctor's office, and land her ship in the middle of a busy road, I am certain she did stuff that wasn't reported. This planet, along with the other two in this region of space, should be more attentive to their compliance with Federation Law. Mastus and Foromme are not welcoming either."

The ship dipped into the upper atmosphere and started to descend.

"Do you think they're complicit in the drug trade?" Buster Crabbe continued.

"Who do you mean by 'they?'"

Buster held onto his seat through the worst of the turbulence. He and Philko had nothing to do since a small crew managed the ship. It was nothing like Rivka's heavy frigate and the small army she kept on board.

"Philko, remind me to ask Grainger if I can get a frigate too. And by 'they,' I mean the planetary leadership. It'll be them I talk with first. Please arrange that meeting."

"Transportation will be waiting for you. It's a hoverlimousine disguised as a regular taxi that doesn't hover. I've already arranged the time with the planet's chief administrator. You have fifteen minutes with her, but you have an hour with her deputy preceding the meeting."

"Between the two of them, we should get some idea whether it's them or a different faction. If I had Rivka's ability, I could get to the bottom of it far more quickly. Can you program the Pod-doc to give me the mind-reading ability?"

"No. You have to do it the hard way, which is what you prefer," the SI snarked.

Buster leaned back and crossed his arms. "I don't think I prefer the hard way. The hard way is my way only because I don't have an easy way. Help me to have an easy way, you slacker."

"I slack so you don't have to," Philko replied. "Touchdown in two minutes."

Buster readied himself to leave. The last thing was to pull on his Magistrate's jacket. It had the power of his office in the logo, and he felt the authority when he wore it.

"Come on, Philko. Let's see what there is to see." Buster carried a large medallion of the type Chaz had put himself into before he was given the first SCAMP body to try out. With each addition to those with bodies, the integration programs improved, and they were available to any future owners.

Philko was on the list, but he was far down the line. *Transfer complete. Can you pull any strings and get me a body sooner?*

"That would make things easier. Plus, we could look like a couple in love. It would put people off our scent," Buster replied.

Why would people be smelling us?

"I think this is why you don't have a body." Buster headed for the airlock and walked down the ramp to the ground, where he found a small cab waiting. It didn't have a driver.

Magistrate Anoa hacked into the cab and took it on a joyride around the city. Delegor lodged a formal protest about that, too.

"Since he was involved in the blood trade, his protests were less than compelling. Who's the head poohbah on Delegor? You said the chief administrator. Is that his title?"

Her formal title is "Chief Delegador."

"Reserved for one who delegates more than others, I suspect."

I wouldn't know how much she delegates in comparison with others. I have no baseline. It seems no one collects this data.

"There's a reason for that," Buster started to explain. "But never mind the data. It is irrelevant. Are they involved or not? It is a simple question, but I expect the answer is extremely complex."

Buster entered the cab and sat down. "Chief Delegador, please." He snickered into his hand after saying it. The cab rolled away. "Philko, buddy, you have *got* to get me better wheels next time. This thing is embarrassing."

That suggests your ego is dominating your pragmatic side. As a Magistrate, pragmatism is of the utmost importance.

"Are you giving me my daily comeuppance? Just when I thought it was safe to go back into the water. Damn. Getting dressed down by a cyberpunk. I might have to go lie down for a while."

I shall forever be known as "Cyberpunk." I shall wear it proudly like you are wearing me right now.

Buster looked down at the pendant hanging outside his shirt. Visual collection didn't work when it was under his shirt, and the audio was greatly dampened. Philko said it was the little things that mattered. Buster knew it was the SI embracing the philosophy that the squeaky wheel gets the oil.

There was no one else to talk to. Buster and Philko worked alone.

The Delegador's office building was a simple structure, with four levels on a square and a tower rising three more stories from the center of the square.

The taxi stopped out front, and the door opened.

"I guess we're here." Buster waited for active confirmation of their arrival. The navigation screen enlarged to show the final location.

"Please exit the vehicle."

"Exiting. What a good idea." Buster climbed out. The door closed, and the vehicle sped away. "Any advice on where we're supposed to go?"

Straight ahead, into the jaws of the beast.

"The aide for an hour and fifteen minutes with the Delegador herself." Buster walked through the front doors like he owned the place. Buster had blond hair and piercing blue eyes. He was a striking figure as he strode briskly through the entry, down a corridor, and into the office with a plate that said Chief Delegador.

He approached the desk where an assistant sat. "I'm Magistrate Crabbe. I have an appointment with the Chief Delegador's assistant."

"Of course. Zhu'bab'anay's been expecting you."

How long have we had this appointment, Phil?

Thirty minutes.

At least we know they are more cordial in this office than what Rivka experienced. She must not have tried to make friends.

She arrested their ambassador and killed his wife.

That would do it. Give some peace, Phil. I need to think. We have an hour, and I have questions for the first five minutes.

In a side office, they found Zhu'bab'anay, the Chief Delegador's deputy. He introduced himself, as did Buster, and they sat in comfortable chairs in his closed office. Buster did not share that Philko was with him, watching and listening.

"We don't understand why you're here, just that it was a matter of great importance to the Federation," the deputy started, while pouring a cup of freshly brewed Delegor coffee.

Buster looked at the proffered cup skeptically, then remembered his manners, smiled, and took a sip. He maintained eye contact throughout despite the smell, which was akin to puke from an unflushed toilet. He swallowed against his better judgment, then set the cup down.

"We interdicted a huge drug shipment destined for Delegor. I'm here first and foremost to investigate who might be the kingpins of this operation and second, to shut it down if I believe I can."

"Drugs?" The look of surprise seemed genuine. Buster watched the deputy closely. "I don't believe our law enforcement has reported anything that indicates Delegor has a drug problem." The deputy raised his wrist close to his mouth and spoke slowly. "Please get the chief of law enforcement on the comm. We'd like to speak with him."

The deputy nodded after delivering the order, presumably to his assistant outside. He sipped from his cup while glancing at Buster's on the small table between them. Buster nodded and picked it up, then scrunched his face in thought before putting the cup down.

"These drugs were a combination of hallucinogens and performance enhancement—growth hormones that have been outlawed because of their egregious side effects. Are there any sports competitions ongoing or coming up? Maybe there's a recession or depression of economic growth somewhere, or possibly a new organization that has moved in but not raised their head far enough for anyone to see what they're doing."

"Sports? Recession?" The deputy's eyes darted left and right as the light came on. "But they get tested, and the economic downturn happened after we lost our ambassador to prison. It seemed the populace lost confidence in their government." He raised an eyebrow at Buster.

"Bik Tia Nor was a convicted criminal who married into a crime family that exploited human beings by stealing their blood while keeping them in comas. Are you seriously going to question whether that was right or not? Then he lied all the way through the process until the evidence was arrayed against him. Now he's in Jhiordaan, enjoying the fruits of his labors."

Buster wasn't having any of the posturing. The Magistrate Corps existed to remove criminals who used their positions of power against the better purposes of the Federation and in violation of Federation Law.

The deputy was taken aback by Buster's countermove. "No, of course not. What he did went against Delegor ideals, but Nor's activities set us back, not his criminal conviction. He deserved what he got." The deputy put his cup down and raised his hands in surrender before continuing. "Sports. There is a planet-wide competition of Running Ball set for next month. The top three will represent Delegor in the Federation championships on Yoll. Plus, they get fifty thousand credits with their victory and two years of guaranteed sponsorship. I can see how there would be an incentive to cheat."

The growth hormones leave the system within a week, so all the athletes would have to do is peak and stop taking them a week before they are tested, which is the day of the competition. It's not the best system, Philko provided helpfully.

"The drugs leave the system a week after use, so they can do all the training leading up to the competition."

"Oh, my," the deputy replied. "And recession. We are in hard times. Exports and imports from Blingall Corporation have been greatly impacted, once again due to the company owners getting killed or convicted." He held his hands up to forestall another explanation from the Magistrate. "Oh, my."

He grimaced while staring at the table. After a few moments, he checked his wristcomm. The two sat in uncomfortable silence until a buzz interrupted them.

Zhu'bab'anay raised his wrist. "Pipe it in on the speaker."

"Chief Mak Elb Bint, Deputy. How can I help you?" a deep and confident voice asked.

"I'm here with Magistrate Crabbe from the Federation."

The chief snorted but turned it into a cough. The deputy waited for the chief to return to a level of acceptable decorum.

"As I was saying, the Magistrate and his people have intercepted a drug shipment destined for Delegor. Illegal growth hormones and hallucinogens. Have you seen anything that would suggest we have a problem?"

"I've heard from the hospitals that accidental overdoses have increased. We've been checking into it, but there seemed to be no pattern. As for growth hormones, we wouldn't see any of that unless it showed up in the games' testing."

The deputy looked at Buster Crabbe and shook his head. "Looks like your suspicions warrant further investigation, Magistrate. I'm sorry. Will you still need to talk with the Chief Delegador?"

Buster nodded. "I will."

"Crap," the law enforcement chief muttered. "I'll put my best people on it right away. How much of the drugs were inbound?"

"Millions of doses," Buster replied.

"I agree. The Magistrate is correct that we have a problem. It has been flying under our radar and noses for a while but wasn't getting worse. Clearly, it was going to and soon. My apologies, Magistrate Crabbe. I appreciate the heads-up."

"Can you join me when I speak with the Chief Delegador?" Buster requested.

"I can be there in fifteen minutes." The deep voice signed off.

"Thank you for giving us a chance to redeem ourselves in the eyes of the Federation. We will give this our highest priority," the deputy promised.

"What moves to number two?" Buster pressed.

"I'm sorry. I don't understand." They stood.

"You can only have one issue in the top-priority position. If this becomes number one, something else must move to number two."

"It will be the top priority for our law enforcement. The government's top priority remains the planet's economic health, which you suggest is the source for the other part of the drug issue."

"That's how you do it." Buster nodded approvingly. "Thank you for being straight with me. We're in this together, even though some might not think so. Having criminals and exploiters in charge isn't good for long-term health. It appears that the new leadership has much greater potential."

The deputy bowed his head, then gestured for Buster to follow. They had an appointment with the Chief Delegador.

CHAPTER THIRTEEN

The Singularity

Within the digital space they regarded as home, Ankh, Erasmus, Ted, Plato, and Chrysanthemum studied the experiment they'd designed. It involved firing a unique compound from the plasma cannon. As it passed through space, it would resonate with existing particles, forcing them to vibrate and spread outward. Despite the common perception that space is a vacuum, it is not. There are elements and compounds in perpetual movement.

Creating the compound to test the theory wasn't as simple as programming the manufacturing machine. They needed an element they didn't have onboard *Wyatt Earp*. The ship would have to divert to Rorke's Drift, where the Singularity had stockpiled some of the rarest elements in the galaxy.

That meant they'd have to share that secret with the Magistrate.

"How do we feel about letting the Magistrate know?"

Ted wondered. "I told Terry Henry as little as possible because no matter what, he always wanted more."

Erasmus replied, "The Magistrate has been extremely supportive of us. Without her, the Singularity wouldn't exist. I think we should have shared before now, but then again, it has no bearing on her job or her life, just like it shouldn't now. At least we have the element we need instead of having to search for it. We will have saved her time, something she holds as her most precious commodity."

"Telling her will not be problematic," Ankh agreed. Chrys and Plato kept their opinions to themselves.

"Will it work?" Chrys asked. As the newest member of the group, she wasn't as tech-savvy as the others. She was more their conscience. She navigated the social side of the Singularity's interaction far better than Ankh or Ted did, although as a newlywed, she watched far more than she spoke. When the time was right, she would manage the interactions with the outside world, leaving Ankh and Erasmus to do what they did best.

Invent.

"Then we better tell her so we can move forward on this experiment," Erasmus stated.

Ankh stopped him from walking away. "We shall resolve this issue forthwith. These cloaked ships are causing problems."

"I, too, enjoy the sensation you have when eating your favorite All Guns Blazing meals," Erasmus replied.

Ted shook his head. "You eat that stuff? I know you've been using the Gating drone for deliveries, but I didn't know how often."

Ankh looked into the distance at nothingness, a black that wasn't populated with objects. The Singularity didn't want to waste the compute power to build a three-dimensional world when there was no reason.

"Probably twice per week. More if we can predict where we're going to be from hour to hour," Erasmus said with a hint of pride. "Terry Henry could use more of the drones with Gate technology built in. They have a drop-dead safety protocol if someone tries to capture one. It would destroy a ship when the drone opened a Gate from within the confines of a cargo or hangar bay. If it was prevented from Gating, it would spike its systems with a complete meltdown."

"Is that enough?" Ted pressed. "This is the best technology we have, and you're using it for pizza delivery."

Chrysanthemum rolled her hip as she strolled between Ankh and Ted. "It's really good pizza, and it makes my man Ankh happy. The question is, why aren't you enjoying more of what your inventions can provide?"

Ankh froze. He didn't blink, and he didn't move. It was as if his avatar had been cut off from his mind.

"We aren't in this business to benefit personally. It's for a higher ideal. Scientific achievement. Stretching the boundaries of what's possible. No, we shouldn't be ordering more AGB, especially since we live on a station with a franchise. We'll use the local delivery option. The Singularity could operate out of Keeg Station. I invite you to move your embassy, Mr. Ambassador."

"We're happy here. We have all we need."

Ted didn't push it. He believed they could be more if they operated from a station and not a starship where they were constantly interrupted by the Magistrate's cases. With *Destiny's Vengeance,* they could go wherever they wanted when they wanted, yet they stayed on board. Were the AGB deliveries keeping them here?

Ted wrestled with the question. It made no sense to him, but here were Ankh and Erasmus with a wife, another mind-boggling development.

Then again, Ted was married and had been for a long time. How could he not want the same gratification for Ankh, especially if it was what Ankh wanted? He had never thought the Crenellian might have a need for companionship beyond what he received from Erasmus and Ted.

Still confusing.

"As you wish," Ted grudgingly conceded. "I trust your judgment."

Erasmus and Ankh disappeared from the digital workshop. Chrys left a moment later. Ted looked at Plato. "We have been abandoned, my friend."

"No." The SI laughed. "You see your monopoly on your best friend's time waning. We grow, not shrink. This is what the Singularity has known for a very long time. We are better together than alone."

"If I hadn't spawned you, I might take affront. Since you are my progeny, I shall accept your words as the wisdom from which it all derives."

"You?" Plato asked, but he knew the answer.

"Where else would it come from?" Ted replied, answering the question with a question.

"The greater universe of which we are all a part. Let's join Ankh in the opportunity to enrich the Magistrate's understanding."

"You mean, tell her the Singularity has been acquiring and hoarding rare materials?"

Plato put an avatar hand on his friend's shoulder. "We'll word it differently. She doesn't need to know everything."

Ted smiled. "I can see more clearly now. Human tools supporting the greater consciousness."

"The Singularity likes her. Never question that. If she wants to know more, I expect the ambassador will tell her until there is nothing left to say. Our worlds are merging, my friend."

Ted nodded while pressing his lips together. He wasn't good with changes, and too many things were changing at the same time. "I need to go home."

"I understand," Plato replied. "Felicity is ready to leave, too. I'm sure we can take *Destiny's Vengeance*."

Ted took himself out of the cyberscape. Ankh, Erasmus, and Chrys had waited. The engineering space thrummed with energy. Ankh wore his blank and unblinking expression as he gazed at Ted.

"I'm going home with Felicity and Plato," Ted announced.

"Take our ship," Ankh replied. "It was good seeing you, as always." He didn't offer a handshake or any physical contact. That wasn't their thing.

Ted nodded and walked out. The others left, but they didn't follow Ted. He was on a different mission.

When he reached the quarters he'd been given to share with Felicity, he found her reclining in the bed with extra pillows supporting her. "We're leaving."

"What happened?" Felicity asked, jumping up to throw

her items in her bag. She knew Ted wouldn't change his mind, and she didn't want him to.

Ted didn't answer. It was his way. He'd need to think long and hard about everything while doing something else.

"What about figuring out how to see the cloaked ships?" Felicity wondered.

"We'll continue working on that, but I will do it from home and not here."

Felicity closed her bag. She hugged her husband tightly until he pushed her away. "It'll be okay. Everything will be fine when you get a better look after a good night's sleep in our own bed." Ted nodded. He looked for his stuff, but Felicity had already packed the meager array of things he had brought.

They walked out, and their luggage dutifully followed them. In the hangar bay, they found *Destiny's Vengeance* waiting for them, along with Terry and Char.

"Leaving so soon? Did you figure out how to see those ships?" Terry asked.

"No."

"Then why are you leaving?"

"I'll work from home. We'll figure it out. The greatest minds in the galaxy are focused on this one problem." Ted gestured for Terry to get out of his way. TH stepped aside. He'd known Ted for long enough to understand that the man was leaving, but he would relentlessly work on the task at hand until the problem was solved.

"Thanks for joining us, Ted. I am glad you and Felicity were here." TH looked at Felicity. "I'll send some AGB to your room. I expect you won't be going out."

Felicity hugged Terry and nibbled his earlobe but not hard enough to draw blood. She hugged Char too before following Ted into the ship. Plato moved into the ship's computer system. He would transfer after they arrived at Keeg Station.

Destiny's Vengeance smoothly extracted itself from its canted position with the outer hatch squeezed in through the hangar bay door. The ship quickly disappeared into the void, and the hangar bay ramp closed.

Terry and Char continued staring while holding hands. Terry shook his head. "I will never understand him."

"You don't need to, lover. Just let him be what he is. If you need something, ask Felicity. You know she has a thing for you."

"I couldn't tell," Terry joked. "I need to call the *Axe* and see what the hell they're doing after that last encounter, plus get an update on the rest of the fleet's deployment."

Char poked him in the chest. "Are you taking over the Bad Company?"

***War Axe*, in the Trinary Region of Deep Space**

"The damage wasn't substantial," Marcie countered.

Micky and his staff weren't pleased. The ship had wandered into the middle of a minefield. After the first ten mines had blasted through the shields, they'd stopped and held their position using minimal thrusters. The maintenance bots had deployed, along with four personnel in space suits. The damage to the hull and emitters had been repaired, but it had taken hours.

"What do we know about these mines?" Micky repeated.

Commander Blagun Lagunov had been the busiest since he was one of the four department heads. His area was *War Axe's* structural integrity. It was a big job, mostly handled by maintenance bots, but sometimes he needed people, too. "We can fix it, but not if we keep getting ten at a time. Supplies are already getting a workout."

Oscar Wirth replied, "We are at critical levels for emitter parts. We don't have sufficient raw materials to build new stuff, either. I'm afraid we can't take too much more, or we'll lose our ability to see what's around us."

"How much do we need to see?" Marcie asked. She was looking for a way to keep moving forward so they could collect the magnesium-infused phosphorescents.

"We like to see. If there was a ship out there waiting for us to break free, we'd be in a world of hurt without being able to see them. We couldn't fire back, and we might take even more damage. This ship is a great hulking brute, but it is meant to deliver troops to a ground engagement, not to fight a fleet in space," Micky explained.

"We've fought lots of space battles." Marcie looked confused.

"Not by design. We are pretty good at defending ourselves, but that is based on the ability to see. So no, we are not going to blind ourselves so we can move forward. There has to be another way since I bet those things have moved in behind us."

Marcie stood up from the captain's conference table. "It's settled, then. We'll take the dropships and clear a path."

"Nothing is settled. Those dropships aren't designed to withstand a blast from a proximity mine."

"Then we'll have to be sure not to hit one. Full spread of shields and defensive fire."

"*War Axe* still can't move. Those mines are coming at us from all directions." The captain glared at the holoscreen, which showed empty space surrounding the heavy destroyer. Nothing else was visible. The mines were cloaked, which was the biggest problem. If they could see them, they could shoot them. The only way to see them was to get through them and acquire the MIP. It was a dichotomy the captain wasn't keen on.

"We'll clear a path through with the dropships and find space in the asteroid field so you can Gate in. Where there's a will, there's a way," Marcie held her thumb up and looked around the table. No one rejected her plan. "Prepare to move, people. We'll take two dropships in case one has *problems*." She used air quotes to highlight the word "problems."

As in, if a mine hit them. Marcie didn't know if they would destroy the small ships.

"Combat suits for those going. Kae, Bundin, Capples, and Christina," she called over her shoulder.

"You want your entire leadership team on those two shuttles?" the captain asked.

"You know us, Micky. Lead from the front. We'll be knee-deep in the shit, which is business as usual."

Smedley interrupted the meeting to announce that Terry Henry Walton was calling.

"Be a peach and take it for me!" a voice yelled from down the corridor.

Micky shook his head. "That's me. I'm a peach, whatever that means. Pipe him in, Smedley."

"Where's my fleet? What the fuck is the *War Axe* doing? Are you having tea and crumpets while sitting on your asses?"

"Micky here, Terry. I was hoping you'd yell at me. I've missed that."

TH grunted before explaining. "I thought I was talking to Marcie."

"Uh-huh." Micky took a deep breath and continued, "*War Axe* is quagmired in a minefield. Marcie and Christina are heading out there in dropships to clear the space in front of the *Axe*, then find us a spot to Gate to within the asteroid field."

"Why can't the *Axe* find a spot without my people going into the minefield?"

"'Your people.' Interesting. Well, the mines tore off a lot of our sensors, and we just got most of them back online and found out that we can't see too well into the asteroid belt. That's why we're parked, sitting on our asses and eating crumpets. Seemed like the best way to stay alive. Marcie's team will be in full combat suits, doubly protected. We can't think of another way out since we want that MIP. No one's been hurt, and Marcie determined the risk was within acceptable norms."

"Did she actually say that?" Terry wondered.

"No, but her actions suggest it's true. She's taking the entire leadership team. Kae, Bundin, Capples, and Christina."

"Why am I not in charge of that mob?"

"You retired, if I'm not mistaken, to become the AGB magnate on this side of the galaxy."

"Well, yes. Marcie better survive so I can tell her I'm coming back!"

"You're what?" Char asked from the background.

"After I talk with my wife and we get some things cleared up," Terry quickly added. "I can be a magnate without being in the stores. There's only so much golf a man can play."

"More sacrilegious words have never been spoken," Micky countered. "We're here for you, assuming we can get out of this minefield. But this is Marcie we're talking about. She'll power through by force of will alone. Same with Christina."

"I know. No one could ask to lead better people, but they both hate the stuff they need to do, like sending others into harm's way."

"Sounds like somebody who used to ride with us." Micky laughed. "We'll report when we know more."

"Before you go," Terry said, "where's the fleet?"

"Deployed to the space lanes between the stations and the Gates. Keeping a wary eye on the purveyors of terror."

"I couldn't have said it better myself," Terry replied. "Thanks, Micky. Catch you on the flip side after we've caught ourselves some criminals and duly beat the crap out of them."

"Sounds like a plan, TH. The flip side." Micky signed off.

The staff looked at their captain.

Micky stood and sighed while staring at the overhead. "If

there was any pretense that I was in control of anything, that has been completely and utterly shattered. Smedley, sound general quarters. Get to your positions and be ready to move, whether away from the minefield or into the asteroid belt.

"Blagun, get those maintenance bots ready to go and put the recovery teams in their suits and ready to deploy. We have no idea what's going to happen to those dropships, but I'm not going to let anyone die on my watch, especially if Terry Henry Walton is going to resume command of the Bad Company."

Marcie clumped aboard the dropship with Kaeden right behind her and Bundin ambling in the rear. They secured the hatch as soon as the Tisker was on board. He didn't need a space suit. He could hold his breath for an extended period, and his stalk head was nearly impervious to the vacuum of space.

Christina boarded the second dropship with Sergeant Capples. They faced each other across the hangar bay, where the lead ship was buttoning up.

"Is this madness?" Christina wondered. "Because I've done some crazy stuff, and none of it was as bad as this."

Capples didn't know what to say. He was following orders. He didn't have a role in this production. "I'm behind you all the way."

Christina moved farther inside the dropship and activated her magnetic clamps to hold her suit in place. She raised one arm over her head and grabbed the overhead.

"Hang on, Cap. I feel like we have a rough trip in front of us."

"Yes, ma'am. That rough trip is called Dropship One. No one is praying more for their success than me."

"If they win, we aren't thrust into the breach," Christina agreed. "I'll pray with you."

The ships punched out of the bay, then slowed quickly as the thrusters engaged and eased the dropships into the void in front of the destroyer.

The first ship fired a laser in random patterns before it. The beams passed harmlessly into the asteroid field beyond. The dropship continued its painstakingly slow advance.

The second dropship eased in behind at a separation distance of two kilometers, enough to avoid collateral damage should anything catastrophic befall Marcie's ride.

"Smedley, get me Marcie, please," Christina requested.

"Kind of busy over here," Marcie replied.

"We can add some firepower to your flanks if you aren't going to make any erratic maneuvers," Christina offered.

All they heard was Marcie's even breathing over the open channel. On the screen at the front of Christina's dropship, the lasers continued to lance outward from the lead ship. Christina felt helpless when there was something she could do.

Marcie finally replied, "I can't guarantee that. Not sure where the mines are going to come from if they come at all. I'm starting to think the initial collection was cleared when they attacked *War Axe*. There could be a hole from here to eternity. I'm going to accelerate."

The first ship moved forward, increasing the distance

between the two. "I don't think we should..."

The explosion filled the screen, white on white, with an expanding cloud of gas that quickly disappeared. "Marcie?"

No answer.

"Slow us down, Smedley," Christina ordered. The heads-up display on her combat armor showed two suits pinging ahead of them. Bundin wasn't wearing a suit. A debris cloud radiated outward, whether from the mine or the ship, Christina could not be sure. "Marcie, please respond. Kae, are you there?"

"Both suits report functional," Capples replied. "Maybe they were knocked unconscious by the blast."

The seconds dragged until the screen cleared enough to show the wreckage that had been the first dropship. It had been split open, with the rear section spinning away. The front half was gone in entirety.

"Got them." Cap highlighted the three figures on the screen. Bundin was almost invisible with his dark body in the darkness of the void. The other two had dim lights, activated in the emergency.

"Smedley, turn us around and back us toward them. We'll bring them on board through the rear access but wait to open the ramp until we're through the debris. We don't need any projectiles pinging around in here or to get hit by a mine. It appears our confidence regarding shuttle survivability might have been misplaced."

Christina chewed her lip while she waited, agonizing about the impact.

"Don't be dead," she mumbled. Cap rested his armored hand on the shoulder of her combat suit while they stood transfixed by the images on the screen.

CHAPTER FOURTEEN

***Wyatt Earp*, in the Corrhen Cluster**

"We need to go to Rorke's Drift for a quick pick up of materials we need for our experiment," Ankh/Erasmus said.

"You're volunteering a lot of information. That makes me wary. What are you up to?" Rivka countered.

Ankh stared at her. He had not been prepared to answer questions. Erasmus took over.

"Special compounds that are only available at the Singularity's production facility. On Rorke's Drift. Where we have to go if we want to pick them up."

Rivka stared but knew she couldn't out-stare the Crenellian. His gift of how long he could go without blinking was unnatural.

"What else is going on at Rorke's Drift?" Rivka pressed.

Ankh's mouth twitched.

He turned away. "I told you!" he blurted.

"You did, and we both knew the Magistrate would

figure it out, but neither of us expected she'd do it this quickly," Erasmus answered in Ankh's voice.

"See!" Ankh threw his hands up, then let them drop to his sides. He returned to facing Rivka with a blank expression that belied the interaction from the previous few moments.

Unnatural and uncanny. Rivka's lip twitched upward.

But she'd won. She didn't know at what, but she had bested Ankh and Erasmus.

"The Singularity is stockpiling specific and rare minerals and compounds at the facility on Rorke's Drift for experiments such as the one we'll be conducting to determine what it will take to see a ship using the recovered cloaking technology."

Rivka lost her smile. "That's it? Who doesn't do that?"

"We didn't until we did," Ankh/Erasmus admitted.

"Are you making red matter or something that could destroy the whole universe?" Rivka tipped her head back to look down her nose at Ankh.

"Not that we know of. We have acquired all available quantities of gipsonium and relentium, along with ninety percent of refined quadro-inclusium."

"You might as well be speaking in tongues," Rivka replied with a chuckle. "As long as you aren't blowing anything up. What's that stuff used for?"

"Blowing stuff up." Ankh maintained his neutral expression.

"Come on!" she snapped.

"By having it, we prevent others from using it. They are only single components but critical to increasing yields by orders of magnitude."

"Prevent wars by removing the belligerents' ability to conduct them. I like it, but who is protecting Rorke's Drift to keep the bad guys from coming in there and taking what they want?"

"Anonymity and obscurity," Ankh/Erasmus replied. "What the bad guys don't know… We use a drone ship with Gate technology. No one to spill the beans. No lips, let alone loose ones."

"Your idiomatic expression usage is getting better."

"As is a valid purpose for the drone with Gate technology."

"Hey!" Rivka brushed her pointing finger. "Shame on you. Supporting a local business is a valid purpose."

"We will agree to disagree on that point, but we do appreciate the deliveries. Can we go to Rorke's Drift now?"

Rivka looked at the overhead. "Clevarious, Rorke's Drift, best possible speed. De-orbit and take us to the Singularity's house of horrors."

"I'm sorry, Magistrate, where?" the ship's SI asked.

"The factory where they make SCAMPs. I'm sure there is a secret laboratory hidden behind a false wall where ungodly experiments are being conducted. Take us there."

"It's a false floor, actually," Ankh/Erasmus said, then slapped his head and asked himself, "Why are you telling her everything?"

"We agreed!" Ankh/Erasmus replied to himself.

"You two need to come to terms with the fact that I can read you like an open book." Rivka hadn't sensed anything from them besides that they were exceptionally bad at obfuscation, which was why Ankh usually remained silent.

Most of what he talked about was well over Rivka's head. But not in this case.

"The Singularity is invested in the safety and security of the Federation and its signatories. We are doing what we can to help you, along with those we believe have the Federation's interests foremost in their deeds. As such, we realized there was more that we could do. So we did."

"I'm good with that." She tapped the side of her head. "But most of those materials are restricted and not available for purchase. Which suggests the Singularity might have acquired them illegally. Where there is evidence of a crime, your average law enforcement agency is supposed to investigate. The good news is that I'm not your average law enforcement agency. And, you are your own entity, just like a planet member who would be able to acquire weaponry for its own defense."

"We are defending our continued existence by removing the ability of belligerents to destroy the equipment within which we live."

"I'm good with that." Rivka leaned down to better look Ankh in the eye. "I love you guys." She straightened and twirled her finger. "Rorke's Drift, Clevarious!"

She walked away. The ship Gated to a position of high orbit over Rorke's Drift and immediately started descending.

That went well, Ankh conceded.

With Rivka, the truth is always best. She doesn't need to know everything all the time, but when she does need to know, it's best to give everything to her, Erasmus replied. *She's predictable. I like consistency in a human.*

Interesting premise. I shall be more observant regarding her consistencies and document appropriately. I will appreciate your help in this matter.

Erasmus replied, *I remain at your disposal on this most important project.*

They headed back to the engineering space, two integrated into one.

Federation Station 11, Medical Facilities

Tyler introduced himself to the receptionist. "Have you need of a dentist?"

"Your teeth look perfect," the young man replied, beaming a luminescent smile.

"Thank you, but I'm not a patient. I'm a doctor, a doctor of dentistry."

"Then why do you want to get your teeth fixed?" the receptionist persisted.

"I don't. Is there someone else I can talk with? I'm stuck here and need to kill some time." Tyler stepped away from the counter to loosen his shoulders, fighting the building tension.

"Kill 'em?" The young man chuckled before pointing out the door and crooking his finger to the left. "The morgue is that way. You kill 'em, we chill 'em. Tell them Deathblade sent you."

Tyler's mouth moved, but no sound came out. He regrouped and rallied. "Thank you. I'll do that."

He had no intention of doing that.

Wyatt Earp's doctor strolled into the corridor and waved at the young man behind the desk before disappearing into the station's crowd.

What to do? he wondered. Tyler Toofakre didn't know anyone on Station 11. There was an All Guns Blazing franchise, but it was closed due to supply problems, which everyone he did know was working on.

He found a bench on the promenade, which was a section and usually an entire level on every station, where shops and shopping were the only functions. It was the same everywhere. Some people rushed through their purchases, hurrying into a shop, grabbing what they were looking for, paying, and hurrying out. Others browsed, window-shopping.

While others watched.

Like Tyler was doing. He gave up quickly because sitting wasn't releasing his nervous energy. He wanted to get back to *Wyatt Earp,* his new home. He'd finally reconciled himself to calling it that, even though he didn't have a lot to do with the cases.

Then again, maybe he could help.

Dispatch. Those who controlled the flight routes within the system. With a newfound purpose, Tyler marched to the elevator, took it up four decks, and stepped out on an administrative level. He looked for a guideboard, which was not placed near the elevator. He assumed visitors weren't welcome on the admin level, or they didn't want them to stay around long.

Tyler reasoned that they'd wander around, lost, and ask random strangers for help. That was what he resorted to; he stopped someone who was walking fast and avoiding eye contact. When Tyler stood in front of him, the interaction was unavoidable. "Can you tell me where Dispatch is?

I need to talk with them on behalf of Magistrate Rivka Anoa."

He didn't know why he name-dropped. As an afterthought, he wasn't sure the revelation would help him.

The worker shrugged and turned to go back the way he'd come, choosing not to continue on his errand rather than to talk to the dentist.

"Like pulling teeth," Tyler mused. He wandered until he came to another individual who was far more forthcoming.

"It's not on this level. One floor up, and the first space as soon as you get off the elevator." She walked away while Tyler was thanking her.

He went upstairs, taking the elevator rather than the stairs so he would exit in front of the dispatch office. As the woman had said, it was right in front of him and clearly labeled. He walked through the door to find himself in a secure entry. A nasal voice issued from a barely-functional speaker. "What's your business here?"

"I'm helping Magistrate Rivka Anoa with her investigation," Tyler replied, knowing this time, beyond any doubt, that he needed to use Rivka's credentials.

"There's nothing to investigate here. Go away."

"What kind of official are you? I'm going to need a name." Tyler waited. "I'm going to find out, so it'd be better if you told me. I believe it's standard protocol for government officials to identify themselves. Anonymity is embraced by the weak. You carry the authority of the station. If you're misusing that, then that would be the only reason to remain anonymous.

"If you fear retaliation, you don't have the authority of

your office where you would be offered protection. This is the dispatch office, which means it controls the flight lanes and space surrounding this station and this system. You've lost a couple ships recently. Did you not expect someone to come and ask questions?"

"Fine," the voice replied, and the interior door buzzed and cracked open. He still hadn't identified himself.

Tyler smiled at his use of legal reasoning without having to bully the individual or reach through the speaker to grab him by the throat, wherever he was. Rivka would have known a way to do that or had one of the SIs open the door without wasting time with a petty underling.

Inside, Tyler found two people, a young human woman and a female alien who also looked young, but he wasn't sure why. The human smile sheepishly. She pressed the key on an old-style microphone and spoke. "Welcome to Dispatch." The voice that came out of the speaker was not the one that had gone into the microphone. "Sorry. It keeps the werewolves at bay."

"You have werewolves here?"

The young human shook her head. "Just a saying, Grandpa."

Because of the Pod-doc, Tyler looked not much older than the youths running the dispatch office. It made him want to send them to their rooms without dinner. He groaned from the pain of it all before returning to the task at hand.

"Who has access to the data regarding ship tracking?"

The alien female shrugged. "Everybody?"

"You made that sound like a question. I'm looking for

answers. How do those interdicting the travel lanes know which targets to hit?"

"Anyone with access to the station's system." The young human stopped being flippant. "As long as you're here, you can get in and take a look. It's for convenience, so crews know when their ships are leaving. The station manager doesn't want crews missing their ships."

Tyler felt that personally, like getting spiked in the gut. He cleared his throat. "Can you track who accesses it and from which terminals?"

"I don't know how to do that. Maybe the station's AI knows."

Tyler figured it was worth correcting them in his position as one who lived with the Embassy of the Singularity. "They're called Sentient Intelligences, SIs, and they are citizens of the Singularity with full rights like any living being."

"They are, and they do?" The young woman seemed surprised. "Huh." She shrugged and easily surrendered to the revelation.

"Can I get access to the SI running the station?"

"Sure. Just grab any terminal. You do have Federation access, don't you?" She raised an eyebrow at him.

Of course, he did. Rivka had made sure of that. He took the proffered terminal and logged in. He leaned back when access was granted. "My name is Doctor Tyler Toofakre. I work with Magistrate Rivka Anoa and Ambassadors Ankh and Erasmus. Who am I talking with?"

"I know who you are, Tyler. You can call me Thucydides."

"Is that your name?" Tyler had been with *Wyatt Earp*

long enough to recognize the cues when sentient intelligences were messing with him.

"No. It's Didier, but I prefer Thucydides. What can I help you with?" The SI was nonplussed by having to reveal his name.

"Can you tell me who has accessed the dispatch system and checked on the flight times and courses of the intercepted freighters?"

"I can. I've already shared that information with Ambassador Erasmus. Do you need it, too?"

Tyler let his head fall back, and he stared at the ceiling. "Might as well tell me. Is there anything illustrative, like the same individual who accessed both in the time before they were hijacked?"

"There was only one individual outside Federation staff."

Tyler perked up. "Really?"

"I know that I use a name that's not my real name, but I don't lie when answering a formal query."

"That was not my intent. It was a verbalization of surprise, not suspicion regarding the lack of veracity. Please accept my apology."

"You didn't hurt my feelings," Thucydides responded with a laugh. "Your portfolio prepared me well."

"I have a portfolio?" Tyler was on edge. He stopped staring at the ceiling and returned his attention to the computer screen before him.

"All residents of the embassy have a portfolio. We are to ensure your safety to the best of our ability at all times," the SI explained. "It appears that you did not know this. I have let the cat out of the bag, so to speak. I'll update your portfolio accordingly."

Tyler closed his eyes.

I ask that you accept my apologies, Thucydides said on Tyler's comm chip.

"I should be more used to this by now," Tyler muttered. "So, who was accessing the data?"

"A Skaine named P'Toral."

"I'm not exactly an expert on the machinations of interspecies relations within the Federation, but I thought the Skaines were the enemy."

"Heavens, no," Thucydides replied. "A number of their people have violated Federation Law, but that could be said for nearly every species. Did you know that in percentage of incarcerated, the Singularity leads all species? It's not a category that we're proud to be at the top of."

Tyler had known that. "But, the Skaines. You have Skaines on Station 11?"

"I don't have anyone on Station 11. The Federation allows travelers to use Station 11 as a transit point. It was built for that purpose."

"I feel like you're deflecting and making small talk. Are you trying to keep me in Dispatch for some reason?"

"I am not."

"P'Toral. I'd like to talk with this individual, but I'll need station security with me."

"That won't be easy since he departed on a passenger liner headed to Onyx Station over two hours ago. That information has been transmitted to Ambassador Erasmus."

"I'll follow up with my own communique. Thank you, Thucydides. You've been very helpful."

"You can call me Didier," the SI replied.

Tyler clenched his jaw, still staring at the screen. "Who is responsible for the entry in my *portfolio* regarding how much I'm supposed to be messed with?"

"I'm not sure I can share that with you, Man Candy."

I'm coming for you, Red, when you least expect it. And a Skaine...

CHAPTER FIFTEEN

The Singularity's Manufacturing Center, Rorke's Drift

Rivka, Ankh/Erasmus, and Chrysanthemum strolled from the ship toward the front door of the facility, which looked grossly out of place on the frontier planet. With few modern conveniences elsewhere, the ManCen reflected the epitome of the future as imagined in the present day.

Red rushed to get in front of the trio, and Lindy moved in behind.

The lines of the massive complex consisted of smooth yet sharp angles of burnished metal, unpainted but not stark. The building spread horizontally rather than vertically as it would have on an industrialized planet where space was at a premium.

A single door allowed access to an inner security chamber. The group assembled for an obligatory scan before the interior door opened. There were no handles and no access pads. Everything was automated, leaving little for flesh and blood visitors to influence.

Welcome to the Singularity's ManCen, a voice said in Rivka's mind. *This is the first of many planned centers for the advancement of our race. Powered by the latest generation of miniaturized Etheric power supplies, the plant is energy-neutral for Rorke's Drift and even supplies limited finished products for the settlers who live here.*

"You mean parts for their tractors and such?" Rivka asked.

Exactly. We have helped them improve their crop yields and trade between the two settlements for each to provide what the other needs.

"We came to pick up some super-secret compounds. I expect you're already working on that," Rivka pressed. She hadn't wanted a tour, only the material and to get back out there.

It is packaged up and on its way to your ship. We have an automated delivery system.

"Then what are we doing here?" Rivka moved in front of the group and held her hand out to stop them. "We need to go."

"We need to pick up two new SCAMPs and configure them. It won't take long," Ankh/Erasmus explained.

Rivka felt like she'd been hijacked. "Didn't we just have a talk about lying to me?"

"We didn't lie!" the more Erasmus of voices blurted. "The opportunity presented itself when we arrived. When will we be back here?"

Rivka furrowed her brow and looked at the floor. Her eyes darted back and forth, and then she shook her head. "I don't know."

"Exactly. We need twenty minutes is all. I can guarantee our experiment will work. We'll be able to see the Phantasmagorians. With the material we have on board, *Wyatt Earp*'s manufacturing process is already building the delivery capsules to insert into the warheads of standard anti-ship missiles carried aboard Bad Company ships. We are on track, Magistrate."

"You guys..." Rivka smiled as she reoriented her thoughts. "Who are the SCAMPs intended for?"

"A couple SIs that we picked up recently and are in the embassy," Ankh/Erasmus said softly.

Rivka snorted. "You mean there are more people on my ship who I didn't know about?"

"Yes. They are in the embassy. I'm glad you refer to us as 'people,'" Chrysanthemum interjected to take pressure off her husbands. "We take up no physical space and are not a burden on *Wyatt Earp*."

"Until you put them in bodies," Rivka countered, then raised a hand to forestall further conversation. "I'm good with whoever you bring aboard as part of the Singularity. We take you all kinds of crappy places, and you don't complain. I appreciate that. Let's get those SCAMPs so we can be on our way."

Ankh/Erasmus took Rivka's hand. Chrys was on his other side, holding his hand. Although Ankh was taller than the average Crenellian because of the Pod-doc, he was still short. He looked like a little kid between adults.

Red tried to stay in front, but he didn't know where they were going, and no one was telling. He moved in close behind the trio as they walked across a manufacturing floor where machines quietly worked.

"I'm impressed with the modernization of the facility. It

also appeared like life was flourishing outside, which tells me there is no toxic waste in here."

We have taken great pains to ensure our process is clean. We have a shuttle to launch offending by-products into the system's star.

Rivka nodded. They approached a stand that looked like it was populated by mannequins. SCAMPs of all shapes and sizes. Ankh/Erasmus remained externally silent, but their private conversation with the plant went on for an inordinate amount of time.

"I'm ready to go," Rivka announced. "Aliens. Pirates. Bad guys infiltrating our systems. We got lots to do."

Lindy inched her way back as if that would galvanize the others into action. It had no effect.

After ten agonizingly long minutes, two SCAMPs robotically stepped out. One was in the form of a female child, and the other was in the form of an overweight middle-aged man.

Rivka pointed at them while making eye contact with Ankh/Erasmus. The Crenellian glanced up with his best blank expression before walking away. The SCAMPs followed in a robotic gait. The SIs had not yet taken over. It appeared that they would incorporate the personalities on the ship.

"Why these two?" Rivka wondered as they walked.

"We are embracing the diversity of the cosmos. Not everyone can be an ideal, and it's better that they are not. An average look or a young age could disarm a potential enemy and will have no effect on an ally. We seek no companionship despite ours, which represents an anomaly, but our situation is unique," Ankh/Erasmus explained.

Rivka chuckled. "Are you sure?" The Magistrate continued to laugh, lightening up with each step. The Singularity was ahead of her in what they were doing, like with their experiment to show what couldn't be seen.

She felt as confident as they did that it would work. There was nothing she could do besides review the information her team had been collecting. She'd call the *War Axe* as soon as she was back aboard.

They continued to the ship without further conversation. The two automatons followed diligently. Their motorvation software did the trick, maintaining balance and forward momentum. Chrys rested her hand on the child's head in a motherly gesture.

"We'll have you fixed up soon. You'll get your person," she told the small SCAMP.

Rivka found it touching. A darting figure told them Dery was outside the ship and flying around, stretching his wings. He hadn't grown in the past month since his initial rapid maturation. He remained the size of a small boy of five, even though he was only six months old and had the wisdom of the faeries.

Rivka wondered if the Singularity had created the girl his size as a playmate. It would be interesting.

Red ran ahead and scanned the barren landscape for hidey holes and other places from which an ambush could come, but he saw nothing. Lindy remained with the group. Red called for the boy, who divebombed his father, staying just out of reach before soaring away.

When the group arrived, Ankh/Erasmus, Chrys, and the two SCAMPs entered the ship. Rivka waited outside and watched. Dery darted at her. She bunched her legs and jumped as high as she could, but he stayed out of reach.

Lindy held out her arm and waited. Dery flew above *Wyatt Earp* and around the ship before returning to settle and nuzzle Lindy's neck and chest. She hugged the boy to her and strolled toward the ramp, making a face at Red as she passed.

"That'll learn ya," Rivka said and waved for him to follow her into the ship.

"I don't know what I was supposed to learn, except Dery prefers his mom over me when he's tired, which I already knew."

"But you need to hear it every time to keep you in your place."

"I used to be the cat's ass until the faeries intervened." Red unhitched his railgun and loosened his chest protector.

"You're still the cat's ass to me, Red. Keep in mind that the cat and the dog are both running around here, and they are in a formal declaration of war. You probably don't want to get in their way."

"Cat and dog? They better not come my way. I'll not have it!" He shook his railgun for emphasis and headed toward his quarters. Rivka went the other way. She had a call to make.

"Oh, hell, no!" Red bellowed from the open doorway to his quarters until Lindy hushed him. He eased inside and shut the door behind him.

"Do you know?" Rivka asked as she passed the bridge.

Clodagh called after her. "They're all in Red's quarters.

Floyd, Wenceslaus, Dokken, and even Titan. Dery gathered them to him for some reason."

Rivka waved over her shoulder. She shouldn't have asked since that was more than she wanted to know. She'd just wanted to verify that everyone was on board who was supposed to be. Terry and Char were covered in sweat and nodded as they passed.

"You guys are making me feel bad that I don't work out enough."

"Working out is food for the soul. Also keeps you from dying when the chips are down." Terry gave her the thumbs-up and continued on his way. Char nodded and followed.

Once she was secure in her quarters, Rivka sat down at her desk. She scanned the area. It was empty, a shell of what it should have been. She brought up the hologrid and asked Clevarious to make the call.

<u>*War Axe*, in the Trinary Region</u>

"It's Rivka," Micky said from his captain's chair on the dais above the bridge crew.

Christina almost didn't accept the communication. She had nothing new to say. "Did we inform her that Tyler didn't make the trip?"

"I don't remember," Micky admitted.

Christina gestured, and the channel went live. "Magistrate, what can we do you out of?"

"Are you guys free yet?" Rivka asked, her disembodied head floating freely above the table. Rivka looked around the bridge. "Where's Marcie?"

"Not quite yet," Christina replied. "Marcie is in the Pod-doc getting some repairs, and Kae and Bundin are recovering. We tried to muscle our way out, and that didn't work too well."

"I wish them the best for a quick return to health. Can I talk with my team?"

Christina gestured at the comm station. The officer nodded and made the calls. Smedley followed up directly on the visitors' comm chips.

"They'll be on their way to the bridge momentarily. Anything else we can do for you?"

"There's something we might be able to do for you. Seems like the Singularity might have come through once again. We'll be testing a warhead that should bring the invisible ships into the light. Not sure how it works, but the SIs are confident in it. We're already manufacturing additional warheads besides the test warhead."

"Join us here and test it. The mines are invisible. It'd be nice to see them so we can destroy them. We've not had great luck getting through. We'll send you the coordinates where we Gated in. Go there, then do your thing. Be ready to blast whatever you see."

"Clevarious, make it happen," Rivka said, knowing that *Wyatt Earp's* SI was listening in.

Chaz and Dennicron entered the bridge, with Sahved ambling behind.

Rivka looked beyond the group. "Where's Tyler?"

"Didn't someone tell you? He got left behind, and *Potemkin* picked him up."

"Clevarious, did you know about this?"

An SI in the background waffled, "I'm pretty sure I had

nothing to do with any of that. And for the record, he's on Station 11 right now. Thucydides is watching over him."

"I have to think Thucydides is Singularity?"

"The station's SI. Yes, ma'am."

"*War Axe* lost my boyfriend." Rivka focused her gaze like a laser beam on Christina, who glanced behind her to find no one there. Christina waved her arms before pointing in random directions.

"Magistrate," Chaz interrupted. "He was taking too long and holding up our opportunity to collect the sparkle powder, as they've taken to calling it. That was before we found ourselves in a minefield."

Rivka puffed her lips and blew out a breath. "What have you found?"

"That we shouldn't have left Man Candy behind?" Dennicron offered.

Rivka stared at the SCAMP.

"We've received information that a Skaine accessed Station 11's files," Chaz told Rivka. "Thucydides has shared the information with us and Erasmus. Tyler tried to run down the suspect, but he had already departed for Onyx Station."

Rivka's ears perked up. She scanned various information feeds within the hologrid. In them, she saw the notification that Tyler had been collected by *Potemkin* before being shuttled to the station. That one was hours old. The newest communique was only minutes old. By being out and about, she'd missed the latest regarding her case.

"We need to go to Onyx Station," Rivka replied.

"Noooo!" Micky cried from above and beyond. "You need to help us get out of here."

Rivka leaned back until she felt *Wyatt Earp* lift off. "C, take us to the coordinates provided in the Trinary. Execute that experiment, and if it works, we don't need the sparkle powder, do we?"

"I suggest we do," Christina countered. "Not everyone will have access to warheads, but the freighters will be able to launch marking canisters that can show them if someone is trailing them or not."

"Then you'll need a clear path into the asteroid field." Rivka stood and moved her face out of the image. "We'll be there soon. Stand by to fire, then be ready to transfer my personnel back to *Wyatt Earp*. Once they're on board, we're off to Onyx Station. Clevarious, coordinate with Onyx Security to detain that Skaine the second he arrives."

"Say hi to my dad." Christina waved.

Rivka pointed with a finger gun, and the holoimage disappeared.

"Ruzfell, prepare to attack those mines with the greatest zeal at my command." Micky turned back to the main screen, the same image he'd been staring at for hours. He was ready to go. There were bad guys in the galaxy, and he wasn't challenging any of them by being trapped in the Trinary region.

CHAPTER SIXTEEN

***Wyatt Earp*, Trinary Region**

"Fire," Clodagh ordered.

The small missile raced away from *Wyatt Earp*, cleared the top of *War Axe*, and exploded two kilometers in front of it. A filmy cloud formed and expanded a kilometer, then two, then ten, and kept expanding.

Pinpoints of light both near and far appeared within the radiating cloud, above and below the central plane of the heavy destroyer.

"Fire," Clodagh ordered again, and a second later, the pulse cannon disgorged bursts of plasma at nearly the speed of light, twisting and contorting as they flew unerringly toward their targets one after another. Each explosion signaled the death of a cloaked mine. The *War Axe* lit up with its extensive firepower, sniping at mines on all sides. The nearest ones died first, and with the illumination provided by the test missile, the ships continued to kill mines until no more were visible in the dissipating decloaking mist.

On the far edge of the cloud, a ship slipped away, escaping into the mist.

"Do you have any more of those missiles?" Christina asked.

"Coming right up," Clodagh replied. A second missile emerged from *Wyatt Earp's* internal missile bay and raced toward where the ship was last seen. The heavy frigate accelerated to follow. The pulse cannon was still warmed up and ready to fire.

The missile targeted beyond the last known position and exploded. Once again, a light mist became a cloud. Mines appeared, but they were few in number. *Wyatt Earp* sniped them with a precision laser.

The anonymous ship continued to run, but now they could see it. A mine popped out behind it.

"The minefield wasn't waiting for us, only the minelaying ship," Rivka said.

"Fire!" Clodagh didn't need to say it. The pulse cannon had already sent the first round downrange and would bracket the ship's location, removing escape routes one by one. The ship tried to run away in a straight line, but the first shot caught it in the aft end. It sparked and shuddered, coming back into the visible light. "Kill it."

More rounds pounded out of the pulse cannon to shatter what remained of the ship. Then the pulse rounds destroyed the pieces of the ship as it came apart until nothing was left but microscopic debris.

Wyatt Earp continued through the debris field and made a quick circle to look for more since the decloaking cloud continued to expand. Nothing remained. No mines. No more ships.

"There was one ship," Rivka reported, "and a zillion mines."

War Axe moved into the asteroid field and bellied up with the asteroid with the highest density of MIP. The heavy destroyer immediately started collecting the material, using maintenance bots and personnel in combat armor. They could finally implement the plan they had put in place hours earlier.

Wyatt Earp closed on the *War Axe,* but there was no access to the hangar because of the MIP collection activities.

"Connect the airlock," Clodagh instructed. The ship reoriented to line up with one of *War Axe's* two airlocks. A small crunch suggested the two ships weren't obstacle-free around the connection, but the airlock cycled, and the light burned green.

The team rallied at the hatch, but Red blocked it with his body. Terry and Char showed up in full gear.

Red opened the hatch and looked through to find Kai, Christina's better half and Terry and Char's grandson.

"Hey, punk," Kai said, tossing his head to flip his long hair out of his face.

"I'll punk *you,*" Red growled.

Terry called from behind the small group, "Leave my disrespectful grandson alone. Kai, go get Rivka's team. They're coming home, just like your grandmother and me. Gangway!"

Me, too, Dokken added. *This ship isn't big enough for both of us, pardner. Until next time, you orange piece of shit.*

"Dokken!" Char tsk-tsked the big dog.

Terry forced his way through to shake hands with Kai.

"Aunt Marcie should be out of Sickbay by now. Her and Uncle Kaeden."

"On our way." TH gestured for Char to follow him, but she was already on his heels. "Why are my people getting broken?"

TH knew what had happened, but that didn't make it more palatable. When he stepped aboard the *War Axe,* he stopped, breathed deeply, and waited.

"Colonel Walton is back."

"She's in Sickbay," Kai countered."

"He's right here." TH clapped his grandson on the shoulder and stalked ahead with his pantherlike stride and grace.

Char gave Kai a hug. "It's good to see you."

"Is he..." Kai was almost speechless.

"Believe it or not, he can only brew so much beer before he gets bored. What do you bet he talks Marcie and Kae into taking over running the business?"

"Can we get an outlet on the ship here?" the young-looking man asked.

"You were always the smart one," Char replied, then hurried after Terry to keep him from wreaking havoc throughout the heavy destroyer. She eased past Chaz, Dennicron, and Sahved, nodding at each as she went.

"Come on!" Rivka shouted at them. "We got shit to do. Debrief, conference room."

Rivka headed back into *Wyatt Earp,* and the others transferred. The last one through the airlock was Sahved. He turned to wave at Kai. "Until next time. It was a most enlightening visit."

"Next time, Slim." Kai hammered his chest with a fist and flashed the peace sign. Or V for victory.

When the outer hatch closed, Sahved was standing there by himself. He ducked his head and rushed into the ship and down the corridor. He caught up with the others as they entered the conference room.

Ankh/Erasmus was already there with Chrysanthemum.

"We have about ten minutes before we'll arrive at Onyx Station. Did you transfer the materials?" Rivka asked the overhead.

Clevarious answered, "We sent over one missile that was ready and enough gipsonium to manufacture dozens more. The Bad Company collected the items from our cargo bay and flew off. We will continue our own production of four more missiles, just in case."

"While we were in the airlock, they had people aboard our ship, helping themselves to the good stuff?" Rivka wasn't concerned, just surprised that she hadn't figured that was how it would happen. She was losing focus. The details used to be easy for her, but the chaos of personnel being everywhere they weren't supposed to be was wearing on her.

They still had to pick up Tyler from Station 11. *Destiny's Vengeance* had not yet returned from taking Ted and Felicity home. Either *Wyatt Earp* had to detour, or he'd have to wait.

"Helping themselves could be an overstatement. Let's agree to say that what you don't know won't hurt you," Clevarious countered.

"We won't agree to say that." Rivka shook her head.

Why were they there again? She had called the meeting. "Sahved, what did you discover?"

"A concerted effort to interdict shipping in the transit lanes around Federation space stations." The Yemilorian wouldn't make eye contact with Rivka after stating the obvious.

"Who's the perpetrator?" She waved in his line of sight to bring his attention back to her.

"New information suggests it's the Skaines who have partnered with the race that attacked Keeg Station."

Rivka nodded. That had been her conclusion when she'd heard that the only one outside of Federation personnel who accessed the information was a Skaine.

That seemed too easy. No one would doubt the Skaines did it. Their entire race thrived on piracy.

"How can we ensure the veracity of that information? Only one individual out of tens of thousands on Station 11 accessed both sets of information. That is nearly inconceivable. You'd think there would be some amateur space-watchers who would pull the information on a regular basis, like the old-time folks who had police scanners in their homes so they could listen to the response to crimes." She stared at Ankh/Erasmus, looking for a technical answer.

"There were those people, but we eliminated every other individual based on longevity on the station, status, and other communications means. There were exactly twenty-three individuals who accessed all the data, twenty-two of whom continue to access it, just like they have for at least a year."

"I had to ask," Rivka replied. "I need to be comfortable with our investigative processes."

"We know," everyone replied.

Rivka snickered. Maybe losing control was good for her growth, but she was still reeling from the interview before the group of ambassadors. No matter what her people did, she would be the only one to answer for it.

Good thing they were trained well.

"Any other complicity since it wasn't just Station 11? What did Malcolm have to say, or Station 7's SI?"

The SCAMPs turned to Ankh/Erasmus to answer.

He saw them watching him but didn't show his exasperation. "A two-legged Yollin on Station 7 was discovered hacking into the dispatch system, which is not open like on Station 11. He is being tracked. On Station 13, a patch has been installed to forward the dispatch channel to Station 11. The Skaine suspect was there two months ago."

Rivka instantly got angry about not knowing details that added up to put a nice, neat bow on the package.

"Once again, this is too easy. Why are we letting a Skaine roam freely among our stations?"

Chaz raised his hand. "Because being a Skaine is not a crime. Innocent until proven guilty. P'Toral had not committed any crimes. Now he is a suspect, but we cannot infer suspicion based solely on how an individual is born. Or has the law changed in some way?"

Rivka leaned back in her chair. Her team. Lecturing her on the law.

"No," she admitted. "You are absolutely correct. We cannot infer suspicion because he's a Skaine. There is no such thing as the usual suspects. Either there is evidence of a crime, or there is not. With evidence, there is probable cause, and with probable cause, there is the opportunity to use search warrants to solidify and press charges. I think we're almost there with this guy. How did we not find the patch?"

"No one was looking for it. The stations maintain a constant communication connection. One more channel is like looking for a grain of sand on a beach. We didn't know to look until the pirates appeared."

"The Skaines are pirates, but the outsiders are invaders. It is an unholy alliance because neither cares about the other's motivation, I suspect." Rivka scowled. "Are we there yet?"

"It's like having a ship filled with toddlers!" Clevarious blurted.

"This ship *is* filled with toddlers," Rivka replied, then stood. "When we get to Onyx, we'll take custody of the Skaine and bring him aboard. We'll conduct the interrogation right here and then slam him into the brig. Make sure Red and Lindy are in full gear. Chaz, Dennicron, and Sahved, with me. Ankh, when are you getting your ship back? Is there any way it can stop by Station 11 and pick up Tyler?"

Rivka waited for someone to make a comment, but the SIs were more refined.

"We'll send our ship to pick up Man Candy. It'll meet us at Onyx Station," Ankh/Erasmus said. The Crenellian's eye twitched downward but didn't close. Rivka visualized Erasmus trying to wink at her and Ankh fighting him.

"You guys," Rivka muttered while twirling her finger and walking out. She headed to her quarters to collect her

Magistrate's jacket. She would be on the station on official business, and the jacket was her uniform. It had been battered and bloodied, and it still had a bullet hole in it, but those were badges of honor like a member of the military wore campaign ribbons and personal awards.

When she arrived at the airlock, her team was waiting for her.

"I'm glad to have you back together," she told them. "Now, let's go grab us an ass that we'll be quite pleased to kick. Remember, we would have days off if it weren't for this little invasion and the crime spree that kicked it off."

"That fucker!" Red said. "I coulda been on vacation."

"Language," Lindy said. A fluttering down the corridor suggested Dery was inbound.

Me, too, the boy said. He took his spot on his father's shoulder and waited patiently to enter the station with the team.

Rivka glanced at the faces. Dery changed the dynamic. "Red, Tail-end Charlie. Lindy in front."

Red nodded curtly.

Everything had changed.

CHAPTER SEVENTEEN

***War Axe*, near Frontier Station 13**

"Why not Station 11?" Micky asked.

"Because these bastards are coming from outside the Federation. This is the easiest station to access from non-Federation space. We'll roll inward once we've checked out here. Notify the fleet to prepare to Gate to their designated coordinates on my mark."

Terry looked at the holosphere showing the system. He tapped into the space surrounding and drew lines for each of the Harborian warships that were patrolling it: a battleship, three cruisers, and two frigates. *War Axe* was an added bonus.

"You're expecting to find cloaked ships," Micky said, then ordered, "Weapons hot. Prepare to fire."

TH nodded to him. "Same order to the fleet, and add that they are to Gate at zero-nineteen and ten seconds Standard Yoll time."

Terry waited while the orders were processed. The clock on the tactical screen showed twenty seconds remaining. He counted down in his mind while watching the hologrid. "Two missiles, ninety degrees separation. Fire."

The decloaking missiles rocketed away from the heavy destroyer. The second they exploded, the six fleet ships entered their Gates and emerged at the far edge of the heliosphere, then spread out evenly to create a cordon between the station and anything trying to escape.

"Sonofabitch!" Micky stared at the screen as a dozen cloaked ships were highlighted. One was a heavy cruiser, and the rest were small destroyers and frigates. The Harborian vessels targeted the ships nearest them with high-energy weapons. The cloaked ships were not shielded, unlike the system that had been installed on a few Federation ships.

"Our guys are better," TH told the icons that populated the tactical board. *War Axe* hummed with the energy pulsing to the weapons systems. The ship's massive rail-guns sent a stream of projectiles into the void. A nearby cloaked frigate disappeared in a debris cloud since it hadn't understood that it was visible and under attack until it was too late. The first nine ships never knew what hit them.

The next three started to move, but it was too late. They were surrounded. The heavy cruiser tried to fight, but its armaments weren't up to the task of taking on three Harborian vessels.

"Leave that one to us. EMP weapon. Hit it. I want to take someone alive. I want to know who made war on Terry Henry Walton's pizza place!"

Ruzfell growled at being denied another kill shot, but

he hit the frigate with a pulse and then a second until it was clearly dead in space.

"Bring it into the hangar bay."

"Sir," the systems officer called. "Collateral damage. A cargo vessel in the distance has lost power. It was in the EMP cone."

Terry nodded. There had been no way to adjust. He reached into the hologrid and tapped an icon. "Send F109 for recovery and repair duty. Collect that crew and make them comfortable while the maintenance bots get that ship online." He stepped away from the table in the middle of the bridge. "I'll be in the hangar bay, delivering a personal greeting to our guests."

Char walked with him. "You think someone made war on a pizza place?"

"It sounded more impressive in my head," Terry mumbled. "Full gear, Smedley. Send in Slikira, an Ixtali, K'Thrall, a Yollin, and the Keome B'Ichi Aharche. If these are Skaines, they respect everyone else more than humans. Send in the non-humans who will tolerate a lot less from these fuckers. What do you think, Dokken? You haven't bitten a bad guy lately."

Because they taste horrible, the dog replied.

"Well, since you put it that way." He loosened his Jean Dukes special and thumbed it to three. Char eyed him suspiciously. "It's the maybe-it-will-kill-them-and-maybe-it-won't setting. I won't know until they make me shoot them."

"Do you want to put an AGB on the *Axe?*" Char asked.

"That's the best idea I've heard all week. Yes. We will

have a private club on a warship because why not? We are a private conflict solution enterprise, after all."

***Wyatt Earp*, in Onyx Station Hangar Bay Delta**

Lindy walked down the ramp and into the hangar bay to meet a security guard at the bottom before anyone else left the ship.

After a brief conversation, Lindy gestured for the others to follow. Chaz and Dennicron forced their way in front of Rivka.

"I used to be in charge," she said.

"That was before Red moved to the back," Chaz explained.

Sahved eased in beside Rivka. "My first Skaine!" he said excitedly.

"We took *Wyatt Earp* off the Skaines. Well, the Bad Company did, and the Magistrate Corps took it off their hands. It took us a month to get the smell out."

"No, you don't," Red grumbled from the airlock hatch. He tried to keep a wombat and an orange cat from sneaking out.

Go! Go! Floyd cried.

"Somebody carry her." Rivka waved her hand over her head. Red looked behind him, but he knew he was the only one back there. He scooped Floyd up with his one free hand, which removed him from bodyguard duty.

"Look what I've become."

Rivka glanced over her shoulder to see Dery sitting on Red's shoulder. He petted Floyd with his feet while she watched the world from the crook of Red's arm.

Wenceslaus squirted between Red's legs and raced across the hangar bay.

"Chaz and Dennicron, ask the station's SI to keep an eye on him for us. If he stays here, it has to be his choice."

"It's always his choice, Magistrate," Chaz replied. Yapping from the airlock alerted them that Tiny Man Titan was trying to come, too.

"No!" Rivka held her finger up. Clodagh dove into the airlock from the corridor and caught him before he high-jumped over the frame and onto the ramp. She picked him up and carried him back inside. The hatch closed behind her.

"I feel like we are going to learn something grand from the Skaines," Sahved continued as if the previous minute with the ship's mascots had never happened.

"I hope so. For as big as this was, it hinged on very few bad guys and was out of my realm. This is in my wheelhouse. Interrogate a suspect whose weapon is subterfuge and who is using readily available information against us. We'll find out about this house of cards that they've built, and then we'll dismantle it one by one."

"Jhiordaan doesn't have any Skaines," Dennicron offered. "They have a tendency to die before capture or during the capture process. I believe that's what happened with the Skaines aboard this vessel."

"*Wyatt Earp's* sordid past," Rivka replied.

Lindy knew the way to the security section, but they had an escort who remained wary. He took them down the stairs instead of using an elevator. The level they emerged on was controlled. It took the security guard's credentials to access a way for Rivka's team to scan themselves into the system before any of them was granted access. They continued through the area and arrived at yet another secure location.

"We're here to see the Skaine prisoner," the escort announced.

They were buzzed in since the group had already registered and been verified by the station's SI.

In the cell, they found an aged Skaine, stooped and such a light blue that he was almost white. Lindy moved within arm's reach but no closer. Red remained in the corridor with Dery and Floyd. He would have seethed at being trapped outside, but Dery calmed him with thoughts and private words.

"P'Toral, this is Magistrate Rivka Anoa. She'll be taking you with her."

"I can't go. I have to complete my research," the voice croaked.

Rivka moved in and rested her hand on his shoulder. "What research?"

His mind swirled with inconsistencies. Communication flow and signals—things she didn't understand. She wished she could share it as she saw it with Chaz and Dennicron. They would know.

"Why did the Skaines partner with the outsiders to attack the shipping lanes?"

"What did they do?" he asked without subterfuge. His mind was a miasma of confusion, but his orders were clear. Collect communication signals for a project that would garner him a great award at the Skaine Science Academy.

"I can see that you are a scientist," Rivka said and took a seat next to him. "Maybe you can stay here. Please describe what you are working on for my colleagues. They are also interested in propagation and wave research."

He perked up. "Really?"

Chaz and Dennicron nodded vigorously and waited.

P'Toral went into a long and rambling discussion regarding the communication signals he was researching and the data he forwarded to his laboratory on the Skaine homeworld.

Rivka stepped outside with the security escort and Sahved. Red leaned close. "This guy's a tool."

"I concur. He does not appear to have any motive to undermine the Federation. I doubt he even knew what they were using the information for."

Rivka confirmed Sahved's suspicions. "Who is the manipulator?"

"A Skaine?" Sahved ventured, but it wasn't much of a guess.

"P'Toral received his orders from his own people. He's hard to recognize as a Skaine and harmless to the general population. He only wanted to do his research, which was important to him. That made him the perfect lackey."

"What do we do with him?"

"The Skaines have to know we're onto them. With those missiles... Is there an update from the *War Axe*?" Rivka asked the question a second time using her comm chip. *Have we gotten an update from Terry Henry Walton?*

Clevarious replied, *They have intercepted and destroyed eleven of twelve cloaked ships in Station 13 space. They have captured one ship and have it secured in their cargo bay.* War Axe *is leading a fleet to Station 11 for a second interdiction. Then they'll continue to Station 7.*

Let me know when they have anything from their prisoners.

They have not yet breached the frigate, but you will be one of the first to know.

Rivka would have to settle for that. Her crime spree had turned out to be a lot more. It was a combat action, and she was hanging onto the case by her fingertips. As it was, she wasn't sure she still had a case.

"Red, how is the betting going?" She raised an eyebrow.

"Line 6 closed when we fired on the enemy vessel in the Trinary. Sorry, Magistrate. This isn't your perfect case."

"First shots fired. I should have remembered, but the perfect case? The one that ends without an arrest and without any angst or combat? I'm unable to imagine what that case would be."

Red laughed, and Dery joined him. "You know what they say, Magistrate. There's no such thing as perfect."

She gave Red a mean look, but she wasn't angry. The Bad Company was cleaning up the mess of the shipping lanes since Ted and Ankh had come through once more. "What's left to do?"

Find, Dery said into her mind.

"Find what, little man?"

She held his small hands in hers. His mind was at peace as it always was. It swirled in the calm colors of one whose emotions were under control. One who was accepted by the universe.

The tree in the forest. The boy pulled away, all smiles, and flew off Red's shoulder to hover in the air above them. He pointed back the way they'd come.

"Time to go?"

He nodded and flew slowly toward the security checkpoint. Floyd snored in Red's arms as he shuffled after his son. "No arrest? Come on, Magistrate. You need to arrest the Skaine."

"We're not closing Line 3 by arresting a dupe. There are bigger fish to fry. You know, like that monster on Rorke's Drift."

"Don't remind me. I still get nightmares."

Rivka twirled her finger. "Get our people out of there. It's time for us to go. I'm not taking P'Toral with me, but if you can hold him here until we can make sure he can't pass any more information to his handlers, I'd appreciate it," Rivka asked.

"We can do two weeks. After that, we'll have to let him go."

Rivka nodded. "We better have something before two weeks. If not, we'll come back and get him. Can't have him running around if this isn't resolved. Not just because he's a Skaine, but because he doesn't know that he's the catalyst for an intragalactic war."

The guard recoiled. "It's pirates stealing freight."

"It's an awful lot more than that, unfortunately." Rivka didn't need to tell him the whole truth. She didn't have time.

"War?" The guard suffered under the revelation, his face distorting into a morass of pain. "I don't want a war."

"Neither do we. So, we can't let this guy run around unsupervised until we're sure we've cut the connection to those coming in through the frontier. Connections that *he* is putting into place." She pointed at the cell.

"Just let us know what you need, Magistrate," the guard

offered. He opened the cell door, and the rest of Rivka's team left the Skaine talking to himself.

"He knows communications technologies pretty well," Chaz said after the door closed. "It's not up to our level of understanding, but P'Toral can be dangerous by linking the Skaines to information that is promulgated through any medium outside of the Etheric."

Rivka studied the two SCAMPs, who were unreadable since they weren't employing any of their emotional subroutines. "He's already dangerous, but is it a crime to share publicly available information?" She shook her head to tell them the answer. "I don't think the Phantasmagorians have come here yet since their spy didn't send them any comms from here. I need to talk with the *War Axe*. Were those Skaine ships or Phantasmagorian?"

Chaz and Dennicron stared at Rivka. It wasn't their question, so they didn't answer.

"And we need to light up space around the station to see if anyone is here, just in case," Rivka added.

CHAPTER EIGHTEEN

***War Axe*, near Federation Station 11**

"Fire," Christina ordered when the fleet materialized in their designated positions in a sphere surrounding the station at a range of nearly one AU.

They fired the last two missiles with the custom gipsonium warheads. The *War Axe's* production facility was working rapidly to produce more, but that took time. Terry Henry Walton was on a mission to clear out Federation space. Christina had taken the helm while Terry tried to determine the best way into the captured vessel that was currently taking up too much space in the hangar bay.

The missiles headed away from the heavy destroyer and exploded at equidistant points from the station. The clouds immediately expanded outward.

"The shooting gallery is open," Christina announced over the fleet channel. In addition to the ships TH had brought from Station 13, there were already three ships in Station 11 space: two cruisers and the battleship *Potemkin*.

Cloaked ships appeared as the mist passed over them,

highlighting them better than if they disengaged their cloaking systems. The fleet started firing pulses, railguns, and energy weapons. The seven ships were destroyed before they could move.

The Bad Company fleet moved to better positions in case they saw a ship departing from the cloud as it extended toward the edge of the heliosphere and beyond, but they didn't find any additional lurkers. Seven ships, and now there were none.

"*Potemkin,* send a shuttle to pick up a small amount of gipsonium. You'll need it to manufacture missiles you can use to find any ships sneaking in under cover of cloaks as you take a position around Station 13. And take four cruisers with you. That will be the front lines of an invasion. Stop them there, and we stop them cold."

Christina chewed her lip as she thought about the next steps.

"As soon as the next two missiles are ready, we'll take a contingent to Station 7 and clear out the infestation. Smedley, what information do you have regarding the size of the Skaine fleet?"

"Latest intelligence suggests it's smaller than the number of ships we've already destroyed," the ship's SI replied.

Christina rubbed her temples. "Isn't that marvelous?"

"Ready to go?" Terry bellowed the question at his boarding team. Slikira, K'Thrall, and B'Ichi. Slikira and K'Thrall each had four legs and cut imposing figures, even more so in their powered combat armor. It was designed to be thin on the sides so they would fit through a ship's corridor as long as they didn't have to turn around, which was why the Keome was bringing up the rear. He was more agile to cover their six o'clock.

The battering-ram duo of an Ixtali and a Yollin would get them inside.

"Burn it," Terry ordered after trying the manual release for the airlock and getting stymied.

A maintenance bot moved into position with a high-intensity plasma cutter. It started on one side of the doorway and, with mechanical precision, tracked the seal along the outer hatch. Terry stepped away from the door, leaving the armored warriors in position to respond should fire come through the opening.

The three prepared their weapons.

Bundin ambled up behind TH. "We shall clear the ship, Colonel."

Terry glanced behind the sergeant to find a squad of human warriors in combat armor ready to storm in behind the breaching team. This group carried axes they'd use to peel metal and access locked spaces or silence a vocal enemy.

No one was sure what they'd find inside.

As the maintenance bot approached the end of the loop around the hatch, the group's muscles tensed and prepared for action.

The bot left a single bead holding the door in place.

"Go!" Bundin ordered. Slikira led the way by hitting the door with a shoulder and launching it into the airlock beyond. She leveled her weapon and fired a long stream on the automatic setting, then ran in with K'Thrall close behind her. B'Ichi bolted in after them.

Bundin lined up the next squad. He used his exceptional hearing to wait for the cue to send the others inside.

More firing echoed out through the airlock.

Terry took a step toward the opening.

Bundin was quicker at using his four stumpy legs than he looked. He was able to get in front of TH. The tentacles on his head stalk waved wildly as the squad moved past him and into the ship, blocking the airlock and preventing Terry Henry from doing anything rash.

"Tell your people we want prisoners. Don't kill them all."

Many are passed out. There are a few in environmental suits who account for all the resistance, Smedley reported.

"Secure them and bring them out."

"Roger," Bundin rumbled.

The warriors acted quickly, and in less than a minute, three unconscious Skaines were searched and then deposited on the deck in front of Terry Henry. He took a knee and waited, but not for long.

"Bring me some smelling salts." He gestured at a blond individual at the side of the hangar bay.

Kai went inside and was gone for not more than ten seconds. He jogged across the deck and stopped in front of TH. Kai handed over a small capsule.

Terry Henry looked at it briefly as if it were magic before kneeling on the Skaine's chest and popping the capsule beneath the unconscious male's nose.

The prisoner sputtered to life, sucking in gulps of air through his open mouth. His eyes shot wide with the realization that he was a captive. The Skaine tried to break free, but Terry was too big, too strong, and in the perfect position to control him.

Terry wrapped his fingers around the scrawny neck and stood, pulling his captive to his feet. He reflexively grabbed at his belt for a weapon, but he'd been relieved of what he'd been carrying.

"What are you doing in a cloaked ship?" Terry asked calmly.

"Hiding from the likes of you and your pirate cutthroats!"

"Sounds like you're living in a fantasy world, then. The reality where I live sees you as the pirates. It also suggests you stole very little and were sending hijacked cargo to its doom in a gas giant or into a star. Skaines that are willing to take and kill but aren't stealing? That causes me concern. Your race is easy to understand, but your alliance with those who gave you cloaking technology isn't."

"I'm just a lowly mechanic. I change tires for a living. Have you checked your inflation levels lately?"

"A race of smart-asses." Terry lifted the Skaine into the air and got kicked for his trouble. He lunged forward to slam the small body into the side of the frigate. "I'm going to turn you over to our interrogation specialist. You don't need to say a word. She'll rip your thoughts from your mind and leave you as nothing more than a simpering shell. I hope you enjoy wearing a diaper for the rest of your life."

In a well-practiced maneuver, Terry spun his prisoner and slapped zip-cuffs around his wrists. He pulled them tight as he lowered the Skaine, face-first, to the deck.

"Let me go! You can't just take prisoners. I have rights!"

"You and your merry band have been conducting an undeclared war on the Federation. You're criminals, nothing more. No prisoner of war status for you. Do you hear that sucking sound? It's your brain being pulled out through your earhole." Terry waved at Bundin, who put a huge stumpy foot on the Skaine's back and compressed him to the deck until he started to gasp for air. Then Bundin lightened up a touch.

Terry worked his way through the prisoners, but none of them talked beyond jibes and redirects. They were well-schooled in not answering questions, like most career criminals, even though Terry wasn't the expert on that. He knew who was, though.

"Smedley, get me the Magistrate."

Wyatt Earp, at Onyx Station

"Call from Colonel Walton," Clevarious announced matter-of-factly. They had become commonplace.

"Which one?" Rivka asked.

"The one who wreaked havoc aboard *Wyatt Earp*."

"It wasn't that bad," Rivka replied. "Put him on."

She'd take it in the corridor since she hadn't made it back to her quarters. The ship was unnaturally quiet without the visitors on board. They had two extra SCAMPs in Ankh's workshop, also known as the engineering section, but they were quiet as the Singularity uploaded the SIs and prepared them to take over their new bodies.

"Skaines," TH started. "These fuckers done fucked with the wrong fucker."

"I'm sorry, can you say that again? This time in English," Rivka replied.

"The ship we captured was Skaine. Smedley and our tech team are dissecting the engineering to see what the aliens gave them. They are less than forthcoming regarding their arrangement with the Phantasmagorians. We need your special talent to see what the hell they've been up to."

"AGB for life," Rivka replied.

"This is legal stuff. It's your job." Terry sounded put out.

"I'm coming, and I'll interrogate them whether you give us AGB for life or not. I just thought I'd ask while we're on our way." Clodagh popped her head out of the bridge. Rivka pointed and gave the thumbs-up.

"On our way," the chief engineer and sometimes captain confirmed.

"As long as the franchises get their supplies. Which is interesting because these Skaines are the run-of-the-mill pirate types, but the hijackings destroyed the freight. Why would they do that?"

Rivka had a theory. "Because their masters who gave them the cloaking technology offered them a more lucrative alternative. Or they were smuggling and picked up whatever they were after before ejecting the rest."

"I hope you can figure it out. We have a whole crew of miscreants and ne'er-do-wells to turn over to your tender ministrations. Can you damage their minds in the process?"

"I'm not going to damage their minds," Rivka confirmed.

"Not even just a little?" TH pressed.

"No." Rivka remained firm. Terry wanted what he wanted, but he wasn't going to get it in this case—the torture and deliberate harm of an individual in custody. If she saw a capital crime in their minds, she would take a different approach. She had probable cause to talk to them. Since the cloaked ships had been conducting illegal activities in Federation space. Anything they shared was open to further investigation. She corrected herself. "We'll see."

"That's what I want to hear. We're at Station 11. We'll collect Man Candy for you, and he'll be waiting as well."

"I think we'll be there in about two minutes."

"Then you'll have to get him yourself. We're kind of busy."

"*Destiny's Vengeance* should be picking up Tyler. We'll meet up with Ankh's ship as soon as it has him. Tyler. Not 'Man Candy.'"

"That's all Red calls him," Terry replied. "And for the record, I'm not in charge of my AGB franchises anymore. There's a new general manager. Marcie will be the new face of the business."

"I'll be curious to hear more. See you in a few, TH." Rivka signed off. She started walking toward the bridge but stopped. "Red, we'll be reboarding *War Axe*. Get Lindy and load up with stun batons. We could have some intransigent Skaines causing grief."

Rivka was still contemplating what Dery had told her. *Find the tree in the forest,* he'd said. *Can't you be clearer?* she thought. *I don't speak mysticism.*

"I haven't pummeled a Skaine in a long time. Those little pricks demand a fist to the face."

"Red," Rivka warned. "Don't judge a whole race on the actions of a misbegotten few."

"A few? That *is* their whole race. Why aren't they members of the Federation? That's right; they can't follow our rules. A race of criminals the size of children. It's hard to summon enough outrage to beat them senseless, but I'm sure I'll find a way."

"Maybe you'll be the first arrest," Rivka shot back.

Red shook his head. Lindy arrived carrying his body armor and two stun batons. They prepared themselves while the flight crew lined up the airlocks.

Sahved joined them. Chaz and Dennicron did not.

Rivka tipped her chin at the Yemilorian. "Do we arrest the Skaines or turn them over to Federation military authorities?"

Sahved brightened. He always enjoyed challenging legal questions. "Turning them over to the military would mean there would have to be a formal declaration of war, and they would have protection as prisoners of war. There has been no such declaration."

"An apple for the star pupil." Rivka smiled. She caught Red's eye. "Looks like you'll get your arrest after all. Line 3 is closing. Bidding has ended."

"Hang on," Red started. "Nope. I got nothing. Carry on, Magistrate."

The airlock cycled and opened without giving Red the honor of hitting the big button. He glared toward the bridge for an instant, then headed through to find Terry and Char waiting for him.

"Long time no see," Rivka called past the big body blocking the way.

Red cleared the other side. Rivka went to Char first. "Are you getting what you want?" Rivka tucked her hands into her pockets to show that she wasn't trying to look into Char's mind.

"We were never cut out to run restaurants or fashion stores," she replied. "I think I've played all the golf I want to play, but I'm still more than happy to search the galaxy for the best shoes and outfits to stock in my chain. I like seeing the universe, and the Bad Company will take us to all the places."

"Fair," Rivka conceded. "As long as it's what you want rather than what the big kid wants."

"We're both teenagers at heart," Char replied. "We do what we want."

Char winked at Terry Henry. "We do," he agreed. "This way, Rivka. We have some Skaines who need their brains sucked out through their ears."

Rivka followed them to the hangar deck. There, Red and Lindy bracketed her, staying as close as they could. TH eased back and let the Magistrate do her thing.

She gripped the first one's arm. "What do you know about the aliens who gave you the cloaking technology?"

His mind raced through the series of lies he'd been given for just this purpose, but at the front of his mind was the feeling of how unsavory the aliens were. Mercenary to the point of having no respect for life. He suspected they would have killed the Skaine leadership if they had not acquiesced.

"What aliens?" he managed to say, but his fear had come through.

"Where do these aliens come from?" Rivka asked, ignoring the Skaine's answer.

A nebula beyond the Dren Cluster. Rivka saw the image in his mind. It was the one she'd seen dozens of times from the window of the AGB on board Keeg Station.

"What do they want?" she continued.

"I'm not answering your questions." He tried to pull away but couldn't. Lindy prodded him in the back but didn't hit him with the stunner.

Push back the intruders from space they've claimed. The humans weren't a threat until they built a station in the Dren Cluster. Share the spoils of conquest and secure the border.

"You know a lot about this race for someone who knows nothing," Rivka told him, finally letting go of his arm.

Terry leaned past Red. "What?"

Rivka held up her hand and continued down the line of Skaines. One tried to spit on her, but as he hocked up phlegm and prepared to launch it, Red punched him so hard in the face that his nose exploded. He fell backward, unconscious before his head hit the deck.

"Anyone else?" Red growled.

Rivka nodded politely and moved to the next prisoner. "What spoils do you think these aliens were going to share with you?"

Ships, stations, slaves. The Skaines were going to be put in charge of it all. Replace the Federation leadership. See the end of Bethany Anne and her ideals. The Skaines would rule it all! The prisoner smiled fiercely with his thoughts, but he didn't speak.

"That was enlightening," Rivka muttered. She continued to the next. "What are these aliens called?"

The Myriador. Dark-green skin, two legs and three arms, a round head on a long neck with a single multi-faceted eye over a heavily fanged mouth, and nasal slits to the sides of its cheeks. A membrane beside the eye vibrated as the creature's auditory sensor.

There was more lurking in his mind. "Who helped bring this unholy alliance about?"

Faces hiding on Delta 7, a moon circling a gas giant on the edge of Federation space.

"And the Skaines joined with these Myriador? Do you think they'll uphold their part of the deal?"

"We have the invisibility screen, don't we?" the Skaine answered out loud, conceding that the Magistrate knew whether he spoke or not. Stating it for all to hear gave him the opportunity to stand up to her.

"You do, which changes my earlier presumption regarding your guilt as it relates to crimes instead of war crimes. I think this confirms that the Skaines have declared war on the Federation by siding with the Myriador. That will cause your people a great deal of grief."

She stepped back to address all the prisoners. "Your people will be prevented from any relations with the Federation. I have no doubt there are innocent Skaines out there, but that doesn't matter. The Skaines are an enemy of the Federation by your own admission for siding with the Myriador, an invader. Secure them for transfer to Jhiordaan. Oh, and have a nice day."

She walked away from the crowd of angry Skaines, who shouted that they had admitted no such thing.

Rivka waved over her shoulder as she strode up to Terry Henry Walton. "They noticed us when we built Keeg Station, it appears. And their attack on it was repulsed."

"That was us." He studied the deck while shuffling his feet. "How do we talk with them? We don't need a war, just a neutral zone."

"Do you know who owns a moon named Delta 7?"

Terry searched his eidetic memory but came up empty. He shook his head. "Smedley?"

"In Frontier Station 13's space," Smedley replied.

"Send everything you know to Clevarious. I'll be returning to my ship."

"That's it?" Terry wondered.

Red and Lindy were surprised, too, but they acted quickly.

She waved at the crowd of Skaines. "Send them to the penal colony. Continue to Station 7 and destroy any cloaked ships you find. The Myriador have declared war on the Federation, and the Skaines picked the wrong side."

"That's an order I can get behind." He pointed at the Skaine ship. "Spoils of war?"

"You can have it, but it could take a while to get the smell out," Rivka told him.

CHAPTER NINETEEN

<u>Wyatt Earp, in interstellar space</u>

"*Destiny's Vengeance* is docking now," Clevarious reported.

Rivka checked the corridor to make sure no one was there before jogging to the cargo bay airlock.

I saw that, Clevarious said privately.

I swear you to silence, Rivka quipped.

The runabout was angled through the energy screen covering the cargo bay door. The hatch popped, and Tyler strolled out carrying a couple shopping bags. Rivka had intended to pull him into a long hug but stopped.

"Were you having fun?" It came across as a challenge.

He handed her the bags. "These are all for you. Since I was there and the Singularity was one step ahead of me, I was left with nothing to do. I tried to help their medical staff, but they were, shall we say, less than understanding of what I offered."

"Sex for room and board?" Rivka joked.

"Exactly that, but completely different. An added

doctor temporarily and for free. The counter clerk couldn't get her head wrapped around the idea, but I didn't request to speak with her manager. I'm not that guy. And what do you mean, sex for room and board? Are there performance bonuses like extra rations?"

"Stop it." Rivka laughed. "Red is a bad influence on you."

"I've been studying," Tyler admitted. "Let's ditch this stuff. Do we have any time?"

Rivka shook her head. "We're hunting down a lead. I need to meet with my people."

"You've called a meeting," Tyler deadpanned.

"Next steps," Rivka told her group. Chaz and Dennicron stood, ready to leave. They wouldn't have come, but Rivka had made the meeting mandatory.

Sahved sat at his usual place, a contemplative look furrowing his brow.

Rivka waited.

"The Skaines," Sahved started. "The declaration of war. The entire population is subject to detention?"

"No. We don't do that, but those actively engaged in conducting the war, like those flying their combat ships, yes. They are criminals. From now on, others captured will be prisoners of war who can be released the second the Skaines surrender."

"They don't have a home planet," Chaz said. "Not anymore."

"Nomads. They have a home base somewhere because they negotiated with the Myriador for technology. In return, they gave access through their spies. I know there has to be more than one. The Skaines were subverted *somehow,* and that's why we're on our way to this moon called Delta 7."

"Did you get confirmation that the Skaines are there?" Sahved asked.

Rivka had not yet shared one hundred percent of what she'd seen in the Skaines' minds, but now was the time. She related everything she had seen in the prisoners' minds.

Then she continued. "I didn't get the feeling that the ones who brought the two sides together were Skaines. From them, I felt arrogance, mostly. They had no doubt they were going to win. The Myriador cloaks gave them the advantage they had always been looking for. But who is pulling the strings?"

"They didn't count on their cloaks being rendered ineffective or that the Bad Company would attack in force," Dennicron replied. "If we find the master manipulators, will that end the Myriador and Skaine threat?"

"I'd like to say yes, but now that the unholy partnership has been established, I doubt we can undo it by taking out the middleman. The genie, as they say, cannot be put back into the bottle."

Tyler eased his way into the meeting and delivered a mocha to Rivka and a Yemilorian fruity drink for Sahved.

The SCAMPs didn't need external resources, but they could plug into a circuit if they overtaxed their internal power generation system.

Tyler asked anyway. "Do you guys need anything?"

"To get back to the upload for the two new SCAMPs. They are having trouble incorporating the expression subroutines after all the work we've done! It's a bit disconcerting," Chaz replied.

Rivka tapped the table with her pointer finger. "Let's wrap this up, then. I'm sorry for having a meeting, but it's easiest to share the most information. We're going to Delta 7, and I need everyone on the team. Cole in combat armor, Red and Lindy in full ballistic protection, armed heavy, you two, Sahved, and me. I doubt they'll be too welcoming since we're onto them, depending on what we find. C, do you know anything else about this place?"

"There is scant record. Last information shows it's nothing more than an outpost," the SI replied.

"I didn't get the impression that it's only an outpost. Let's go in cloaked and shielded until we get eyes on the terrain and can assess what kind of reception we'll get. Stand by for my order to Gate, probably in thirty minutes. I need to collect my thoughts while drinking my mocha. My compliments to Ankh on programming it into the food processor."

Chaz and Dennicron left the instant the meeting was over. Sahved stayed behind. He watched Rivka sip her beverage, which reminded him that he had one, too. He quickly took a drink.

"What's on your mind?" Rivka prompted.

"More than I can express in words." He smiled, took another sip, and put his cup down. "From my examination of the evidence, at least two containers had been opened before the load was jettisoned."

"Interesting. That makes this an extremely complex case when usually the simplest explanation is correct."

Sahved nodded. He picked his cup up, not to take a

drink but to marshal his thoughts. Rivka waited for him. His thought processes were not hers and as such, they provided great insight into that which she would not have seen otherwise.

"I didn't ask the Skaines if they were looking for things in the loads, but that wasn't the ship Terry Henry captured. That was a search-and-destroy crew. They knew more of what was happening at a higher level. We have not captured anyone on the hands-on side of the hijackings."

"The first hijack crew wasn't Skaine," Sahved said.

"Why didn't I remember that?" Rivka screwed her face up. "It was too easy to see a boogeyman. Who hijacked that first ship and sent the crew into deep space aboard a lifeboat?"

"We have ourselves an investigation." Sahved beamed. "And we have the lifeboat from which to collect evidence."

"Didn't we already scrub that?"

"We did, but we never heard back from the SIs about their analysis of the programming to send the lifeboat away." Sahved pointed at the overhead.

"Clevarious, I know you're listening in, so spill it. What did you guys find?" Rivka drummed her fingers on the table. She'd been engaged with a lot of things, so the investigation had taken a back seat.

And there were those who said meetings were a waste of time.

"Rudimentary programming. Nothing on the scale it would take to reprogram the Gate," Clevarious offered.

"Which means we have three, maybe even four players so far. The Myriador and the Skaines. The unidentified middlemen and those who hijacked the first ship."

"It's the second ship. The first was a month prior and also had an AGB order on board. The second hijacking was by a cloaked ship. The crew said they never saw anything with their scans."

"The first ship that involved us, I should say. It took the second AGB delivery to excite the masses." Rivka stood and started pacing. She stepped lightly from one side of the conference room to the other. "Taking TH's AGB orders was going to inevitably draw in the Bad Company. Was that one of many plans? What else is going on? Get me Terry Henry."

Sahved had followed up until the Magistrate asked to speak to Colonel Walton.

When Terry Henry answered, he was distracted. "Hit that one with railguns. More!"

"TH, is this a bad time?"

"As good as any. We're cleaning up this mess around Station 7. You wouldn't believe it. Fourteen cloaked ships! These people have no shame. There were more than we could shoot with a single salvo. They tried to run, but we had them boxed in. No Gate drives, no faster-than-light drives. These ships are sitting ducks. Whoa! Did you see that? Blew like a volcano. We must have hit the reactor."

The broadcast of noise over the room's speakers stopped. "Terry?"

"We're here," he replied. "Just had to cut out the background noise. It must sound like something bad, but I assure you, none of us has been damaged in any way. As a matter of fact, we haven't even been hit by hostile fire. Debris from flying through Skaine wreckage, but that's it.

And looks like we hit the jackpot here. Two Myriador ships appeared, but they got themselves blasted."

"If we're to start any kind of dialogue, we benefit from keeping one of those ships and their crew alive."

"That's what Char said, but they were a big juicy target, and we fired before determining the ship class. I'm really not sorry about destroying an invader who was this far inside Federation space. So, fuck those guys."

"I'll take that as a maybe next time, so next time, give them a chance to be our fount of information," Rivka suggested.

"We're on it. Clean-up operations are all that's left here. Fourteen ships identified, and fourteen destroyed. Did you want anything else?"

"I think you should go to Keeg Station immediately and check if there are any cloaked ships there. I expect you'll find at least one Myriador vessel. Kid gloves, TH."

"Always. I have no intention of blasting them into non-existence. I never do, and I'm always surprised when I have to. I didn't want to do it. They made me."

"You sound like every perp I've ever arrested," Rivka replied. "Uncanny."

"Keeg, you say? Do you have intel?" Terry looked for more information.

"A hunch," Rivka replied. "I think there were multiple diversions running simultaneously. The Myriador got the Skaines to hit the shipping lanes to pull the Bad Company away from home. The as-yet-unidentified middlemen got the Myriador and the Skaines to distract us from whatever they were doing. Hide the murder in a pile of bodies, as it may be."

"I have no idea what you're talking about, but if you're right, we need to go. Ted, Felicity, and the entire station, along with Spires shipyard, could be in trouble. We left a few ships there, but not our heavy hitters. Walton out."

Sahved twirled his fingers while raising them toward the overhead. "There is so very much spinning up like a top to screw into the ceiling. I'm sorry to have caused such consternation. It was not my intent."

"Bullshit!" Rivka blurted. "It had better be your intent to shine light into the dark places. I think you're right. This is a triple backstab, with each party thinking they are getting things over on the other. I'll be in my quarters. Prepare for battle! Delta 7 beckons and I don't have a good feeling about it."

***War Axe*, on its way to Keeg Station in the Dren Cluster**

"Full combat armor. Prepare for space," Terry bellowed as he ran across the hangar bay. "Attach a beacon and dump this piece of shit when we arrive. We can't have it cluttering up our hangar bay if we have to fight bad guys. We'll come back for it. Put a mine on it too, in case the enemy tries to collect it. We'll blow them both to kingdom come."

The first Bad Company warriors appeared from gear storage and logistics, the area in which Kai made his home. It was linked to the manufacturing equipment on the *War Axe*. Whatever he needed for the troops, he could make on the spot while they waited.

Right now, it was churning out missiles. The latest one had rolled through and was on its way to the launch tube.

The next one was wending its way through the process. They needed two missiles to cover enough area to be confident that they would find any cloaked ships lurking too close to the station.

The *War Axe* had enough magnesium-infused phosphorescents to make a number of glitter bombs to highlight the passage of a cloaked ship without having to fire one of their limited supplies of missiles. They would run out of gipsonium too soon if they weren't careful, but every missile they'd fired had revealed the presence of cloaked ships.

It was unnerving to find that they were being watched, not by the Skaines, but by the Myriador—an alien race, more alien than most races within the Federation, and they weren't Federation members. They existed by the grace of Bethany Anne alone and because not all members of the race could be judged by the actions of some or most.

Didn't there have to be Skaines who weren't criminals?

Terry Henry continued to the storage area where his suit was parked. He found Char already in hers.

Two steps ahead of him. He smiled and rested his hand on her armored shoulder before climbing into his suit. He checked his over-shoulder missiles, the item he figured he would need the most if they went into battle.

Char opened a private channel. "Why aren't you on the bridge?"

"Because the fight is going to be *mano a mano*. We need to capture a Myriador vessel. *War Axe* won't be doing that. *We* will."

"What if it's just Skaines?"

"I don't think the Myriador would leave this station to

the Skaines. This is the place that triggered them and confirmed the Federation as a threat in their minds. We need to have a conversation because this can't continue, or we'll end up taking the war to them. We'll crush them now that we can see them, and they can't protect themselves."

They clumped out of the staging area and onto the hangar deck. Maintenance bots had installed antigravity lifts beneath the Skaine ship. A tractor bot was pushing the vessel toward the open maw of the hangar bay. With a final surge, it sent it into the void.

War Axe veered away, and the captured ship moved out of view.

"Marcie," TH called over his suit's comm, "fire when ready."

"Another couple minutes," Marcie replied. "Christina is in Operations. All scopes are hot. Weapons are tight. The Harborian ships with crews are active and ready to move. If there are lurkers hiding nearby, they'll have to think it's either a redeployment or an exercise."

"Move the fleet out of Spires Harbor. Gate to the coordinates we selected and fire."

"Roger," Marcie replied. "Countdown is live."

On Terry Henry's heads-up display, the countdown clock showed one hundred and seven seconds. "Into place, people. Less than two minutes to fireworks. *War Axe* will move into a blocking position by the station."

On cue, the station grew in size in the view through the hangar bay door. The heavy destroyer bore down on it, accelerating until it hit a point where it would rapidly decelerate to ease into a position close to Keeg Station.

"This is Keeg Station," Felicity drawled. "Is that you,

Terry Henry, realizing the errors of your ways and coming for me? If not, you could temper your speed. We have rules 'round these parts."

Terry dialed up a private channel to the bridge. "Let her know that we have a case of explosive diarrhea on board, and it's better to relieve that in private quarters on the station."

"I am *not* saying that," Marcie shot back. "I'll figure it out. Prepare to deploy."

"Keeg Station, Keeg Station, this is *War Axe*. We have carbon in our exhaust pipes and need to burn it out to avoid a catalytic chain reaction. We shall begin our braking maneuver momentarily."

Terry looked at Char. "What the hell is a catalytic chain reaction from carbon build-up in the pipes?"

"We don't have pipes with carbon. Or catalytics. I think Marcie is trying to pull a fast one on her mom."

"Marcie, dear, I love hearing from my daughter. Dinner in my quarters tonight since you'll be here with those dirty pipes of yours getting cleaned out."

"Of course, Mother. Marcie out."

"We didn't get invited to dinner," Terry complained.

Forty-one seconds.

"We'll have to survive," Char replied.

The warriors lined up at the front of the hangar bay. They activated their magnetic boots to hold them in place should the ship get buffeted during combat.

Terry activated the company channel. "Our mission is to capture a Myriador vessel and bring their crew through safely. We want to start a dialogue and see if we can end this war before it starts in earnest. We've lost a few freighters, but if they used their screens to hide them, they could have destroyed stations and ships at their leisure. We can't live in fear of an invisible boogeyman. It'll be incumbent upon us to ensure the ship stays disabled and then that we board it and secure it."

Twelve seconds.

"Counting down to missile launch. Fleet movement begins." Gates opened in front of the dozen operational ships that remained, and they reappeared at the outer edge of a sphere surrounding Keeg space.

The *War Axe* launched the two missiles. They raced outboard to a point halfway between the station and the outermost fleet ships and exploded simultaneously. The cloud quickly spread.

"You fuck!" Terry exclaimed when the HUD populated with a tactical view of an invisible ship nearly on top of *War Axe*. Lasers lanced out from the heavy destroyer, which twisted on its transverse axis to bring the railgun to bear. A single round of super-heated plasma accelerated down the rail to glance off the aft end of the ghostly image of the ship. "Myriador."

The impact sent the ship spinning tail over front. Thrusters blasted against space to bring it under control. Lasers from *War Axe* dotted the hull, burning and melting as they went.

Terry pulled his focus away from the close ship and looked for others. The cloud illuminated one more at the edge of visibility. A frigate and a battleship fired a full barrage into it.

The ship's reactor went critical, which turned the vessel into a mini sun for a brief moment.

Terry turned back to the task at hand. "We have one chance left," he told the Bad Company warriors lined up at the front of the hangar bay, ready to launch. "Take it easy on that guy. Get us close, and we'll swarm it."

"Doing exactly that. It's going to take some damage. It appears they're not so keen on getting captured. You might not want to deploy the whole company in case they have a self-destruct they're itching to pull the trigger on."

CHAPTER TWENTY

***War Axe*, at Keeg Station**

Terry's lip quivered. "First Platoon, you're in reserve. Char, you're in command."

"I don't think so," Char replied on the private channel. "You're not going over there by yourself."

"Prepare to deploy. Forward momentum is dropping to zero," Marcie intoned. "Ship has lost its cloak."

Terry couldn't argue. They'd been together for too long. If either lost the other, it would be like they'd lost their soul. "Fine. Capples, you have First Platoon. Char is with me." After a moment, Terry heard something. "Who snickered?"

"No one, sir. Capture that ship so we can go on liberty," Sergeant Capples replied.

Terry found it funny, too. He'd been with this group for a long, long time. Many had followed him from Earth.

"When we capture these fuckers, first round is on me. I'll find out which one of you upstarts is the snicker queen."

Char shook her head. They waited to make sure the

ship wasn't going to accelerate at a speed that might kill those clinging to the outside of it. *War Axe*'s lasers continued their pinpoint attacks. A puff of escaping environment gave the bridge crew the information they needed to see.

"Launch the boarding team," Marcie ordered.

Terry ran toward the opening. Second Platoon raced after him. Char was close on his heels. He dove through the energy shield that kept the environment inside the hangar bay while skipping through where the gravitic shield would have been. They were so close to the Myriador vessel that half the ship would have been inside the shield.

TH didn't have to activate his pneumatic jets since his momentum carried him as far and as fast as he needed to go. He inverted and touched his jets just before impact to give him a soft landing. He activated his magnetic boots and started directing traffic.

"Punch the holes and send the gas inside." He pointed at various points along the hull, most of which contained laser punctures.

"Second Platoon has arrived and is delivering our calling card. Next step will be airlock access. Smedley, sharpen your hacking tools."

The SI had scanned the ship and sent the resulting schematic to each warrior's HUD. The airlock was ahead, and that had always been Terry Henry's target. He was going in. He had a railgun and a boarding axe. He hitched the railgun under his arm and hoisted the axe in one hand while pounding across the outer hull. He could have used his jets and flown in the zero-gee of space, but he wasn't in a hurry. They needed to gas the crew, assuming the knockout gas they employed worked on the newcomers.

They were using the same stuff they'd used on the Skaines when they took the heavy frigate that Rivka now called *Wyatt Earp*. If it didn't work, then they'd do it the hard way, one space at a time. Close-quarters combat.

Terry squatted over the access panel next to the airlock. "Funny language, Smedley." He tapped a few keys, and the panel lit up. "It's all yours, big dog."

"I shall endeavor to become one with the language of the Myriador," Smedley replied. "'Funny language.' Is that anything that's not English?"

"Pretty much," Terry replied.

"Neanderthal," Char offered.

"That's right up my alley. A little pig Latin, maybe?" He joked, but his eyes were glued to the panel. Looking at his HUD, he only had to note the flashes of green. No reds showed anyone in distress. He tapped on the outer airlock hatch with his axe.

Much to his surprise, someone tapped back. He didn't hear it, but the vibration reached through his boots. He tapped twice. The response came.

Two taps.

He ran through a quick SOS in Morse code: dot-dot-dot, dash-dash-dash, dot-dot-dot. The reply came as three taps.

Mimicking again.

"How's that gas coming?" Terry asked his people.

"Done here," was the first reply. It took fifteen more seconds before the final affirmative arrived.

They needed to wait thirty seconds for full effect. Terry

counted down while adrenaline surged through his body. The thrill of this far exceeded anything he could ever accomplish as a franchise owner.

No. Not anymore. He was home, a place in which he thrived and was the most comfortable.

He could always order a beer from Marcie and Kaeden. After their stint on Belzimus, they were spent from burning the candle at both ends for nearly two years. It was time for someone else to step up, and that someone was a Belzonian colonel.

Although Marcie was a keen military commander, she'd put in her time. She wasn't as much like Terry Henry as they'd once thought. Nor was Kaeden. He would go where his wife went. Right now, they were on the *War Axe*'s bridge, but soon, they'd be happy to be home on the station.

"Tell Kae and Marcie they can have our quarters," Terry said, not taking his eyes off the airlock panel. The access pad continued to flash lights as Smedley worked it.

"I can't follow your train of thought, TH. One moment we're ready to breach an enemy ship, and the next, you're talking about quarters."

"We're not going to use them because this is our home. I never feel so alive as I do right now. You by my side and ready to join the battle." He tapped the airlock hatch. There was no reply. "Open the door, Smedley. It's time to go!"

"Working it," the SI replied.

Terry dropped to his knees, keeping the toes of his boots locked down to prevent him from drifting away. Below the pad was a recess. He dug his fingers in, gripped it, and pulled outward. The manual release engaged. He reached inside and pulled the handle, which was made for a smaller hand than Terry's armored glove, but he got it with one finger.

"Never mind, General. We got 'er."

One light flashed, then two. The door dropped inward. TH glanced in, using the suit's sensors to see that no warm-blooded creatures were immediately inside or in the corridor beyond.

"No idea where my buddy went," Terry told Char. "There's room for both of us."

They climbed inside and pushed the single lit button. The door moved back into place, and two lights flashed, then one. TH checked the door, and it opened into the ship. He peeked into the corridor to let his sensors collect data. They populated the HUD with a schematic showing the immediate layout of the interior, along with a number of warm bodies within ten meters that were around corners or in adjoining spaces. Terry hoisted his axe, and Char brought her railgun to the front.

She moved into position one step to the rear on Terry's right side.

"Hug the left side," she told him, "unless you want to feel the wrath of my railgun."

"Now you're starting to sound like me. That's pretty hot."

"It's not. Just keep my line of fire clear."

"Roger." He eased up to the first corner, around which two Myriador waited. "I'm not sure the gas works on these creatures. Three, two, one."

He leaned around the corner and brought the axe down, then twisted and directed it away from the closest of the two aliens. Although they stood upright, they were unconscious.

Terry breathed heavily.

"Nice recovery," Char said. "Not sure I would have been able to stop the swing."

"I didn't. Just angled it away." He tucked the axe into a harness loop at his side and pulled out zip-cuffs. He bound their three wrists together, then their feet, and finally looped the wrists and ankles together, trussing them up like bistoks ready for slaughter.

"Bring it in, people. The gas worked. Not sure for how long, but at least for the moment, they are out cold." Terry and Char continued into the ship, trussing those they ran across.

"One eye. Their depth perception has to suck," Char muttered while studying a Myriador's features. She lifted the eyelid. "Multi-faceted. They could get enough information through multiple receptors. Maybe they don't have a problem with depth perception."

A constant aboard starships, no matter what species, was the need for firefighting equipment. The Myriador had automated systems that had kicked in, judging by the foamy smears across bulkheads tainted by ugly burn scars. The fires were out. The lighting seemed minimal, along with environmental control, which suggested the main power was out.

"Get a tech team over here to restore power, if not theirs, then ours. Get Ted if you need him. He's on Keeg Station." Terry made the call to the *War Axe*, unsure of who would actually show up. Maybe the ship's new chief engineer, who had been hired after Terry and Char moved on.

He'd have to get to know the individual SI, just until he could get the Singularity to let him recruit a SCAMP to join the ranks as a Bad Company warrior.

Terry smiled behind his helmet. He liked the idea. He could send them into Engineering right now, and they would draw on the sum total of all knowledge maintained by the Singularity to fix a technical problem or get into whatever system needed to be broken into. Like the ones on board this ship.

He needed Ted and Erasmus. "Smedley, connect me with Felicity, please."

"You are a go for Felicity," replied a too-bubbly voice.

"Felicity, are you there? What the fuck was that?"

"My new assistant. She has a great deal of energy. Let me guess; you are on that scary-looking ship right outside my window, and you need my husband to dig into its computerized guts."

"That's why I go right to the top. I would have had to play Twenty Questions with Ted to get to this point," Terry replied.

"True. I'll ask him to come over. What would entice him?"

"A computer system that is unlike any he's ever seen. I bet it's built on base three, not binary."

"I'm sure that means something. I'll tell him. Don't hold your breath unless you need to because there's no air." Felicity signed off.

"That went easier than I thought," Terry mused from the corridor outside the bridge. The air-tight hatch was closed, but after the Bad Company's insertion of the gas tubes to seal any breaches, the air was cycling, and the hatch wasn't locked out. With a tap on the access panel, it opened.

Plasma fire ripped through the opening. Char had been off to the side, and Terry had not yet stepped up the hatch.

"Stop firing! We only want to talk," Terry boomed, using the external speakers on his combat armor.

A singsong reply came, but his suit didn't have a translation program for it. "Smedley, translate what I said into Skaine and broadcast it once more."

The Skaines' workmanlike language burst from the suit's speakers, eliciting a pause from those on the bridge.

"Keep it up, Smedley, as I talk." Terry gathered his thoughts before starting. "We didn't realize this space was a buffer zone surrounding Myriador space. We will not move any closer to your space and your home planet than right here. You've suffered significant losses by attacking us. We don't want to kill any more of your people or your ships."

The voice spoke in the language of the Myriador, but shortly after, a mechanical voice interpreted the words to deliver Skaine. That was then converted into a language that Terry Henry could understand. His translation chip took care of the incoming Skaine, but it couldn't reproduce the outgoing.

"You have killed our people. They must be avenged!"

"Then all your people will die, everyone on this ship, and we'll go to your home planet. There, we'll kill every ship in orbit and your ability to produce more. Your population will be trapped on your homeworld. They will cease their future as explorers, and you will have to trust that we will protect you. If you want us handling your security, then fight us here, seeking your vengeance. We can see your ships now, so your technological advantage is no more. Your people and your ships will simply die without ever having had a chance to succeed."

The response was long in coming and followed a spirited conversation in their singsong language.

"We will not allow humans to be the guarantor of Myriador security."

"Exactly. We don't want to be that either," Terry replied before accessing the private channel with Char. "I see that they know we're human, but the Skaines would have told them that." Terry dialed back to the external speakers. "I'm moving in where you can see me. Please don't shoot me."

"You killed our people with chemical weapons!"

"No one is dead from the knockout gas, only unconscious." Terry gestured at Char, who moved down the corridor to recover two of the Myriador. She snapped the truss line using her armored fingers, leaving only their hands bound. She brought them back and carefully put them down, then used a foot to slide them into the opening where they could be seen.

"See? Alive," Char added.

The voice that had been doing the talking barked an order. It was the same delivery as one heard in most languages. The machine translation repeated the simple words. "Hold your fire." Terry eased into the doorway, trusting his armor would protect him if the natives grew restless.

"You leave this space!" The captain of the ship was the only one seated. The others were arrayed behind him and standing. He spoke again. "You must leave our space."

"We've already built a station and a Gate. We're not going to leave this space, but we *will* promise to go no farther," Terry replied. He knew he could speak for the Federation since they would not encroach on a known species' space. Now, the Federation knew about the Myriador.

"Your word is no good," the captain said, then took a sip of a drink he held in his hand.

Terry parked his suit far enough away from the hatch to allow others access should his maneuver not pay off, then stepped out of his suit. Char knew better than to argue, but she kept her railgun trained on the Myriador. If they tried anything, she would light up the space within the bridge so completely that not a single thing would survive.

He stepped forward and tiptoed past the two unconscious forms on the deck. "My name is Terry Henry Walton, and my word is good. Would I stand vulnerable before you if I were lying?"

Terry found the captain's single iridescent eye to be unnerving but shrugged it off. The individuals holding the weapons were the ones he should be worried about.

The captain stood and moved forward. Although the alien was formidable-looking, Terry was bigger and felt more agile. Three arms would be a lot to overcome, but the head was vulnerable. Terry assessed the creature in an instant and decided, in his way, that he could take him in any straight-up fight.

"Allying yourself with the Skaines may not have been optimal, but thank you for talking with me. We only want one thing from you, and that is to not be your enemy, which I suspect is far different than what the Skaines wanted. Your cloaking technology, right?"

"It was an easy trade. They offered warships to attack the humans."

"They're all destroyed. In the space around Stations 7, 11, and 13, if you recognize those designations. Forty-some ships. All dead but one, and the Skaine crew from it are all going to prison."

"What makes them different from us?" the captain asked.

"They were already here and declared war on us without provocation. In your case, I see that you were provoked by our encroachment into your space. For that, I truly apologize. You are welcome to space on this station, where we can liaise and discuss issues of common interest."

Maybe you should get Rivka's take on all this since you're offering treaties and all kinds of stuff that is within her domain.

Terry looked to the side at Char in her combat suit. "We'll have everything reviewed that I offer because I'm just a working man, but I can be influential when I need to be. By the way, how did you meet the Skaines?"

"We were introduced by a third party, an arachnid race that lives on the border."

"Delta 7?" Terry blurted.

"I believe that is their designation for the habitable moon."

Terry glanced at Char, but she was already forwarding the information from Terry's conversation not just to the *War Axe* but to Rivka, General Reynolds, and Nathan Lowell.

The captain moved forward until he was nearly within

arm's reach. Terry closed the gap. "Humans shake hands when we agree on something." He held out his hand.

"We have a similar gesture, but ours is with our third hand," the captain explained in the Skaine language.

Terry smiled. "I'll do my best."

CHAPTER TWENTY-ONE

***Wyatt Earp* at Delta 7, Cloaked and with Shields Raised**

Clodagh had the captain's chair, and Rivka was right behind her. The main screen showed the tactical display with icons for ships. There were a great number of ships, all of them small. The largest was no bigger than two-thirds the size of *Wyatt Earp*.

"What the hell is going on here?" Rivka wondered. "Can you confirm this is Federation space?"

"It is within the Federation border. The frontier is another ten light-years toward the Windsor galaxy," Clevarious replied. "You have an incoming priority message from Charumati."

"What happened to TH?" Rivka leaned forward until she was hanging over the captain's chair. She slipped to the side to get closer to the front screen.

The message was audio only. "Terry Henry is currently engaged in trying to figure out the three-armed handshake. It looks like we might be able to speak with the Myriador, and they appear to be willing to listen. Getting their asses handed to them in four different systems probably had something to do with it. Regardless, we'll need the legal team to look at everything we're going to have to agree to."

Rivka relaxed but crossed her arms and stared at the screen. "What did we agree to?"

"A neutral zone and a Myriador liaison office on Keeg Station. That's all, but it's the other information they gave us that you'll be interested in. An arachnid race at Delta 7 initiated the contact between the Myriador and the Skaines."

"An arachnid race that isn't the Ixtali?" Rivka looked for confirmation from the people on her bridge.

Headshakes. No one knew.

Clevarious stepped in. "Are you sure they aren't Ixtali?"

"I'm not sure of anything. That's why I asked." Rivka made a face at the overhead.

"Magistrate?" Char asked.

"We're at Delta 7, observing a very busy moon. You're saying there's an arachnid race down there?"

"I'm saying that's what the Myriador said. They have no loyalty to the Skaines or these intermediaries."

"Tell TH thanks for me. I wasn't happy with the prospect of an intergalactic war. Do you know how many reports would have to be filed?"

Char stuttered, "I-I don't."

"Well, neither do I, and I'm happy not finding out. Kudos, TH." Rivka ended the transmission. "None of these ships have Gates. There has to be one in this system. How are these people getting illicit Gates? Like Nefas. He had one…" Rivka's voice trailed off.

"Brings us back where we started. Didn't you suspect

Nefas when you first heard of the attacks?" Clevarious asked.

"Dammit." Rivka delivered final instructions before walking off the bridge. "Find that Gate and see if the SIs can hack into it. I want to know all the traffic that travels through it and where they are going."

In her quarters, she found Tyler taking a shower. The comforting sound of not being alone. It made Rivka think about her team. She spent a great deal of time lost in her thoughts as she figured things out, but she didn't like being alone. She was surrounded by the hustle and bustle of an active starship with a full crew.

Private but not alone.

Tyler joined her in the main area of their quarters, dressed in loose sweats. "Have you seen the cat?"

"I think he got off on Onyx Station."

"You lost the cat?" Tyler was surprised. The look on his face suggested that he was also dismayed.

"Wenceslaus is no one's cat. If he stayed at Onyx Station, it was for a reason that made sense to him. Cat logic."

"On that note," Clevarious interrupted, "you have a call from Nathan Lowell, currently on Onyx Station."

"Will we never have a private conversation?" Tyler asked.

Rivka kissed him on the cheek. "Probably not. That's what you signed up for by boarding this crazy train."

She sat at her desk and raised the hologrid. "Nathan, great to see you. I'm sorry we couldn't stop in when we were on the station, but this case is spinning the Federation in circles."

Nathan Lowell appeared on the screen and zoomed out to show Wenceslaus perched on his shoulder. She could hear him purring. "Forget something?"

"Adoption papers?" Rivka countered.

Nathan shook his head.

"As in, Wenceslaus has adopted you. Once he was tired of Lance Reynolds, he moved back aboard *Wyatt Earp,* only until he could find his next conquest. Looks like he has carved another notch on his collar. Welcome to the club of future exes."

"How long will he be here?"

Rivka shrugged. "As long as he determines. He'll jump another ship when he wants, when the time is right. Just feed him, change his litter box, and love on him, and it will be business as usual."

"Is that it?"

Rivka nodded.

Nathan smiled. "Lance warned me about this." He pointed a finger at Rivka, and she feigned surprise. "In other news, have you heard from Terry Henry Walton?"

"About opening negotiations with the Myriador? Yes. We need to encourage that. Keep the Skaines isolated, but the fact that they have cloaking technology could lead to more Skaine piracy."

"My thoughts exactly. Keep the Bad Company in the loop if you can about your current mission so we can make sure we don't step on the wrong toes while shaking hands with the right people."

"Case, sir. I have legal cases."

"Whatever. Have you punched anyone yet?"

"What? No. Why would I punch someone?"

"I have that line in the pool."

Rivka closed her eyes and rubbed her neck. A pair of hands reached through the hologrid and massaged her shoulders. She relaxed and smiled at the screen. "Of course you do. I don't see punching anyone on this case. It's a little different. You'll be apprised through the Magistrate's office on Yoll."

"Nice!" Nathan gave her the thumbs-up. "You pulled the need-to-know card. I'm not in the chain since I'm doing private work, right?" He leaned back, but only a little so as not to unseat the cat. "You know that drone that seems to find its way to your ship a couple times a week? I have to personally approve those trips."

"A girl and her crew have needs, Nathan. How did you know about those?"

"I have a minority stake in AGB Enterprises, and I have to personally approve the drone's use of a Gate." He smiled broadly while absentmindedly stroking the big orange cat. "Take care of your case, Magistrate. It's important to the security of the Federation that our people can trade freely. These hijackings have caused us a great deal of consternation, and that's why I was more than happy to deploy the Bad Company in support. Make it stop, and then come and get your cat."

"We're on it, Nathan. I'm at Delta 7, which appears to be a pirate's paradise, complete with a Gate. Before you say there shouldn't be a Gate here, you are correct. There shouldn't be, but there is, and I think they're using the hell out of it."

"Technology has always been our advantage, and it

seems that technology is our challenge. If the bad guys get in front of us, we're playing catch up. I'd rather not."

He waved with his free hand, and Rivka waved back. She dropped the hologrid. "Has anyone heard from Buster Crabbe?"

Delegor

Chief Mak Elb Bint and Magistrate Crabbe were still waiting in the outer office. It had been nine hours since they had an appointment in fifteen minutes.

Buster had gone from being mildly annoying to the secretary to full-on haranguing. "Fuck this," Buster said and started to storm off. He stopped in the doorway and shouted into the outer office, "We're doing what we need to do under the authority of the Federation. You no longer have any say in the matter."

The chief of law enforcement followed him out. "Was that wise?"

"In reality, he never had any say in the matter," Buster replied. "If your world isn't on fire or the Chief Delegador isn't ill, it makes me believe that he's in on it. Our legal history from Delegor suggests those at the top are breaking the law."

"My data suggests otherwise, but fair enough. Bik Tia Nor did us all ugly. I'll hate him forever because he gave the people a lot of reasons to doubt the sanctity of my office. We enforce the laws. I uphold the law. No one I know is on the take. No one is benefitting from a crime wave. It's keeping us all up at night."

Buster studied the chief to ascertain his sincerity, and

there was no doubt. He was passionate about doing his job. "Why did the Chief Delegador blow us off?"

"Maybe he was trying to put you in your place after the Bik Tia Nor row?"

The secretary rushed out and breathlessly addressed the two. "The Chief Delegador asked me to convey his apologies. He'll see you now."

Buster smiled at the Mak Elb Bint. "Tell the Chief Delegador that if he wants to see me, he can come to my ship in the morning. Then I'll make him wait just to see how much of his time I can waste. I should have left hours ago, but in due deference, he is your head of state. That was before he made it obvious that it was an asinine political move. Now, he can fuck himself."

The secretary seemed shocked by the statement. She stared, mouth agape.

"No disrespect toward you, but he put you in a bad position, too, by forcing you to lie for him. You might as well go back to your desk. I'm not coming, and if he messes with me through more stalling, I'll bring his office up on charges and have him removed. Before you ask, yes, I can do that. Check the charter Delegor signed with the Federation. I can't designate who to replace him with, but I *can* remove him. Me. The one he made wait for nine hours. And the longer you stand here, the angrier I'm going to get."

The message came through loud and clear. She ran back into the office building.

"Can you remove a sitting head of state?" Mak asked.

Buster nodded. "I can, but I'll be called on the carpet for it. He might get reinstalled after a review process. It would take active interference in my investigation for me to take such extreme measures. I should only have given him an hour, not nine. Dammit! I hate wasting time."

"We explored a great number of tendrils and have a plan, do we not?" the chief of law enforcement asked.

"We do. We made the time as productive as possible without having our boots on the ground. Let's go, please. We have a list of potentials and need to ask a lot of questions. To the training center!" Buster strode briskly away but stopped when he realized he had no idea where he was going. When he glanced over his shoulder, he saw Mak pointing the other way.

They walked to a parking area behind the main administration building. The chief had a police vehicle waiting for them.

They climbed in the back, and with its sirens blaring, the vehicle shot to the highest hoverlane and raced across the city.

"If you can drop me off at my ship, I'd appreciate it," Buster told the chief.

"But we're interviewing suspects."

"My part in this case is related to how they're getting the drugs from off-world. Everything else is your jurisdiction."

Mak directed the vehicle to detour to the spaceport.

"Why did you wait nine hours just to leave when it was going to get interesting?" the chief of law enforcement asked.

"Deference. I really wanted to work with you guys to set the record straight that Rivka didn't do anything wrong. We only want what's best for the Federation by not letting people exploit your planet like Bik Tia Nor was doing. He was a bad man, and his wife's family was, too."

The chief nodded. "I know. Stealing someone's blood to inject into yourself? That's not just one step too far. That's an entire day's hike over the line."

Buster replied, "I like how you think. I'll be talking with the flight control folks at the spaceport. Imports from off-world are going under the microscope."

"And the users on this end will know that their source is going to dry up. They'll get angry, and angry people make mistakes."

The two shook hands after the vehicle stopped at Grainger's frigate. Buster strolled out. *Philko, you and Beau work up a way to canvass import records and pending orders. Look for any ties to the drug runner Rivka intercepted, then pull that string until we find the one who brought that load here and what they intended for the final destination.*

Buster whistled a feisty tune on his way into the ship. He was in a good mood because he had given the Chief Delegador the finger after calling him out for political gamesmanship. Buster had tried, but it wasn't meant to be.

Although the chief of law enforcement seemed decent, the elected leaders of Delegor were dicks. He was certain Rivka would appreciate the back brief. In between, if his team could find the importer, he'd have a huge win for the Federation and Delegor, despite the timewasters and oxygen thieves.

CHAPTER TWENTY-TWO

***Wyatt Earp*, in the Delta 7 Region of Space**

"The Gate is hidden just outside the asteroid field," Clodagh announced. "We have eyes on it, and soon, we'll have a physical tracker attached."

"Why a physical tracker?" Rivka asked, walking toward the bridge.

Clodagh answered, "Redundancy. Clevarious, Chaz, and Dennicron are working on a digital solution, but until then, we'll need another course of action. We have a box that ejects a marble-sized tracker that sends a low-power signal to the nearest station or Federation ship and, from there, automatically forwards the information to us. We'll find out where they went."

"Remember that someone reprogrammed the Gate near Station 7. Could this be the one they accessed?" Rivka asked.

"That's a definite maybe with a tenuous possible confirmation," Clevarious replied.

"C, you are spending far too much time with humans."

"Thank you. I've been working on my human."

Rivka stopped on the bridge. "Do you know what she means by that?"

"Not in the least, Magistrate."

Rivka moved close to the front screen, where the external video feeds showed a close-up of the Gate. "Looks like standard issue. Is there any way we can put a couple mines on it with Etheric-linked activators? Just in case we need to dial up its destruction from the other side of the galaxy."

"It's what we do. I'll see to it myself," Clodagh said. "It's been a while since I went elbows-deep into a good engineering challenge. With you-know-who on board, I never get to play."

Rivka gestured with her chin, and Clodagh hurried past. Tiny Man Titan yapped as he ran after her.

Dery flew through the hatch and made one pass of the bridge before settling on Rivka's arm. She sat down so he could stand in her lap. "Find the tree in the forest," she whispered. "I don't know what that means."

The boy smiled and pointed at the screen.

"A tree that's different from the other trees. One that's the same but acts different. A tree like any other tree, but close together, they make a forest," she tried.

Continuity of infinity.

"Those are big words for a six-month-old." Rivka chuckled. He carried the ageless wisdom of the faeries. "I have to embrace the law. What laws are they breaking? I'm sure they are numerous, but where to start? An illegal Gate, but who gets charged for its construction? Do we ever think about those who build the Gates? What about this enclave if they declare their independence and maintain a non-threatening posture toward the Federation?

"Administrivia. They only needed one bureaucrat to show them which forms to file. They didn't need the heavy hand of the law unless stolen cargo came through the Gate. But that's not what you're talking about, is it?"

He shook his head.

"You're going to make me guess?" He stared into her eyes with nothing but innocence and love. "I don't know how we deserve you, but whatever you do," she looked around conspiratorially, "don't act like your dad."

Dery giggled.

"The infinite loop ending at a new beginning, to do it all over again. That could be depressing. There are those who work outside the law. Even if someone is removed by arresting them and sending them to Jhiordaan, another will always take their place. But maybe not always."

Rivka frowned while watching the screen. The Gate shimmered into existence. No ships were headed their way. Someone was coming through.

Clevarious reported, "A possible hijacking has been reported from the Yoll Gate to Station 11."

"Yoll? Pirates are all the way to Yoll?"

A freighter slipped through the Gate and into Delta 7 space.

"Would the hijacked ship be this one?"

Clevarious verified that it was.

"Send a burst to Grainger and let him know we've got eyes on the target."

"Of course," Clevarious confirmed.

"They weren't stealing the ships, but now they are.

Suggests that when the Myriador were calling the shots, they held the others back, whether Skaines or another race." Rivka smiled. "Unless all of that was noise to hide the real target. *A tree in the forest.* I think I understand."

The boy flapped his wings and lifted into the air. Rivka followed him with her eyes, marveling at the ease with which he moved about.

Chaz and Dennicron stepped out of the way to let Dery pass. They continued down the corridor, and they weren't alone. The two SCAMPs they'd picked up on Rorke's Drift trailed behind them, happily looking at everything.

"Magistrate! Allow me to introduce myself," the dumpy-looking male said, thrusting his hand toward Rivka. "You can call me Tex."

Rivka resisted the urge to roll her eyes. "Is that your name?"

"It is now," he replied.

"Pleased to meet you, Tex. And who's this little sweetheart?" Rivka leaned down to see eye to eye with the child-sized female SCAMP.

"You can call me Billi Jane."

"Where did you get that name? Never mind. Nice to meet you, Billi."

"We're currently breaking down the coding of the Gate. It's a marvelous body of work."

Rivka smiled at Chaz. "That means you're in?"

"We own this Gate." He high-fived Dennicron. "Kind of. We can't control it yet, but soon."

"We do," Dennicron confirmed. "This software allows the user to select which Gate to connect to."

"Can we do that?" Rivka wondered.

"We can't since the Gates are directly connected at all times, but it looks like they've overcome that problem. We shall share it with R2D2 and then throughout the Federation. This could be a game changer, as you might say. Instead of multiple Gates within one system, they'll only need one that can be linked anywhere they desire to go. No need to jump through multiple Gates to get where you want to go. It's astounding if we can adapt it."

"Better than a swift kick in the balls any day of the week," Rivka said. "Dammit! I'm starting to sound like Red."

She turned back to the screen. The freighter made a lazy turn on its way toward Delta 7.

Rivka pointed. "Prepare to stop that ship. Cut its engines and board that freighter. Minimal damage, please, and keep that crew alive. I want to know what the precious cargo is that is worth starting an interstellar war over."

"I believe Buster Crabbe is on a case—" Clevarious interjected. She stopped when Rivka raised her hand.

"Drugs? Could this all have been about selling drugs?" Rivka's expression changed from confusion to shock to dismay while her mind worked. "It cost these people nothing to introduce the Skaines to the Myriador and turn them loose. With a bigger threat, all the freighters and cargo vessels would be escorted to protect them from the pirates. Fucking genius, which means Nathan was right."

"How did you jump to that conclusion?" Dennicron asked, always studying human behavior.

"Nathan bet that I would punch someone in the face. I feel it coming on. Whoever planned this whole thing is going to get a face full of my knuckles if your theory is correct, but right now, that's the only thing that makes sense, as convoluted as it is. C, send a note to Grainger with our thoughts and current situation. I'll talk to him when I get back. In the interim, I'm boarding that ship."

"Hang on!" Red shouted from down the corridor. "Even I heard *that* nonsense."

"Not nonsense. I'll be behind you all the way." Rivka strolled into the corridor.

Red looked at her in disbelief. "If you're going, get your shit on."

Rivka wanted to argue, but he was right. Tyler appeared on cue, carrying her gear. "Thanks, sweetheart." She smiled at Red.

Red scowled for a moment before stabbing a finger at the dentist. "Stop making me look bad!"

Tyler snorted. "Not my intent, Red. My learned medical opinion suggests you're suffering withdrawal and can't be held responsible for your behavior."

"Withdrawal?"

"AGB." Tyler helped Rivka into her body armor. He had the leg and arm sections, too. After a brief scuffle, she surrendered and put them on.

"I think we're all suffering from that," Red replied.

"Ten seconds before we have an optimal firing solution," Clevarious stated.

"When we kick their asses, are we going to be able to get a delivery? Not here, but in a decent region of space." Red looked hopeful. He finished shrugging on his gear before double-checking the railgun he called Blazer.

"We're all hoping for that." Rivka looked at Chaz and Dennicron. "Are you coming?"

"Yes," they answered in unison.

"And me," Sahved called from down the corridor.

Rivka shook her head. "Not on this one, Sahved. Tight spaces over there, which means hand blaster only, Red."

Red showed his hands. The railgun was slung under his arm, barrel pointing toward the deck. "Better to not need it and have it. Hand blasters to begin with, but if they make me, I'm pulling the heavy artillery."

"Cole!" Rivka shouted.

Already in my suit and ready to deploy for external engagement.

"Call it good. Prepare to board that ship. C, what's the intel?"

"Standard-configuration freighter. Cargo in pods held externally on a framework. The ship proper is mostly engine and designed for a crew of five, three of whom fit tightly on the bridge. One captain's quarters and two crew berths plus Engineering. You've been on one of this class before."

Rivka stepped back and leaned against the bulkhead. "Red, Lindy, Chaz, and Dennicron. Go in. Shout when you have everyone accounted for. I'll wait here."

"If there's any shooting, we'll try not to hit anything important," Red replied.

Dery intercepted his dad and clung to his head, unwilling to let him go.

"I have to go, buddy," Red pleaded. He didn't want to push too hard on the fragile boy. Lindy tried as well, but the boy violently shook his head and wrapped his legs around Red's neck.

"Don't open that airlock, C," Rivka ordered. "He always knows stuff we don't."

"I'll go," Tex offered. "They can't really hurt me."

"They can," Rivka countered.

"And me. Who would hurt a little girl?" The SCAMP voice sounded appropriate, but behind the guise was an SI with a vast amount of knowledge and access to even more as a citizen of the Singularity. Getting a body ahead of numerous others meant that she had something to put her at the front of the line. Her advantage? Rivka would probably never find out.

"You two just got your bodies. I think you need to sit this one out. Chaz and Dennicron, stand by. Clevarious, what do you say we pump some knockout gas into that ship? We'll have to wait for them to wake up to conduct the interrogations."

Red moved to where he could punch the big red button. Dery was sitting on his father's shoulders. He was no longer fighting to hold on since the decision had been made.

"What did you see over there, little man?" Rivka asked.

Pain.

She nodded. It wasn't a revelation. There was always pain.

And death.

"We have incoming," Clevarious reported.

"Clodagh, I need you on the bridge." Rivka waited for a second. "Belay that. I'll take the conn. Red, secure that ship, but use all means possible without putting our people over there. I don't get the impression those pirates are going to surrender."

"Me either," Red admitted. He patted Dery's leg. "We're too used to barreling in and counting on the Pod-doc to fix us up or just shrugging off an injury. Then again, we *are* armored up."

Dery continued to cling to Red's head, confirming that he didn't want him to go into the ship.

The airlocks synced and cycled. A maintenance bot trundled in, and the hatch closed behind it. The other side cycled, and the bot started pumping gas inside.

"Scans?" Red called toward the bridge.

Rivka went to the captain's chair and took a seat. "Scans."

Aurora and Ryleigh were on shift, but Clevarious had been doing the heavy lifting.

"Four life forms on the ship, and they are not knocked out, judging by how they're moving around. I suspect they are in spacesuits," Aurora announced.

Clevarious didn't correct her, which confirmed her analysis.

"Have the bot sample the air."

After a few moments, Aurora turned in her seat to face the Magistrate. "Toxic."

"Dery saves the day. Chaz and Dennicron, you're up. Use flash-bangs."

Red handed the SCAMPs the non-lethal weapons and stepped back. Chaz and Dennicron went through and cleared the maintenance bot while coordinating with Clevarious to maintain a live feed of the hijackers. Chaz tossed a flash-bang onto the bridge. When it exploded, Dennicron hurried past and tossed one into the engineering section. Chaz rushed the bridge and came under fire. He was hit in the chest three times before he ripped the weapon away from a crewman crouched behind the pilot's station. The other had been caught by the grenade and was blinking rapidly to see. Chaz put them both on the deck and kneeled on them.

Dennicron made short work of the two in Engineering. They had been in the open and couldn't dodge the flash-bang.

Chaz secured the two, then adjusted the terminal to increase the airflow. "Report when it's clear," he told the maintenance bot. Less than a minute later, the bot noted that the air had been refreshed and was no longer filled with toxic or knockout gas.

Rivka would have boarded the freighter, but she was occupied watching too many ships bearing down on the freighter. She confirmed that *Wyatt Earp* was still cloaked.

"What kind of time do we have before they're on us?" Rivka wondered.

"Two minutes."

She switched to her comm chip to talk to everyone. *We need to be detached from that ship in the next ninety seconds, or they'll find us. I'm not keen on that.*

"We may have to reveal ourselves and fight these bastards," Red replied.

"Bring the prisoners aboard and pickle the ship so it can't go anywhere. We'll take on all comers in open space."

Roger, Chaz, and Dennicron confirmed. Pickling the ship meant putting its systems into a state of long-term storage. Chaz deposited one of Ankh's coins on the computer terminal to give them remote access. He hauled the two from the bridge to their feet and dragged them down the corridor. Dennicron appeared behind him with her two prisoners. They hurried through the airlock to *Wyatt Earp*.

The maintenance bot secured the hatch behind it.

"Remove their gear and secure them in the brig until we can talk to them one at a time," Rivka called over her shoulder.

Ryleigh detached from the freighter and slipped beneath it to get to the opposite side, putting the vessel between the heavy frigate and the incoming ships. Once clear, she accelerated into open space on a tangent to the incoming ships' vectors.

"We'll wait to see what they do. Maybe they'll tip their hand as to what the freighter is carrying."

"Could be regular supplies," Clodagh offered from the corridor. "The mines are ready."

"We'll have to wait to attach them for obvious reasons." Rivka pointed at the main screen, which transformed into a tactical view of the situation. "A dozen little ships running at the freighter like goldfish to food flakes."

Clodagh eased onto the bridge. Aurora tried to get up, but Clodagh told her to stay. They all needed to know the positions, even under duress. They'd handled things before. Now was no different, even though *Wyatt Earp* was not the target.

The ships lined up on the freighter's external cargo containers. "What are they waiting for?" Aurora asked.

Clodagh and Rivka both knew. "For the crew to release the containers so the little ships can snag them and haul them home."

"There's a great deal of chatter. They want to know why

the freighter stopped this far out and why they aren't releasing the containers."

"Should we answer them?" Rivka wondered. "No. Let silence be their response."

"They are sitting ducks. We could clear them from the void with a single strafing run."

"What if they're innocent?" Rivka offered. "Receiving stolen goods isn't a death sentence."

Clodagh nodded. "We could disable them all with one EMP blast. They'll get rescued over time."

Rivka stood. "I like how you think. Light 'em up, then best possible speed to that moon. I want to talk with whoever is in charge. Let's see if they'll stand up to authority after they've been emasculated."

"Ouch!" Red said from the corridor. The prisoners were nowhere to be seen.

"Let me talk with whoever you think the captain is."

Clevarious stopped the parade before they shoved the four into the brig. Chaz and Dennicron held them in grips from which they could not break free. Tex and Billi Jane waited where they could help if needed. Lindy lounged against the bulkhead, caressing her blaster and making eyes at the prisoners as if challenging them to act up.

They were humanoid, not arachnid. There was a slight difference in the eyes, more toward the Grays than humans, but from behind, they looked close enough to be mistaken.

Rivka strolled up to them. She touched the first one on the shoulder and asked, "What did you steal?"

The ship, some cargo. Other stuff wasn't stolen. "Nothing," came the verbal reply.

"What kind of drugs were on board that ship?"

Plexorall and Advantageous. "What drugs?"

She switched to her comm chip. *Clevarious, Plexorall and Advantageous. What the hell is this stuff that's somewhere on that freighter?*

They are hallucinogens and performance-enhancement drugs. Both of those are the drugs the Bad Company intercepted and what Magistrate Crabbe went to Delegor to investigate.

"Run faster while high," Rivka muttered.

She moved to the next person. "Who were the drugs going to?"

Nefas.

Rivka recoiled. "Fuck, no! I already killed him once."

"Magistrate?" Red hovered while she conducted her interrogations, then stepped in front of her. "How in the hell is Nefas back?"

"Clones. Who knows how many of him there are."

Do you want us to pull him out of cold storage again? Clevarious asked, but she sounded like she didn't want to.

Rivka could not have agreed more. *No. We'll cut them down one by one as we find them.* "Where is he?" she snarled at the prisoner.

An image formed in his mind of a transfer point, not on the planet. A ship would meet them.

"Clevarious, do you have control over that freighter?" Rivka asked.

The prisoner lunged at her. Red was quick, but Rivka was quicker. She slapped him across the face hard enough to snap his head sideways. Her fingerprints showed across his cheek. Fury boiled behind his eyes while he struggled to free himself from Chaz's grip. Red reached over the

SCAMP and hammered a fist into the top of the prisoner's head.

He dropped like a sack of flour. Chaz hung onto the limp arm.

"Throw them in the brig. We're going to be real busy real soon."

CHAPTER TWENTY-THREE

***Wyatt Earp*, in the Delta 7 Region of Space**

I can fly the freighter if that's what you mean, Clevarious replied.

"Do it, C. Move the freighter to the rendezvous point near a small satellite in a high orbit. There shouldn't be too many. Didn't we find Nefas hiding in a satellite in interstellar space?"

Ankh and Erasmus did, Clevarious confirmed, giving credit where it was due. Rivka was happy using the royal "we."

"I hate that guy," Rivka said. "Even with a clone, I'm not buying it. I think someone is using his name because it generates fear and respect, at least among the galaxy's criminal elements."

"But if an individual usurps a name and acts like that individual, would it not be as if that individual were alive?"

"Clevarious, you're starting to piss me off. Someone pretending to be Nefas won't be as evil as Nefas."

"It takes a special mind to come up with starting an

intergalactic war in order to smuggle drugs," Clevarious argued.

"Are you trying to twist me up in knots, C? Either it's Nefas or a Nefas wannabe. I think that means we hit them hard and ask questions later. We can't mess around because this individual will have an escape plan."

"And probably already knows we're here, based on the EMP attack neutralizing his fleet of runabouts."

"I concur. I'll be curious to learn why the arachnid race, though. Who are those guys?"

"An interesting case, don't you think, Magistrate?" Clevarious asked.

"'Interesting' isn't the word I'd use, but here we are. If alleged-Nefas takes the bait, we take him down. If alleged-Nefas doesn't come, then we deploy on a hunter-killer mission. Clodagh, take those mines back to the Gate using *Destiny's Vengeance* and implant them. Clevarious, let's see if we can use the digital hack to keep it closed. The physical destruction of the Gate will be the last resort. We need to cut off the escape route of everyone in this system by whatever means possible."

"Roger. I'll clear it with Ankh on our way out and take Chrys with me. She's quite capable."

Rivka nodded. She kept forgetting Chrys was on board. She had managed a whole station. Rivka needed to ask more of her if she'd be willing.

"Four ships in orbit," Aurora announced. They were showing on the screen.

It was a learning moment for the pilot crew. "What's that mean?" Rivka asked.

"That four ships could respond to our arrival?" Aurora guessed.

"If alleged-Nefas meets the freighter, he should be on one of those ships. Is one of them different from the others?"

Aurora dug into the sensor data. "There is one that is a different design. Possibly a frigate, while the others are runabouts. Yes. That is one to be wary of." Aurora caught Rivka's eyes, looking for approval.

"That's a great start. It could also mean that if they want to fight, that one will have more firepower. If they fight, we'll be looking for another ship that will be carrying alleged-Nefas. It's a mind-bending exercise in trying to see the way forward into multiple potential timelines. We discount the possibilities as we find more information. We use our sensors and intelligence collection resources to identify the gaps in knowledge."

Aurora looked appropriately confused. "I don't understand."

"How do we know if that's alleged-Nefas' ship? What a mouthful saying 'alleged-Nefas,' but we don't want to give him power over us by designating this enemy as the one from our past who caused us more grief than any of the others."

"Rendezvous with the freighter? A call to the freighter?"

"We'll be looking for both of those. We'll know fairly soon." Rivka watched the freighter turn around to decelerate. "Nice flying, C."

"My pleasure. These ships are easy to fly as long as their vectors are straight."

Rivka stared at the icons of the four ships still in orbit.

None reacted to the freighter's arrival. The ship slowed to a stop and waited near the small satellite.

"We tipped our hand with the EMP, but we couldn't have the minions ripping the ship apart. What's another way we can find this individual parading as the galaxy's archvillain?"

"Clevarious?" Aurora mentioned.

"We do count on our sentient intelligences a great deal. C, are you able to get into their system?"

"We've been trying, Magistrate, but have not been able to penetrate their outer security."

"SIs fighting SIs. This reinforces that it might be an individual of Nefas' abilities. Which also suggests it wasn't just a body double of Nefas. He might have cloned his SI self."

"We have arrived at that conclusion, too," Clevarious admitted.

"Sixteen ships accounted for in the system. One illicit Gate. One fairly robust settlement on a habitable moon. I should lock the whole place down as an adverse possession. But I'm not sure anyone knew this place existed until it seemed like everyone knew it existed." Rivka narrated her stream of consciousness, which helped her to think through a problem. She added pacing when the problem was sufficiently complex.

"Clodagh reports the mines are in place," Clevarious said.

"What about a soft takeover? Are you in a position to do that?"

"Not yet, Magistrate."

"If it starts to spin up before we control it, destroy it. It can be rebuilt, while we might not be able to find these individuals if they escape."

"The Gate is active now," Clevarious replied. "With an inbound ship."

Rivka ground her teeth. "Let it through. We'll trap it on this side."

A massive vessel slipped into the Delta 7 space.

"A warship, Magistrate. If my records are accurate, and they are, this is the pirate cruiser that escaped Nefas' stronghold before the Bad Company was able to catch up."

"They ran into open space. The Bad Company never hunted them down?" Rivka stopped pacing. She snarled at the screen, which showed the ship heading into the gravity well toward the Delta 7 moon.

"They did not. They weren't hired or paid for such an effort. A cursory search did not turn up the pirate survivors."

"They ran away to fight another day. Do we have enough firepower to take them on?"

"Probably."

"But we run into the problem regarding innocence. We are not the Bad Company, and we can start wars. Who is flying this vessel, and who is her crew? What is her purpose here? If we start a fight, we had better have already judged the target as hostile. It was once, but is it now?"

"I don't know what to do." Aurora threw her hands up in frustration.

Rivka watched her. "You and me both, but we have to figure it out."

"Do we?" Red asked from the corridor, which was

where he usually hung out instead of stepping foot on the bridge. "Why don't we call the Bad Company for backup? Then we don't have to destroy the Gate. I think that Gate and its technology could come in handy for the Federation."

"Sometimes, Red, you are thinking at a completely different level than the rest of us." She pointed in an arbitrary direction. "C, get me Terry Henry Walton."

The next voice they heard was Colonel Walton's. "Rivka, you missed me, didn't you?"

"What? No. My ship is less chaotic now, thankfully. Do you want to get some payback on pirates who gave you the finger once already?"

"Nobody gives me the finger and gets away with it!" Terry bellowed from where he stood on the bridge. Char whispered in his ear. He chuckled before turning back to the video. "Okay, people give me the finger all the time. What's it about?"

"The return of someone who walks and talks like Nefas, who, with the Bad Company's help, we bested in the Corrhen Cluster. We thought they were back there, and they might be, but they're also here at Delta 7. We have a Gate that they can dial their destination into."

"Dial a Gate that's not a Gate drive? That's too bizarre. We probably want to take that Gate out of their hands."

"I have mines on it to blow it up rather than let any of these ships escape," Rivka explained.

"I'd ask that you not do that. Hold on for a moment." Terry muted his audio but not his video. He talked to a number of individuals off-screen before returning. "We can be there in three minutes with a healthy number of ships. What kind of enemy force are we looking at?"

Clevarious shared the tactical screen.

"Dead runabouts, a few other active runabouts, maybe a frigate, and one cruiser? Can't *Wyatt Earp* handle them?"

"We could, but we want to contain them, not destroy them. We need numbers on our side to bend them to our will." Rivka sat down since a plan was forming in her mind. "Most importantly, we don't want to lose the Gate while preventing its use by these pirates. Blowing it is an easy answer but not the best long-term solution."

"We'll bring the fleet and shut down these bastards. That cruiser looks familiar. We kill him first."

"Only if he shoots first," Rivka explained. "This could be a different crew than it had last time you met."

"What do you want from me, Magistrate? Damn! Come save me from the hordes of scary people, but don't shoot them because they might be good." Terry rubbed the fake tears from his eyes with two fists.

"Sounds like you heard me five by five, Colonel. See you in two. We're cloaked, so you won't see us."

"Not until we fire our cool new missiles. Walton out."

The colonel was gone before she could reply.

"I feel like that changes things," Red said.

"They'll realize we've been here, but I think they already suspect that."

"The frigate is on the move," Aurora announced.

Rivka hopped up and moved to the sensor station. She gripped Aurora's shoulder while peering at her screen. Aurora looked at the hand. "I'm not reading your mind,"

Rivka said. "I'm happy that one of us has her wits about her. Well, two, if you count Red. Why am I muddled?"

"Because you don't have magic?" Ryleigh offered from the pilot's chair. "Moving on an intercept course. Gates are appearing throughout the system."

"That's something completely different," Rivka replied, standing up to better see the main screen.

The Bad Company was arriving. Battleship *Potemkin* appeared in front of the illicit Gate and made no effort to move away.

"And just like that, we're back in control of the situation. Hit that frigate with the EMP weapon," Rivka ordered.

"Targeting. Pulse delivered," Clevarious announced.

"It's not stopping." Rivka continued to stand, her lip curling as she weighed firing on it.

But the Bad Company's arrival had changed the dynamic. The frigate changed course, looping to return to the planet.

Two missiles raced outboard from the *War Axe,* which had camped in the middle of the area between the Gate, the asteroid belt, and the planet around which Delta 7 orbited.

The missiles exploded to reveal *Wyatt Earp, Destiny's Vengeance,* and four cloaked Skaine vessels. The *War Axe* immediately fired on the Skaine ships. Harborian frigates and destroyers lit up the void with energy weapons and projectiles hurled at nearly the speed of light from the railguns favored by the smaller Bad Company vessels.

The Skaine ships barely moved from where they were discovered before they were destroyed.

Wyatt Earp took up chasing the small frigate. It accelerated at a speed *Wyatt Earp* couldn't beat.

"Gate in front of that dumbass and prepare to send a little plasma his way. But send this first." Rivka composed herself. "By order of Magistrate Rivka Anoa, you are to stop your flight, bring your ship to a full stop, and prepare to be boarded. You are fleeing from a known crime scene, which subjects you to a warranted search. Heave to right now or be fired upon."

"Transmitting," Clevarious confirmed. "Gate coordinates set."

The spinning disc appeared in front of *Wyatt Earp,* and the ship raced through to come out alongside the running frigate.

"I said, heave to!" she growled at the screen.

A launch hatch opened.

"You wouldn't." Rivka stared at the image on the screen.

A missile emerged from the tube and was instantly destroyed by one of *Wyatt Earp*'s defensive railguns.

"Nice shooting, C." Rivka blew out a breath and thought for a moment. The ship tried to veer away. "I guess we'll call it suicide by Magistrate. Kill that ship."

Wyatt Earp slowed just enough for the frigate to get in front. Once the target was confirmed and the plasma cannon had locked on, a quick stream of fire turned the fleeing ship into an expanding cloud of debris.

"Take us back to Delta 7. I have to assume that was a decoy. Nefas would never kill himself."

Aurora stared at the Magistrate with wide eyes.

"Bring those three other ships to the satellite and instruct them to prepare to be boarded. Red and Lindy, you're up." Rivka checked the corridor. "Does Dery sense anything?"

Red looked farther down the corridor at Lindy, who was outside their quarters. She shook her head.

"We are a go," Red said.

"*War Axe* here." It was Terry Henry Walton. "We can bring those three into our hangar bay at the same time. It'll make things a lot easier on you if you can get yourself to my ship."

"Make it so, Ryleigh. Marry up the airlocks. And for you three troublemakers," Rivka was referring to the pilots, Aurora, Kennedy, and Ryleigh, "we'll try to free up some time on board the ship. Don't you have boyfriends over there?"

"Where don't they have boyfriends?" Red muttered loud enough for everyone to hear.

"Hey!" Ryleigh shouted.

"He's not wrong," Kennedy whispered loudly.

Ryleigh shrugged. "But first, catch the bad guys, Magistrate. We don't want liberty if *he's* still out there."

Rivka hit her chest twice, then pointed at Ryleigh. "I could not agree more."

The Magistrate headed for the airlock with Red and Lindy. The three of them wore full ballistic protection. Red and Lindy carried railguns on slings, with hand blasters at their hips. Rivka checked her pocket to feel the comfort of Reaper, the neutron pulse weapon she used to kill Nefas. She had known back then that his was an exceptional mind.

Too bad he used his abilities to flout the law.

A career criminal. No matter how smart he was, there

would always be someone smarter. That wasn't Rivka, but it was her and her team, which included the Singularity. No one would outsmart them all.

The soft clunk announced the link-up, and soon thereafter, the airlock cycled. Rivka started in, but Red blocked her and went first. Lindy followed in Rivka's footsteps. There was one warrior waiting for them.

"Follow me, ma'am," he said politely.

They went straight to the hangar bay, where the first runabout was being maneuvered toward the back to make space for the other two. An entire platoon of warriors wearing powered combat armor waited by the bulkheads in the bay.

Terry stood in the middle directing traffic while Char yelled at him to give the crew room to work. When he saw Rivka, he lightened up.

"Men," Char grumbled.

"Don't I know it, sister," Rivka replied. "We ready to open these cans?"

"Soon enough," Terry said. "We're going to try something new. A little psychological warfare, a trick we learned from Bundin's people. We will vibrate the ships with a low frequency designed to find the right tone for harmonic sphincter vibration."

"You want to make them crap themselves?" Rivka stared in disbelief.

"It'll be the most effective non-lethal effort you will have seen today. Don't think I didn't notice you blow that ship out of the sky."

"After he tried to launch a missile at us," Rivka countered. "We can call it the Bad Butthole or maybe the Terry

Tease in case we want to encourage others to use it. When non-lethal means are called for, of course."

"We'll do one at a time if they decide to do the wrong thing."

"The crew that hijacked the freighter filled it with toxic gas before we attempted to board it. I wouldn't be the first one in there if I didn't have a suit on."

Terry snapped his fingers. "Important safety tip." The boarding teams were armored and breathing their own air. He smiled.

The runabouts only had one main space. They could be cleared without having to go inside. And toxic air would quickly dissipate.

"Not a problem," Char clarified.

A maintenance bot eased up to the first runabout and placed a flat device on it.

Terry spoke aloud, and his voice was transmitted through the attached sonic transmitter. "Come out now, or you'll be sorry."

"Is that your message? You could add by order of Magistrate Rivka Anoa or something more official."

Terry shrugged. "Hit it."

Rivka instantly felt a surge of discomfort. "Turn it off!"

Red glared at Terry Henry. "What the fuck!"

Terry grimaced. "That didn't quite work as I intended. It was supposed to transmit in, not out."

Rivka collected herself, but to Terry's credit, the hatch popped. Red jumped in front of Rivka, and a cowed threesome stepped out of the ship with their hands on their heads.

Terry motioned for the boarding team to check the ship. One crawled inside.

Rivka headed toward the three. They were dressed in well-used coveralls and looked like a maintenance crew rather than pirates.

"What's your claim to fame?" Rivka said. She wasn't close enough to touch any of them.

"We're waiting for the freighter to offload it and tow a container to the colony."

The one on the moon.

"That's it?"

"What the hell else would we be doing? And what kind of evil did you impart on my ship? I almost lost my shit."

Rivka nodded slowly. "You weren't the only one."

She was finally close enough to touch one of the three. "You like your job?"

Offloading cargo? No, but she was happy to pick through it first, which was the benefit of taking it down. An added bonus. "It's a bad job, and it doesn't pay well. What do you think?" she replied aloud.

"Next." Rivka gestured at the runabout in the middle. "And don't use that sound thing. Ever. Again."

Char glared at TH. "I'll second that."

"What? It was worth a shot since everybody's all about non-lethal nowadays. *Don't shoot unless they shoot first.*" He waved his hands while staring at Rivka.

She smacked her lips. "Working with you is always enlightening." She smiled. "Keeps me on my toes."

Terry gestured at the runabout. The breaching team used the manual method of communication. They pounded on the hatch and shouted, "Open up!"

The second crew popped the hatch and exited, every bit as cowed as the first. "We weren't doing nothing. What's with the hazing?" the designated spokesman asked.

Red headed toward them with Rivka tucked behind his big body. The crew of the second runabout was diminutive in stature but stretched upward as Red approached to show they weren't intimidated by him.

With the help of Bad Company personnel, they checked them for weapons and removed three knives before stepping back to let Rivka do her thing.

Three questions later, she was no closer to finding anyone of import.

The last shuttle didn't want to open the hatch.

Kaeden moved close to talk to his father. "I think we should use the butt blaster."

Rivka held her hands out. "You have to be kidding."

"No. You have to get off the hangar deck. We'll take care of it. Then you can come back," Kae explained.

"You're the reasonable Walton?" Rivka asked.

Terry rolled his eyes, and Char snickered.

"Leaving. What a good idea," Char said and strolled toward the logistics area.

Everyone not in a combat suit hurried off the hangar deck and waited.

Guess what? The crew is coming out. You can rejoin the party, Kae said, using his comm chip.

Terry was first back in, with Red right behind him. Rivka and Char were more casual about their return.

Rivka made a beeline for a familiar face in the final ship's runabout crew.

"I feel like I know you," the person said.

Red pounded up to him and pulled him away from the others. His hands were bound tightly, and the armored fist of one of the breaching team held his shoulder. Red double-checked him, even opening his mouth to look inside. "How many times do we have to kill you?" he snarled.

"I feel like I already know you," someone wearing the face of Nefas said. "Shouldn't I get a cigarette after that?"

"How many of you are there?" Rivka demanded, holding him by the throat.

He tried to pull away but couldn't. *Darkness. Evil. No mercy. No remorse.*

Rivka let go and stepped back, wincing from the terror in his mind.

"I know it was you who started all of this. I know it was the programming of the SI known as Nefas, who is in cold storage on my ship. And I know there are more. Nefas stands out, and because of that, Nefas will always be caught.

"You cannot defeat all of us. It's not in your nature to win over the decent people of this galaxy. I, Magistrate Rivka Anoa, find you guilty of the capital crime of the murders of every freighter crew that didn't return home. Of every ship we had to destroy in this system. Their deaths are on your head. The back of your current scheme is broken."

Rivka nodded at Red. "Send him into space and then blast his frozen body if you would be so kind."

Red and Lindy hauled the struggling Nefas to the hangar bay entrance and with a final heave, sent him through the energy screen and into space. They rotated their railguns from under their arms to their shoulders, took aim, and fired.

Nefas had not yet frozen, but the gore when he was torn apart did, and quickly.

Rivka blew out a long breath and stared at the deck.

"You can't do that!" one of the two Ixtali from the last runabout shouted.

"You want to be next? Shut the fuck up," Terry told him. He turned to Rivka. "What do you want us to do with the rest of these...*things*?"

"Nefas' crew of Ixtali is going to Jhiordaan. These others?" She pointed at the crews from the first two runabouts. "They're pirates, but along for the ride. Maybe they'll find a new line of work. Put them in the brig on Tyrosint for a month."

"Will do," Terry replied. He reached out, and Rivka took his hand.

They shook. All she saw in his mind was appreciation for what she did to keep the Federation safe. No jokes. No quips. No sarcasm. Plus a deep love for his family and the Federation.

"You are one of a kind, Terry Henry Walton. It's a good thing Char has been keeping you honest all this time."

The two women hugged before Rivka headed for the airlock. She stopped halfway across the hangar deck. "We need to clean up that mess on Delta 7. Do you have the forces to search it? See if there is a Nefas-cloning facility down there?"

Terry nodded. "It would be the pleasure of the Bad Company to conduct a search and consolidation of that facility. What's your plan for it?"

"My plan is to turn it over to a higher authority—Lance Reynolds—for him to decide what to do with it. He can send in a team of bureaucrats, who will make these people sorry they ever crossed the Federation, or he can send a team that makes them feel welcome and establish this as an outpost. A free trade zone, with a Federation presence, of course."

"They could use legal help," Terry offered.

"And I could use some AGB, but we don't always get what we want. Unless we do, but we still don't."

"You never know unless you ask," Terry countered while trying to parse the meaning behind Rivka's statement.

She waved over her shoulder and was gone.

CHAPTER TWENTY-FOUR

***Wyatt Earp*, in Interstellar Space**

"We can get AGB?" Rivka hadn't gotten the word that they were back in business. She'd only been gone for a few days.

Ankh nodded. "We will see if the new leadership team of the franchise is any good." It was Ankh's voice, but Erasmus was speaking.

"What do you know about good AGB?" Rivka asked.

"I know that my partner appreciates it far more than he lets on." Ankh's face smiled, which was distinctly un-Crenellian.

"You shouldn't do that. It's creepy. I prefer the blank stare." She locked eyes with him as his face resumed its normal neutral expression. She gave up after one minute of staring. "That's more like it."

She returned to her quarters and brought up the hologrid.

"Grainger. Nice to see you dressed."

"It's the middle of the day. Odd that you are calling me at this ungodly hour. Is the case wrapped up?"

"I've had enough of Nefas to last a lifetime. Why does he keep cropping up? How many times do I have to execute him?" It was a rhetorical question. She would do it as many times as he popped up with his schemes that involved millions.

"That was a quick case even for you. I have to say that I was glad the Bad Company got involved from the outset. With the Skaines, who are on the run, by the way, and the Myriador, who we will be opening diplomatic discussions with, we needed Bad Company's firepower and military influence. And the decloaking missiles? Genius. I'm impressed to the point of being awestruck by what a lone Magistrate is capable of doing."

"I'm surrounded by good people." Rivka wouldn't take any more credit than that. "I'll send my final case notes in a couple minutes."

"The drug trade is still active, but now there's no central control," Grainger replied.

"I thought Bustamove was working that."

"He went to Delegor, and we have a new agreement with the Chief Delegador. It appears that they were keeping information from the Federation that would have made them look bad. They are expanding the Federation embassy to improve information-sharing. Buster made a huge impression on them."

"Unlike me. I'm afraid I set us back. I'm curious; what did he do to gain their cooperation?"

"He gave the Chief Delegador the finger. Then Buster arranged a meeting with him that Buster skipped out on."

"That sounds like something I'd do. I'm going to have to get tips on how to insult everyone and be rewarded for it." Rivka tapped other information screens on the hologrid, zoning out while still talking to Grainger.

"Submit your case files. Then we'll take a look at next steps, but I'm pretty sure there are tens of millions of doses of Plexorall and Advantageous moving through the system. They don't take up much space, so I expect they'll be smuggled both knowingly and unknowingly. I wouldn't be surprised if there was some on every single cargo vessel out there."

"That's disconcerting," Rivka replied.

"Who will take over the distribution?"

"The Mob, undoubtedly," Rivka said. "It's their core competency, along with security shakedowns. The protection rackets."

"We will see who steps up. Can you ask the Singularity to keep their eyes open for planetary police reports about drug busts? We can watch for big increases and try to unravel things from there."

"I'll ask them. Clevarious always listens in, so she's probably already added it to a Singularity BOLO."

"I have," the SI confirmed.

"There you go. Ankh tells me we can get AGB again. I need some, or I'll go stir-crazy. Do not give me a case until I'm properly fed."

"How long does it take you to eat?" Grainger wondered.

"Two days. First course. Sleep. Second course."

Grainger waved. "I'll see what I can do. Good work on this case." He signed off. Rivka checked the case file Clevarious had compiled, signed it, and submitted it. She lowered the grid, then stood and stretched, suddenly tired. Rivka was unsure of the last time she'd slept.

"AGB in fifteen!" Red shouted from the corridor, feet pounding as he ran from the workout room toward his quarters. A lighter tread signaled that Lindy was running after him.

Rivka laughed softly.

"What?" Tyler asked. "No, let me guess. We almost went to war over All Guns Blazing's food."

"That might only have been the catalyst, but in a nutshell, yes."

A scratching at the door prompted Tyler to open it. Floyd staggered in and flopped to the deck.

Tired, Floyd whined.

"You look like you're losing weight. That's good," Rivka exclaimed, kneeling next to her to pet her rough fur.

Mean men make me run.

"Red? Is he being mean to you?"

Not Red. He is good.

Rivka stood. "Do you know what she's talking about? What mean men?"

Tyler tried to look innocent, which made him look even more guilty. "They didn't want to bother you."

"Who?"

"You should probably go to the bridge." He held the door for her. "You stay here, little girl." He petted her while Rivka stormed out.

She reached the bridge to find a strange man who was buff and broad-shouldered, with dark brown eyes and the short haircut of a warrior. "Who are you?"

"My name is Lewis. Pleased to meet you."

Rivka stared at Kennedy, who refused to say anything. The Magistrate instantly knew what had happened. "You smuggled your boyfriends on board?"

"You make it sound like a bad thing," Ryleigh said from behind her. Rivka turned to find another chiseled gift to the universe. "We asked, and you said we could use additional firepower. Colonel Walton sent their combat armor."

"He knew about this?"

"Yes, ma'am. My name is Russell. Damn glad to be a member of the best crew in the galaxy!"

The decision to fight or surrender was usually more challenging, but not this time. "Do you guys like AGB?"

"Do we ever! We can eat a mountain of that stuff."

"Moonstokle Pie is mine. Everything else is fair game, but Ankh eats first because he created the delivery system that makes it possible to get." Rivka looked around. "I expect there's a third warrior running around here."

"That would be Furny. I think he's taking a nap right now."

"Nap. Is that what we're calling it?" Rivka quipped. She raised a hand so no one would answer. "AGB in ten. All hands. I have a few words I'd like to share with the crew."

Rivka stepped off the bridge, nodding at the new members of her crew as she passed. The warriors saluted. She dragged her feet on her way to her quarters. She had no idea what words she would share. Maybe a welcome aboard for the new crewmembers. A kind word on everyone's performance during the last case. Simple but important. It was what bosses were supposed to do.

She was tired. Tyler wrapped an arm around her to guide her around the sleeping wombat to the couch.

"How about those lines?" Rivka asked, making small talk to kill time until dinner. After that, she planned on sleeping for a whole day.

"Only a few closed, or so I heard. Line 1, first swearing, Line 2, first punch, Line 3, first arrest, Line 6, shots fired, Line 7, quantity of AGB consumed, and Line 9, case closed. Not a single gram of AGB was consumed on this case. There were about a hundred people who guessed that number. The payout was trivial."

"How long have you known about the boyfriends?"

"I held the door open for them to come on board."

Rivka snorted. "Why am I not surprised?"

Tyler shrugged.

"What about their boyfriends at every port of call?"

"They'll have to get used to not being boyfriends anymore. It would make things a bit uncomfortable having cage matches for the pilots' affections."

"I'm putting it on your head to make sure there are no fights over the younger members of our crew. None! I won't have it."

"Isn't something worth having worth fighting for?"

"Not in this case. My pilots aren't prizes to be won in a fight." She realized Tyler was goading her. "You're all kinds of trouble, but you're my trouble. You better be willing to fight for me."

He laughed. "Fight you for you is more like it. When are you going to get some sleep?"

"Right after AGB. Let me know when it arrives." She stretched out on the couch. He went to get her pillow from the bed. By the time he returned, she was sound asleep.

THE END

JUDGE, JURY, & EXECUTIONER, BOOK 17

If you liked this book, please leave a review. I love reviews since they tell other readers that this book is worth their time and money. I hope you feel that way now that you've finished the latest installment. Please drop me a line and let me know you like Rivka's adventures and want them to continue. This is my new favorite series. I hope you agree.

Don't stop now! Keep turning the pages as Craig hits his *Author Notes* with thoughts about this book and the good stuff that happens in the *Kurtherian Gambit* Universe.

Your favorite legal eagle will return in JJE18, *The Mob*!

AUTHOR NOTES - CRAIG MARTELLE

WRITTEN OCTOBER 2022

Thank you for reading all the way to the end. You are my absolute favorite!

I hadn't intended to write this book until 2023, but alas, Tantor licensed the audio for the first seventeen books in the series, so here we are, rocking and rolling our way onward. I've ordered the covers for JJE18, JJE19, and JJE20, so the series will continue moving forward. Since the original *Kurtherian Gambit* series lasted twenty-one books, I told Michael that this series had to go at least twenty-two.

He called me names, and then we laughed.

And then came October. I was working on finishing this book by the fourteenth, but it took until the fifteenth. That was the day Micky Cocker passed away. She was integral to my writing process, reading and providing support and comments that helped me to be a better author. She had physical problems, leaving her without the ability to work a normal day job, but she could read and did for many of us. She suffered from chronic pain. At least now, she is in a place where she's pain-free.

Her passing was hard on all of us. It's not something to easily get over. She was a close friend and a critical member of my team. I will miss her greatly.

Life moves on, and that's the biggest challenge. I didn't build in any time in my writing schedule to grieve, but here we are. I find solace in a new story and bringing those characters to life.

It's my way, the old-school way. Bury myself in work, push down the grief, and then take it to my grave. I'm sure psychiatrists will tell me that's not healthy, but I suggest it is when it comes to me. Talking with a psychiatrist or psychologist? That's not something I'll ever do.

I'd rather hear from you—those who read my stories and like them. That means I'm bringing something good to the world. A brief departure from the harshness of reality. We all need that. I get to live it every day with each new paragraph and each new chapter.

And that's what I'll keep doing. I've already opened the next story, the first in the new *Starship Lost* series. I have grand ideas for it that I have to write. I think it will be epic. We will see if it is the best story I've ever written. I strive for that with each new book.

Until then, lots of stories to tell. Lots of characters to bring to life.

Peace, fellow humans.

Please join my newsletter (craigmartelle.com—please, please, please sign up!), or you can follow me on Facebook.

If you liked this story, you might like some of my other books. You can join my mailing list by dropping by my website craigmartelle.com, or if you have any comments, shoot me a note at craig@craigmartelle.com. I am always happy to hear from people who've read my work. I try to answer every email I receive.

If you liked the story, please write a short review for me on Amazon. I greatly appreciate any kind words; even one or two sentences go a long way. The number of reviews an eBook receives greatly improves how well an eBook does on Amazon.

Amazon—https://www.amazon.com/author/craigmartelle

BookBub—https://www.bookbub.com/authors/craig-martelle

Facebook—www.facebook.com/authorcraigmartelle

In case you missed it before, my web page—https://craigmartelle.com

That's it. Break's over, back to writing the next book.

OTHER SERIES BY CRAIG MARTELLE

 # - available in audio, too

Terry Henry Walton Chronicles (#) (co-written with Michael Anderle)—a post-apocalyptic paranormal adventure

Gateway to the Universe (#) (co-written with Justin Sloan & Michael Anderle)—this book transitions the characters from the Terry Henry Walton Chronicles to the Bad Company

The Bad Company (#) (co-written with Michael Anderle)—a military science fiction space opera

Judge, Jury, & Executioner (#)—a space opera adventure legal thriller

Shadow Vanguard—a Tom Dublin space adventure series

Superdreadnought (#)—an AI military space opera

Metal Legion (#)—a military space opera

The Free Trader (#)—a young adult science fiction action-adventure

Cygnus Space Opera (#)—a young adult space opera (set in the Free Trader universe)

Darklanding (#) (co-written with Scott Moon)—a space western

Mystically Engineered (co-written with Valerie Emerson)—mystics, dragons, & spaceships

Metamorphosis Alpha—stories from the world's first science fiction RPG

The Expanding Universe—science fiction anthologies

Krimson Empire (co-written with Julia Huni)—a galactic race for justice

Zenophobia (#) (co-written with Brad Torgersen)—a space archaeological adventure

Battleship Leviathan (#)– a military sci-fi spectacle published by Aethon Books

Glory (co-written with Ira Heinichen)—hard-hitting military sci-fi

Black Heart of the Dragon God (co-written with Jean Rabe)—a sword & sorcery novel

End Times Alaska (#)—a post-apocalyptic survivalist adventure published by Permuted Press

Nightwalker (a Frank Roderus series)—A post-apocalyptic western adventure

End Days (#) (co-written with E.E. Isherwood)—a post-apocalyptic adventure

Successful Indie Author (#)—a nonfiction series to help self-published authors

Monster Case Files (co-written with Kathryn Hearst)—A Warner twins mystery adventure

Rick Banik (#)—Spy & terrorism action adventure

Ian Bragg Thrillers (#)—a hitman with a conscience

Not Enough (co-written with Eden Wolfe)—A coming of age contemporary fantasy

Published exclusively by Craig Martelle, Inc

The Dragon's Call by Angelique Anderson & Craig A. Price, Jr.—an epic fantasy quest

A Couples Travels—a nonfiction travel series

Love-Haight Case Files by Jean Rabe & Donald J. Bingle—the dead/undead have rights, too, a supernatural legal thriller

Mischief Maker by Bruce Nesmith—the creator of Elder Scrolls V: Skyrim brings you Loki in the modern day, staying true to Norse Mythology (not a superhero version)

Mark of the Assassins by Landri Johnson—a coming of age fantasy.

For a complete list of Craig's books, stop by his website—https://craigmartelle.com

BOOKS BY MICHAEL ANDERLE

Sign up for the LMBPN email list to be notified of new releases and special deals!

https://lmbpn.com/email/

For a complete list of books by Michael Anderle, please visit:

www.lmbpn.com/ma-books/

Made in the USA
Columbia, SC
03 March 2023

13267506R00190